Praise for

Close Your Eyes

"Ward writes in the language of families, capturing their penchant for loss and the possibility of redemption. . . . Main character Lauren spends the book delving into her memories of her father . . . who has been convicted of murdering her mother. Ward has a deft hand with crafting endearing characters."

—The Huffington Post

"Troubled and achingly human . . . both an absorbing mystery and a stirring journey to redemption."

—*People* (four stars)

"With *Close Your Eyes,* Austin novelist Amanda Eyre Ward puts another jewel in her crown as the reigning doyenne of 'dark secrets' literary fiction."

—*The Dallas Morning News*

"Ward's strength lies in her insightful characterizations. Lauren and Sylvia are deftly and lovingly drawn as each struggles with her pain, eventually finding courage and, ultimately, hanging hard onto shards of family and hope."

—New Orleans *Times-Picayune*

"[Ward] possesses an ability to dig deep into her wounded characters' psyches and express their grief, confusion and frustration in lyrically effective prose that is spare and direct."
—*San Antonio Express-News*

"With the deft hand of an assured storyteller, Amanda Eyre Ward has concocted a dark yet tender tale about two grown siblings struggling to forge normal lives in the wake of an unimaginably shattering crisis: the conviction of their father for the murder of their mother. It is a tale of twists, turns, secrets, and surprises—all the more engaging for its finely drawn characters. Ward understands just how our flaws betray us and how redemption always comes at a price—yet her deep empathy makes this, ultimately, a story about the power of trust in the people we love."
—JULIA GLASS, author of *The Widower's Tale*

"*Close Your Eyes* is a pitch-perfect exploration of what happens when grief meets guilt and anger in a dark alley—or, in this case, a bright Austin suburb. It's lonely and compelling and strangely lovely. Amanda Eyre Ward got it just right."
—KELLY BRAFFET, author of *Last Seen Leaving*

"Amanda Ward's *Close Your Eyes* is electrifying, a literary whodunit of the first order—breathless and disturbing and hopeful and true. You won't be able to look away. People will be talking about this book."
—JUSTIN CRONIN, author of *The Passage*

"*Close Your Eyes* is a wonder. Amanda Eyre Ward has given us a finely spun mystery with complex, absorbing characters and lovely prose. A true literary page-turner in the best sense of the word."
—Katie Crouch, author of *Girls in Trucks*

"*Close Your Eyes* doesn't hook you as much as it spins a delicate but powerful web around you. Amanda Eyre Ward goes straight to the heart of her complex, nuanced characters, and with empathy and insight she lays them bare. As a reader, you're powerless against the elegance of her prose and the emotional honesty of her story. You'll close the cover on this book, but you won't forget it."
—Lisa Unger, *New York Times* bestselling author of *Fragile*

"Amanda Eyre Ward has given us a book that is both beautifully wrought and intensely gripping. I was transfixed by this story of a woman haunted by loss but making her brave, difficult way toward truth."
—Marisa de los Santos, *New York Times* bestselling author of *Belong to Me* and *Love Walked In*

ALSO BY AMANDA EYRE WARD

Love Stories in This Town

Forgive Me

How to Be Lost

Sleep Toward Heaven

Close Your Eyes

Close Your Eyes

A Novel

AMANDA EYRE WARD

BALLANTINE BOOKS TRADE PAPERBACKS

NEW YORK

2012 Ballantine Books Trade Paperback Edition

Published in the United States by Ballantine Books, an imprint of The Random House Publishing Group, a division of Random House, Inc., New York.

BALLANTINE and colophon are registered trademarks of Random House, Inc.
RANDOM HOUSE READER'S CIRCLE & Design is a registered trademark of Random House, Inc.

Originally published in hardcover in the United States by Random House, an imprint of The Random House Publishing Group, a division of Random House, Inc., in 2011.

Library of Congress Cataloging-in-Publication Data

Ward, Amanda Eyre
Close your eyes: a novel/Amanda Eyre Ward.
p. cm.
ISBN 978-0-345-49449-8
eBook ISBN 978-0-679-60508-9
1. Family secrets—Fiction. 2. Psychological fiction. I. Title.
PS3623.A725C57 2010
813'.6—dc22 2010021115

Printed in the United States of America

www.randomhousereaderscircle.com

2 4 6 8 9 7 5 3 1

Book design by Caroline Cunningham

A sister is . . . a golden thread to the meaning of life.

—Isadora James

This book is for my sister, Sarah, with love.

Prologue

August 1986

I can remember the taste of ocean, and the dark smell of impending rain. Our parents had given us reluctant permission to spend the night in the tree house. From our perch, high in an oak tree, we could see a faraway sliver of Long Island Sound. I can almost see myself—the way I looked before: a sweet girl, just eight. I was sturdy, like my father, with his dark hair and olive skin. My mother brushed my hair into pigtails, and I wore sundresses with bare feet, so I could climb.

My brother, Alex, had stolen a can of Tab from the pantry. We drank from plastic teacups, remnants of my girlhood set. Clouds moved over the moon. My L.L.Bean sleeping bag was too warm, and in the middle of the night, I slipped one leg outside the heavy fabric and touched my brother's foot with my own.

The tree house was a small structure shaped like a pirate ship. My mother used to laugh and say it had taken longer for my father to build the damn thing than it had for her to grow and deliver a baby, but by the time I was two and could climb the ladder to the top, it was finished.

We had a large, grassy yard; from the tree house, you could barely see the peeling paint on our back door. No matter what happened inside, as it turned out, you wouldn't hear a sound.

That night, our parents had given a small party. Alex and I often hid during their gatherings, and watched the adults drink wine and act strange. My father grilled elaborate Egyptian dishes on the Weber—rice-stuffed pigeon, rabbit with mint—and my mother sat with her friends at the picnic table and smoked cigarettes furtively, the embers lending her face an angelic glow. The guests that night were Phil Salinas, an investment banker; Jessica Salinas, his newest wife; Adam Schwickrath, an orthopedic surgeon; and Donna Halsey, my piano teacher.

My father teased my mother about Adam Schwickrath. He was the man she should have married, my father said, his words edged with bitterness. Dr. Schwickrath was wealthy and well dressed, usually wearing khakis and a button-down shirt. Some evenings he and my mother would talk to each other in soft tones, my mother laughing and lifting her head to expose her throat.

Dr. Schwickrath had given my mother a wrapped package that night, though her birthday had been weeks before. "Better late than never," he'd said, almost bashfully. As my mother opened the box and took out a pair of high-heeled shoes, I'd looked at my father, who was staring, his jaw set. He had written my mother a birthday poem, made her a pan of walnut brownies. "I just thought of you when I saw them, Jordan," said Dr. Schwickrath.

"Are they the right size?" asked my father.

My mother had peered at the strappy shoes. They were a silvery color, more expensive than anything we could afford, I knew. "Adam, how did you know I was a size seven? They're beautiful!" my mother had said. She held a shoe to the light, admiring. But her hand fell when she saw my father's face. "Oh, never mind!" she said brightly, dropping the shoes back in their box and placing it on a chair. "Let's have some appetizers, why don't we?"

Alex and I snacked on corn chips, answering stupid questions about soccer, long division, and what we wanted to be when we grew up. Alex, who was ten, wanted to be a fighter pilot and I, a ballerina. At long last, our parents said we could take our leave.

We climbed the ladder quietly and lit the candle we'd taken from the sideboard. The caramel light made the tree house seem otherworldly. It may have taken him a while, but my father had built our hideout with care, lining up each board, framing windows.

My father loved to tinker in his basement workshop. My mother earned the money to pay for our real house, but my father took bits of driftwood or discarded lumber and assembled other dwellings. Besides the tree house, he made me a dollhouse that I called the Fairy Lair. He told me long stories about the fairies who lived inside, and sometimes I would come home from school to find a new piece of furniture: a bed made of daisies or a bathtub carved from wood, painted with flowers. He made birdhouses and gave them to friends as gifts.

My father. He smelled like cigarettes and cardamom. When I was small and wanted comfort, he would put down the wooden spoon when he was cooking, or the pen when he was writing. Always, he would halt what he was doing and crouch down. I would press my cheek to his warm chest. In his arms, I was safe.

The sleeping bags nearly filled the tree house. Alex poured the soda, and I heard my mother's laughter as I sipped. Sometimes, when I concentrate, I can still hear her.

We pretended we were on an adventure and talked about where we were sailing. I said, "Alexandria, Captain!" and my brother told me he saw the great port outside the tree house window. The pyramids were in the distance, and the sphinx.

At some point, our parents called to us. I remember my mother saying, "Good night, my loves!"

"Good night!" we cried, waving to them. They stood below us, next to each other. My father, as always, was disheveled, his hand in my mother's long hair. As they walked to the house, I saw him wrapping her hair around his dark wrist: a golden bracelet.

This was the last night I dreamed. The last night, anyway, that I remember any dreams. Now I don't sleep very well, and I am scared of midnight visions. I take pills that lower me into slumber cleanly, and ebb away until morning, when I wake fuzzy, my mind pleasantly numb until after a few cups of coffee.

That night I dreamed of dolphins, of riding a dolphin in a warm sea. I slipped underwater and was scooped up again. Then a bolt of lightning cracked in the sky and my dolphin disappeared under the waves for good, leaving me alone. Rain hammered the ocean; I felt water on my head, driving me down.

My house was underwater. I swam across the lawn and floated upstairs. There were terrible noises coming from my parents' room. I saw bad things—it is a blank now, a black hole of memory—and I fled the house, back to Alex.

When I woke, my father and brother were sitting on either side of me on the floor of the tree house, tearing into cinnamon buns. My father often took us to the Holt bakery for pastries—this morning he had risen early and gone himself, he said. He held the bag open for me, and I selected a bun, took a bite sweet with frosting.

We finished our breakfast and walked to the house to get our swimsuits. I was rummaging in my room for my red one-piece when I heard an awful sound—a cry like a screeching cat.

There was a long carpeted stairway in the house on Ocean Avenue. I was halfway up the steps when Alex slammed my parents' bedroom door behind him and rushed to me, grabbing my shoulders.

"Turn around," said Alex. His face was white as milk.

"What—"

"Turn around!" he screamed.

I fought, straining to find out what had happened, but Alex was stronger. He grabbed me by the wrist and pulled me back outside. I asked him what was going on, and he said, "Shut up. Just shut up! Just shut up!"

I was dizzy and too hot. I clutched my bathing suit in my fist.

A police car arrived—flashing red lights and sirens. An ambulance followed. Brawny, stone-faced men rushed inside our house. When they came back out, they were no longer in a hurry. They bore a heavy stretcher.

My father emerged on the lawn with two policemen. I heard him shouting about his children, *Find my children.* The men put my father in a patrol car, shut the door, and drove away. Alex and I waited to see what would happen next.

Book One

AUGUST 2010

1

"A road trip," said Alex, sounding hopeful for the first time in a long time. "To see Gramma. We can visit her and then go to the beach. We can rent a cottage in Galveston. We can rent a condo."

"A condo?" I said, clamping the phone to my ear with my shoulder as I gathered tomatoes in the produce aisle.

"I have some news, Lauren. Can you get away this weekend, so we can talk?"

"I don't know," I said. "It's a hundred and ten degrees. I have three open houses on Sunday. What do you mean, news?"

"Well, at least you have your priorities in order." My brother sounded like he was pouting. I remembered the way he would hide under the kitchen table when our parents fought, refusing to come out.

I placed tomatoes on the scale, printing out the price and pressing it to a plastic bag. It was August in Austin, and the cost of tomatoes was rising with the temperatures. "Oh, Alex, I don't know," I said. "Just tell me the news. Is it good news?"

"I get it," said Alex. "Mr. Cheapskate won't let you out of his sight?"

I shut off my phone and stowed it in my handbag. I picked out a bunch of bananas, just a bit green, then gathered organic baby spinach, fresh thyme, and new potatoes. In the meat department, I asked for lamb and a pound of ground chuck. I passed the lobster tank, grabbed a six-pack of Lone Star and a bottle of cheap white. I tossed two boxes of strawberry granola and a pint of Mexican vanilla ice cream into the cart. Cheddar cheese, skim milk, bagels, baguette, warm tortillas, chocolate-chunk cookies. I was shopping for a family of five, it seemed, though it was just Gerry and me in the one-bedroom rental. I smiled when I thought of Gerry: the slight curl in his auburn hair, his broad shoulders. Gerry had been a wrestler in high school and still had a rangy, stocky build. He was my height, and when we swayed in the kitchen to a slow tune on the radio, we fit together like wooden jigsaw pieces. Like Illinois, nestled next to Missouri in my old puzzle of the United States.

By the register, I grabbed a lemon soda and a bouquet of tulips. I paid with my MasterCard, my shock at the total assuaged by the knowledge that I was earning a hell of a lot of airline miles. Besides, what was money for if not sumptuous evenings with your boyfriend? By the time Gerry finished work—or "work," as he labored for himself, and what he was doing in the shed in his sweatpants was nothing I recognized as taxing or taxable—I would likely be curled in bed, asleep, but hope sprang eternal, and romance (I believed) was about faith and expensive groceries.

Though I had finished squiring around a couple named the Gelthorps by four, dropping them at the Four Seasons for dinner and discussment (Mrs. Gelthorp had assured me she'd call in the morning with an offer on either the Tuscan-style palace in Pemberton Heights or the Provençal villa in Westlake), it was already dark as I wheeled my booty out of Central Market. I angled the cart toward my Dodge Neon. I had hoped for a glamorous convertible, but Gerry had been firm, armed with a stack of old *Consumer Reports* and Epinions printouts. I unlocked the car, opened the trunk, and screamed when someone tapped me on the shoulder.

"I'm sorry," said my brother, panting in the cool evening.

"How did you—"

"You had that calm *I'm buying foodstuffs* tone," said Alex. "I rode my bike over."

"From the hospital?"

Alex nodded. He wiped his forehead. "I came to say I'm sorry," he said. "I didn't mean to insult Gerry."

"It's okay," I said. "He *is* Mr. Cheapskate, after all."

"I just think a trip would be fun. The two of us. We need to visit Gramma—and I'll reserve the campsite, or condo, whatever. We haven't camped since . . . since we were kids, you know? I'm feeling a bit mortal."

My older brother filled me—always—with bafflement, irritation, and gratitude. He had never recovered, not really, from that morning. I had not made it all the way upstairs, so in some sense, I had been spared. By the time I saw my mother, she had been cleaned and made up, slipped into her favorite dress. He had taken care of me ever since. Instead of parents, I had Alex.

"When are you thinking?" I said.

"How about tomorrow? We can leave first thing in the morning."

"Tomorrow! Can you help me with these bags?"

"Time's wasting, sister," said Alex, grabbing bags roughly and tossing them into the trunk.

"What does that mean?" I said. "Be careful—that's wine!"

Alex placed the paper bag down gently. He turned around and held me by the shoulders. "Have you heard of Doctors Without Borders?" he asked.

"Oh, God," I said. "I have a feeling I'm not going to like this news."

"I applied last year," said Alex. "And I just got my assignment. I'm going to Iraq, to Baghdad."

"You . . ." I said, trailing off. I felt as if I had been sucker-punched. "You can't leave."

"I'll go in a few weeks," said Alex gently.

"What about me?" I said.

"Lauren, this has nothing to do with you."

In the Central Market parking lot, beneath the CITRUS FRENZY banner, I began to cry. "I'll be all alone," I said.

"Lauren, you're thirty-two," said Alex. "Get ahold of yourself."

"Go to hell." I threw the last bag in the car, slammed the trunk, and went around the side to the driver door, wiping my nose with my arm. I felt alarmed, woozy. I opened the door and tried to breathe evenly.

Alex ran to me and grabbed my elbow. "I knew you'd freak out," he said.

"It's so sudden," I said.

Alex hugged me, smelling of sweat and fast food. "Let me just lock up my bike," he said. "I'll come over for dinner."

Gerry and I lived in French Place, a historic neighborhood on the wrong side of the interstate. Fault lines made foundations crack and shift; while many houses looked great up top, there were problems under the surface. As opposed to Hyde Park, where professors and rich hippies lived, French Place was for the young and working-class. I loved it. Our landlord had painted the wood siding purple, which would not have been my choice—I preferred sage green—but the trim was a soothing yellow. Some people in our neighborhood went all out, with giant metal roosters or actual chickens in their yards, but we'd splurged on two lemon-colored chairs and a café table from Zinger Hardware and called it a day. When we had our fabulous pumpkin-carving party every year, nobody minded sitting on the steps or on one of the blankets we spread across the lawn.

Our street, Maplewood Avenue, was situated behind an elementary school. In the mornings, I could sit on our sagging front porch and watch kids arrive for school, their hair still mashed from bed, small fists rubbing their eyes. We had a house of bike messengers on one side of us and an elderly couple on the other side. Gerry and I often shared a cold six-pack with the neighbors.

When I turned onto Maplewood, I could see that the lights in our purple shed, which was now called "The Studio," were still on. "How's that all going?" asked Alex. "The, uh, podcast or whatever."

I shrugged. Gerry had lost his job at Dell six months before, and after a week or so of moping around, he had declared his life's dream. I thought my boyfriend's "life's dream" was finally getting me to marry him (he had been asking for years), but no. In his boxer shorts and a DELL BOWLING '08 T-shirt, Gerry had stood in the living room and announced that he was going to start a blog and begin calling himself "Mr. Cheapskate." Wild-eyed, he showed me elaborate plans scrawled in a notebook he'd bought at Walgreens in the middle of the night.

"There's this guy who loves wine, okay?" Gerry had said the next morning as I edged my way into the kitchen and began spooning coffee into the French press.

"Okay," I said. I had to admit that he looked absurdly attractive with his unshaven face, his eyes alight.

"So he makes podcasts, YouTube videos, the whole nine yards. He talks about wine. And now he's rich! And you know how I always wanted to be a stand-up comedian?"

"I thought you wanted to perfect neural networks," I said.

"Before that, before that," said Gerry. "When I was in high school, I wanted to be a stand-up comedian. I won talent shows, the whole nine yards."

"You don't really tell jokes or anything," I ventured.

"ANYWAY," Gerry snapped, "my point is that I have personality."

"I'll give you that," I said. I put the kettle on to boil.

"So, and I'm cheap," said Gerry. He *was* cheap, of this there was no doubt. Gerry refused to order coffee when we went to a coffee shop, insisting he could sip from my cup. He fished newspapers out of the trash and exited airplanes scanning the seat backs carefully, hoping for free magazines. He had a plastic accordion folder for coupons, he knew every two-for-one night in Austin, and he was happy to buy three cans of a Campbell's soup flavor he didn't especially like (broccoli cheese, for example) because the fourth can came for free. Tea bags in his wallet, a favorite free parking place downtown that required me to walk twenty minutes every time we went to hear a band, a house filled with crap from Freecycle. Yes, my beloved was cheap.

"I am going to be Mr. Cheapskate," said Gerry. "I've already bought the domain name."

"So you're going to write about . . . about saving money?"

"Oh, hon," said Gerry, "that's just the beginning." As I drank coffee and nibbled a stale scone, Gerry talked about blog ad revenue, webcasts, social networks, and later, T-shirt sales and personal appearances. He outlined his plans for the dilapidated shed, which was to become the center of the cheapskate empire. He was never going to work for "the man" again. In fact, he was working *against* the man!

I nodded and smiled, hoping against hope for an upturn in the real estate market, acknowledging with more than a little fear that my boyfriend might be turning into my deadbeat father.

Still, I felt a measure of pride as Alex and I pulled into the driveway and could see Gerry through the grimy shed window, his face illuminated by the halogen bulb he'd installed. "Still at it, eh?" said Alex.

I sighed. "He's working really hard."

Leaning against the car with our arms full of groceries, we watched Gerry gesticulate. His voice rose in the balmy night. "And they'll *tell you* you have to get two of the *same burgers* to get the Hut's two-for-one deal. But I'm here to give you the inside scoop, people. Your wife likes a cheeseburger, and you're a plain-beef guy? Bring a slice of cheese in your pocket! And *that's* the Mr. Cheapskate Secret Scam of the Day. So do good work, people, play hard, and BE CHEAP!"

"Whoa," said Alex.

"He actually has a medium-sized audience," I said.

"That's great," said Alex, starting to walk toward the house with his bag.

"It's wonderful," I said insistently. My dog, Handsome, came bounding out of the house to greet us, and I knelt down to scratch behind his ears.

Alex gave Gerry the big news as he made himself at home, opening the wine, pouring himself a glass. Then he said, "Before

I go, I'm dragging Lauren on a road trip." Gerry, unpacking the groceries, turned around to meet my gaze questioningly.

"It's my final wish," said Alex, taking the box of cookies out of Gerry's hand and helping himself. "She can't refuse me. Besides, we haven't seen Gramma since after the Astros game last spring."

"Please don't be morbid," I said. I sank into the couch, suddenly both ravenous and exhausted. "Or is it *moribund*?"

"Alex," said Gerry, "I want you to know I really admire what you're doing."

"Jeez, Gerry," said Alex, "thanks."

"I think it's ridiculous," I said. "Doctors Without Borders? What's wrong with borders? That's what I'd like to know. I like borders. They make sense to me."

Both Alex and Gerry ignored my commentary. As they ate the dinner I had so carefully prepared, they talked about how Alex would get to Iraq (Austin to JFK, then through Jordan, which had been our mother's name and so seemed portentous, foreboding), what he was bringing (clothes, medicine, and lots of music), if perhaps the love of his life was also packing her stethoscope to join Médecins Sans Frontières (not likely but not impossible). I ate silently, then said I was headed to bed. No one seemed to mind.

I took two Tylenol PMs and lay on the memory-foam mattress I'd bought after I sold my first house. I listened to my brother and my boyfriend talk: a sweet lullaby.

"You're still in your clothes," said Gerry, unbuttoning my blouse.

"Is he going to die?" I said. "Do you think he wants to?"

"He didn't *pick* Iraq," said Gerry. "Doctors Without Borders could have sent him to Mexico or Thailand." He put his warm hand on my stomach.

"But they didn't," I said.

Gerry kissed me. "I think a road trip is a great idea."

"You do?"

"He's really jazzed about it."

"I know," I said.

"Besides," said Gerry, "I just checked: they're having a special at Beachview Cabins in Galveston. You can write about it for Cheapskate on the Road."

"I don't even want to know."

"Cheapskate on Holiday?"

I touched my boyfriend's cheek. "You really love this, don't you?" I said.

"Yes," said Gerry.

"I'm glad."

"So you'll attach a tripod and camera to the Dodge?"

While trying to think of a witty protestation, I fell deeply asleep.

2

As a medical student working through his residency, Alex had very little time for messing around on the computer. Nevertheless, he arrived at my house with hours of downloaded music and *This American Life* episodes and the adaptor cords and hookups that would enable his iPod to connect to my car's meager sound system.

"I wish I could come with you guys," said Gerry, pressing firmly on the six-inch suction cups that he believed would hold a large video camera to the car. "But you know, being a webpersonality is a round-the-clock job."

Luckily, being a real estate agent in a terrible economy was not. The Gelthorps had decided to hold off on buying, and a prospective client from Los Angeles had canceled. "Maybe it's time for a career reevaluation," I'd said to Gerry that morning.

"What about massage-therapy school?" he said.

"Honey, somebody's got to have an income."

Gerry rubbed his left shoulder. "I'll go back to programming," he said. "I know I'll have to eventually."

"No, no," I said when what I meant was *I'm so glad you know.*

"A man's got to support his . . ." said Gerry.

"His lady?" I said brightly.

"His family," said Gerry. "I was going to say *his family.*"

I looked at the floor and bit my bottom lip. I couldn't meet Gerry's eyes, couldn't bear to see the frustrated hope in them.

Gerry watched as Alex and I pulled out of the driveway for the three-hour drive to Houston, and then he went back into the shed to begin the day's programming. (He had made us a list of the least expensive gas stations en route, adding a star next to the Austin Valero Mart, where we could get jumbo coffees for the price of small.)

Alex, in the passenger seat, looked jaunty and cheerful, fresh-shaven for the first time in a while. His hair, like our father's, was dark and curly. It was endlessly frustrating to me that while my swarthy coloring and thick locks were the bane of my existence, on Alex they were alluring to women, sexy, irresistible.

It hadn't been easy to grow up as a half-Egyptian girl in Texas. Really dumb classmates thought I had something to do with the Iran hostage crisis—on the day Ronald Reagan was sworn in and the hostages were released, Austin Phillips wrote SAD DAY FOR MUSLIM GIRLS in Magic Marker on my locker—but many more just thought I was unappealing, an outsider. They called me names, asked if my parents worked at the 7-Eleven or were terrorists. All I wanted was to fit in, or at least to be ignored.

Even teachers paused sometimes when discussing the Middle East and turned to me as if expecting I had words of wisdom to share, a Muslim point of view. *My grandparents are Houston Jews!* I wanted to shout, but I stayed quiet and fiddled with my pencil.

It wasn't until I moved into Jester dormitory on the University of Texas campus—a dorm giant enough to have its own zip code—that I could be anonymous, invisible, and free.

"So what have we got?" I said, reaching for Alex's iPod.

"I'll put on 'Road Trip,' " said Alex. "I've got U2, Led Zeppelin, AC/DC, Ozzy . . ." He started the playlist and leaned back in his seat.

"McDonald's!" I said, pointing. "They have two-for-one McSkillets."

"My my," said Alex as I pulled in.

"Don't make fun of me," I said, smiling.

As I drove out of the city, I began to feel my spirits lift. I had always loved the quiet stretch of road that emerged when you left Austin behind. It would be over an hour before the sprawl of Houston began. As we passed a farm, a cow lifted its head to watch us. Alex sang along with the music, his eyes closed.

We entered Brenham, where the Blue Bell creamery was located. "Ice cream before noon?" I said.

Alex considered but shook his head. "On the way home, how about?" he said.

"Sure."

We kept driving, and then Alex spoke. "I think we should talk about Dad," he said. "Just in case . . . in case something happens to me while I'm abroad."

I gripped the steering wheel tightly. "Stop talking," I said.

"What?"

I began to feel light-headed, my heart beating too fast in my chest. "I don't want to hear you saying things like that! What's going to happen to you?"

"Lauren—"

"Stop talking, *please.*"

Alex looked out the window. The blazing summer temperatures had drained most of the color from the landscape; the passing shrubbery was wilting in shades of yellow and brown. In midmorning, the sun was piercingly bright and oppressive, the heat shimmering above the road in waves. Despite the car's desperate hiss of air-conditioning, my thighs stuck to the vinyl seat, hot and damp.

We listened to U2's "I Still Haven't Found What I'm Looking For." Finally, Alex said, "I just need . . . I need to . . . there are some things you should know."

"Not listening," I said.

"Lauren, please."

"What does a panic attack feel like, by the way?" I said. Alex described the symptoms, and I nodded. "That's what's going on," I said. "I'm definitely having a panic attack."

"Pull over," said Alex.

I took the next turnoff, stopping the car a few yards down a dirt road. "I'm having a heart attack," I said. "And a panic attack. At the same time."

"Jesus," said Alex, getting out of the car and coming around to my side. "Put your head down. Has this happened to you before?"

I moved into the passenger seat and put my head between my knees. "Once, in college," I said. "Before the a cappella singing-group audition. Which I bombed. I shouldn't have tried to sing Billie Holiday. That was the end of my singing career."

"Shhh," said Alex, settling into the driver's seat.

"I'm dying," I said. "Honestly, I feel like I'm going to pass out."

"You need a therapist. Or Valium. Maybe both."

"Don't leave me," I said.

"Jesus Christ!" said Alex. He put the car into gear roughly, pulled a tight U-turn, and hit the gas. As we barreled onto the road, we listened to the sad strains of Joshua Redman's saxophone. "I love you," said Alex. "I'm always here for you, Lauren, but I have to live my own life, too, you know?"

I laid my head back and remembered hiding in the tree house after the police had taken our father away. After what seemed like hours, an officer had climbed the ladder to tell us we were going to the Feldmans' for a while.

Kevin and Jayna Feldman were still in their pajamas, eating Pop-Tarts and watching *Saved by the Bell*. Their living room was enormous, carpeted wall-to-wall with blue shag. Ronnie Feldman had hooked the television up to speakers, and I remember the loud sitcom and a strawberry Pop-Tart, a cozy place on the leather sectional, laughing at nerdy Screech. I was a nerd myself at Holt Elementary. My looks differentiated me from the cool fifth-grade girls, who all had hair as straight and thin as silk—hair like my mother's.

The night before she died, my mother had promised to take me to the Stamford mall. She couldn't stand the mall, preferring to order from catalogs, but I had been anticipating the shopping trip all week. My mother's salary had to support our whole family, but she indulged me. She must have known that expensive clothes and lip gloss helped me feel confident. After a bit of shopping, we usually ate cheeseburgers at Friendly's, my mother happily ordering the fried mozzarella sticks, never flinching when I ate heartily, joining right in with me, saying, "Come on, lovebug, just a little sweet something," when the waitress brought the dessert menu.

I was eight—too old to hold my mother's hand, to love her so much, but I did it anyway. By the time I was an angry teenager, there were only my grandparents, Merilee and Morton, to rebel against, and instead of fighting back, they sent me to boarding school in Austin with a trunk full of nylon sweaters and name tags that read LAUREN M, as if I could hide my last name, and my history, so easily.

I loved my grandparents, and I was thankful for them. But I never felt as if they wanted me around, not really. My grandparents were worn out and sad. They took care of me perfunctorily, as if I were an endless to-do list. I had clothes, check. I had food. I even had a psychiatrist for a year, but I refused to talk about my mother, and eventually, Alex and I convinced our grandparents that we were fine.

Maybe we were fine. Alex had believed from the start that my father was innocent. As appealing as this idea was, my logical mind couldn't quite believe it. I didn't remember what I had seen in my parents' bedroom, but a terror stayed with me—it had been something horrific. They fought often and wildly; it was not impossible that my father had simply gone too far. My grandparents told us with drawn faces and in sober tones that our father was not a bad man, but he had done a very bad thing and would spend the rest of his life in jail. There was no evidence of a break-in. My father had no alibi. The facts just added up, for me.

Alex and I talked about that night once in a while, but I grew impatient with his exceedingly elaborate fantasies, his plans to prove our father's innocence. I hated Alex's weak spot—his belief in our father. I needed for Alex to be the strong one, the one who took care of me. He was the only other person in the world who understood my strange orphanhood. Only Alex and I knew how fragile the world really was.

Over the years, I refined my fake story to effectively erase my father from the picture. My parents were killed in a plane crash, I told friends. Throughout boarding school and into my freshman year of college, I checked my mail infrequently and tossed any letters from my father into the trash.

Alex, who wrote to Izaan regularly, even visiting once when Morton agreed to accompany him to New York, told me he had asked our father to keep copies of all the letters he sent to me. "Mark my words," he said (Alex was prone to such professorial statements; he had a doctor's authority before he even graduated from high school), "you're going to want to read them someday."

It was during my senior year at UT when I finally reached the end of my rope with Alex. He had arrived with some Harvard buddies during a Tri Delt mixer, charming all my friends with his blather and homegrown weed. After spending the night with the daughter of a Dallas judge, Alex took me out for pancakes and suggested we spend spring break in New York. We could go to some awesome parties, he argued, and then "hoof it upstate."

Something broke in me. "He killed her," I said, startling the waitress, who slid our plates to the table quickly and did not return even after we emptied our coffee mugs. "He's not . . . a good person."

"He didn't do it," said Alex.

Sadness curdled into fury, and I put down my fork and knife. They were coated with syrup from cutting my pancakes into shreds. "I can't even look at you," I said. "You're so stupid. You know as well as I do what happened, you stupid fuck."

"I was there," said Alex.

"But you didn't see anything!"

"No, I didn't. Did you?"

I bit my lip. "I don't remember . . ." I said. I had not even told

Alex about my dream, about swimming into my parents' bedroom in the middle of the night.

"Lauren, I know him. I'm telling you, he didn't do it. He couldn't have done it," said Alex.

"Oh, really?" I said, sounding a bit unhinged even to myself. "You know what an asshole he could be! He was angry about those fucking shoes from Dr. Schwickrath, I bet." I held my breath, having finally voiced my theory, which I had never mentioned to anyone before.

"He isn't capable of it," said Alex, sounding rehearsed. He seemed not to have heard my idea, or perhaps he had chosen to ignore it. "I know it, Lauren. I know him."

"Then who killed her?" I asked.

Alex didn't answer, just looked at me pleadingly. "Who the hell did it?" I said, too loud. A football player was sitting at the next table with his parents, all of them staring, and I was both enraged and humiliated. I bent close to my brother and whispered, "I never want to see you again." Then I left the International House of Pancakes, crying all the way back to my room at the sorority, telling my roommate I was hungover to explain why I spent the rest of the day in bed.

Alex graduated from Harvard and sent blank postcards as he traveled from Europe to India to Africa. We did not speak for three months.

Remembering the sadness of the time without him, the move to Houston with the wrong boyfriend, the small room on West Campus—I had been so forlorn I finally bought a turtle just to have something to say *good night* to—I put my hand on my brother's shoulder.

"I'm sorry," I said. "I love you."

Alex set his jaw and looked at the road. I sighed. He didn't want to believe it, but the facts told the truth: our father had hit our mother in the head with a glass decanter, cracking her skull. He had left her to die on the bedroom floor. It was a crime (the prosecution said) of passion. It was what could happen if you were a certain type of person, and you fell too much in love.

3

Gramma was disappearing. Pops, my grandfather, had been gone for seven years, and it was as if Gramma just wasn't interested in a world without him. She was with us bodily, but she often wore a preoccupied expression, as if she were listening to terribly important things happening just outside our range of hearing. She had been diagnosed with Alzheimer's, but it seemed to me like Gramma was living in a better time, a time when she was a young mother with her life ahead of her. To live there fully, I guess, Gramma had to abandon the present day. She was leaving us slowly, maybe to make up for my mother's abrupt departure. I missed her.

After the three-hour drive, Alex parked at Cypress Grove Retirement Village. When I climbed out of the car, the heat flattened me immediately. In Houston, the humidity made summer an absolute hell. If you could help it, you didn't go outside at all. The beach would be sweltering and miserable. Worse, oil residue in the water turned into tar balls that stuck to your skin after swimming. Most hotels had tar-removal wipes next to the little shampoos and lotions, and I'd known girls in high school who took two bathing suits to the beach: one for swimming and a clean one for sunbathing.

That aside, I did love the Shrimp Shack. We had been to Galveston a handful of times during our childhood, and Alex and I had always begged for dinner at the Shrimp Shack, followed by ice cream cones on the beach.

Alex was searching around in the trunk of the car. "What are you doing?" I asked. I was agitated—though I loved Gramma, it was so hard when she didn't recognize me or—worse—thought I was my mother. I looked nothing like Mom, nothing at all.

"Here it is," said Alex. He stood, holding a dented Whitman's sampler. "She loves chocolate."

I felt guilty that I hadn't thought to bring something for Gramma, too. "You're so nice," I said.

Alex shoved my shoulder. "Move along," he said.

Gramma was in her room, a generous single with windows overlooking the man-made water feature that partially blocked the view of a Best Buy next door. Alex knocked and called, "Where's my beautiful grandmother?"

She looked up from her *Cosmopolitan* magazine, her face growing animated. "Hello!" she said brightly.

"We brought you some chocolates," said Alex, handing her the box. I stood in the doorway, trying not to look as ill at ease as I felt. My grandmother's white hair had been recently set, and she wore a pink dress I had always admired. I remembered her arriving at my choir concert in the dress, a dozen years ago.

"Well, how lovely!" said Gramma. She opened the box and selected a truffle.

"Are you having a nice day?" I said, too loudly.

"We have got to water the azaleas," she said, taking a dainty bite of her truffle. "I *told* your father."

My mouth was dry, and I couldn't think of anything to say.

"Do you mind if we sit and visit for a bit?" said Alex. He acted so normal, relaxing into a chair, smiling at Gramma.

"Not for too long," said Gramma. "But that's fine, young man." She touched a gold circle pin on her dress.

"I like your pin," I boomed.

"You'll get it someday, Jordan," she said. "Never you mind."

"I'm not Jordan," I said. "I'm your granddaughter. I'm Lauren."

"You're growing up so fast," said Gramma. "You'll be going to prom before you know it."

Alex wheeled his chair close to our grandmother, putting his hand on her hand. He sat quietly, patiently, though my stomach twisted with anxiety. Gramma's room was filled with pictures of my mother. On the bedside table was a photo of Mom holding me as a newborn, gazing into my crimson face.

Alex talked with Gramma for a while about his trip to Iraq. He promised to write. She listened with an expression of polite bewilderment. He told Gramma that he thought I should marry Gerry, as if I weren't even in the room. "She's afraid to be happy," said Alex.

"I wholeheartedly agree," said Gramma, nodding. She offered the box of chocolates to Alex. He took a fat one with nuts.

"I'm sitting right here," I said, reaching for the chocolate-covered cherry.

"Of course you are," said Gramma, swatting my hand away.

"I'm sorry," I said.

"You can have the white chocolate," said Gramma. "I know those are your favorite."

"No," I said. "Those were my mom's favorite. I like the cherry."

"Quite a mouth on her," said Gramma to Alex. She raised the area where her eyebrows had been. What could I do but laugh?

"I love you, Gramma," I said.

"And I love you," she answered. "What a lovely coincidence!"

When the sun had dipped below the Best Buy, Alex gestured to his watch. We were still an hour from Galveston and wanted to have our feet in the sand by nightfall. I nodded and stood. When I kissed Gramma goodbye, she reached up to cup the back of my head. "My baby," she said into my hair. "My baby girl."

Galveston Island had once been a major shipping port city, as grand as New Orleans. It had the first opera house in Texas, and the first telephone. In 1900 the island was decimated by a hurricane, and although many of the elegant historical buildings were rebuilt, the city never really recovered. Still, the faded grandeur of the historic district and the seedier beer joints both held allure for me. As a child, I believed there were ghosts in Galveston, and I enjoyed walking down the tree-lined streets, pretending that the sounds of the waves were ghostly murmurs.

Beachview Motel was nowhere near the historic district. It was cheap, but there was no beach view. Alex pulled into a parking space at the mauve-colored building and said, "Well, this sucks."

"I was hoping for a bit more ambiance," I said. "Or even a bit *of* ambiance."

"Oh, look," said Alex. "Here comes a truck."

We watched as a Toyota Tundra with oversize wheels pulled into the lot. A man in overalls—just overalls, no shirt underneath—climbed out, followed by two friends holding cases of beer.

"Ah, Galveston." Alex started the car again. "We can find something else," he said. "I have faith."

We drove to the Shrimp Shack on the seawall, claiming a wooden table under a skeleton wearing a pirate hat. When the waitress brought our beers, Alex said, "Excuse me? Can you recommend somewhere to stay in town? Or out of town?"

The girl evaluated us, biting her lip. "What sort of place are you looking for?" she asked.

"A cottage, maybe?" I said.

"My uncle has a bunkhouse," said the girl. "He calls it the Starry Night. It's on the bay side, but it's real romantic."

"We're not looking for romance," I said, grimacing at Alex.

"Whatevs," said the girl. "Do you want me to call him?"

"That sounds great," said Alex. The girl nodded and walked off. "Whatevs," said Alex.

"I'm so old," I said.

"We're not old. Just middle-aged."

The bunkhouse was available for seventy dollars cash, and after we ate platters of shrimp, finishing up with key lime pie, the waitress took off her apron and told us to follow her car. She smoked as she drove along the seawall, her arm dangling out the window. We headed out of town for about fifteen minutes, passing brand-new mansions on the water next to ruined homes that had never been rebuilt after Hurricanes Katrina and Ike. We turned off the pavement and bumped along an uneven stretch of sandy road, reaching a cottage. The waitress parked and let us inside, showing us the bunk beds and the small kitchen. When she left, she said, "Hope you like cats."

"I don't really like cats," I said to Alex.

"I do." He was in high spirits. "I like cats. Bring them on."

There were two wrought-iron chairs outside the cabin, and Alex sat in one and pulled a flask out of his backpack. I settled into the other chair and watched the sky. It was cooler now that the sun had set. "It's so quiet," I said.

"I love it," said Alex.

"I guess I'm more a city girl at the end of the day."

"You used to love camping when we were little, remember?"

"Until that night at Black Bear," I said.

Alex exhaled. "Here we go."

"It was terrible," I said. When I was six or seven, our parents had taken us to the Black Bear campground in upstate New York. We'd gotten a late start, as our mother hadn't been able to leave the hospital until afternoon. By the time we reached Black Bear, it was the dead of night, and the only campsite left was a fifteen-minute walk through the woods. Our father was angry but couldn't say anything—after all, our mother was the only one with a paying job. This was a common strain, exacerbated by our mother's drinking wine on the drive up, and our father smoking in the car, which we all hated. We were silent during the hike to the campsite, nursing our disgruntlements.

When we reached the site, my parents began to argue. I can't remember what the fight was about, but it dragged on. Alex and I set up the tent and crawled inside with flashlights and books.

My father's voice rose in volume. I pushed the nylon tent flap aside and peeked out. I saw my father shove my mother. She fell hard and cried for a while. My father stormed off in the direction of the car. A long time passed, and then my mother said, "Alex?"

"Mom?"

"I think my ankle's broken."

We crept out of the tent and found our mother, her face tear-streaked. "I'll carry you, Mom," said Alex.

"Sweetheart," she said, "just go get your dad. Little One will stay with me." I remember feeling nervous as Alex went down the path, but also happy that my mother had chosen me for company. I told her a long story about my new friend Julie and Julie's pet snake, both to keep her mind off her ankle and because I had a captive audience. She stroked my hair. Leaves whispered in the trees above us, and the air smelled fresh and damp, like moss.

My mother must have been in terrible pain, but she said, "Do you want a snake?"

"No," I said. "I want a turtle."

"A turtle! Really? I'll have to remember that on your next birthday, Little One." She looked at me with such love that I felt like a pet myself. Maybe what I wanted, I remember thinking, was not to *have* a pet but to *be* a pet. Alex returned with our father, who carried our mother to the car. All the anger was gone, and he waited on her for weeks while she healed.

"It *was* terrible," Alex agreed now.

"I know he didn't mean to break her ankle," I said. Alex took a sip of his whiskey, watching the ground. "I know," I went on. "There's a big difference between pushing someone and . . ."

He raised his chin to meet my gaze.

"What does he say?" I asked. "In the letters, what does he say?"

"Why don't you read one," said Alex. He drank again. "He says he loves us."

"What's it like?"

"What? The prison?"

I nodded.

"All of a sudden you want to talk about this?" asked Alex. I had refused to discuss my father for years. As Alex investigated every avenue, trying to find a way to prove our father's innocence, I grew more and more resistant to discussion. The past was over. I wanted to hope for something better and felt only anxiety at the prospect of sifting through old memories. I loved my father. I hated my father. I was scared of my father and what he had done.

"I don't know," I said.

"It's really cold. He's in solitary, he's got lots of books. A mattress, a toilet . . . you can imagine what a cell looks like." We were quiet, and then Alex said, "Can I talk about him? There's more." His voice was drowned out by the sound of my blood pumping in my ears. I gasped for air. "What the hell is the matter with you?" said Alex.

"I can't breathe," I managed.

"It's another panic attack," said Alex. "Put your head down." He touched my hair with his fingers. "It's okay."

"I really don't feel well," I said. "Maybe there *is* something wrong, Alex!"

"Shhhh," he said.

"Okay," I said. When I rested my head on my knees, I could breathe more easily.

"I met someone," said Alex after a few minutes. "Her name is Suzy."

"Hey, that's great," I said. Alex was right: if I focused on something other than my body, the terror receded and my heart stopped its wild thudding.

"We've been together a few weeks," said Alex. "But last night she told me it was over. The whole Iraq thing—she's just not up for it."

"Alex . . ."

"What if I never find her?" said Alex. "Listen to me: Mr. Melodramatic. But really, what if I don't? I'm tired of watching *Without a Trace* by myself."

"That *is* pathetic."

"On Halloween," said Alex, "I was biking through Hyde Park, and there were all these parents pushing strollers. All these kids in costume, monkeys and bumblebees. And the light was so nice. Dusk, whatever you call it."

"Hey." I took his hand. "You'll find her. You will." I tried to figure out how to ask my brother why he was going to Iraq. A suicide mission? Some misplaced sense that he should sacrifice himself? I said, "Alex . . ."

"I want my life to mean something," said Alex. "That's why. I didn't ask for Iraq, but I did ask Doctors Without Borders for something to . . . to do with myself. I don't know how to explain it."

"No, I mean . . . that does make sense, I guess."

"I know you don't feel the same way," said Alex. "Maybe nobody does. Suzy, she . . . she didn't understand why I can't stop thinking about . . . what the point is. Why I'm here. And normal people, I guess, they don't think this way. But I don't want to stop being myself. I'm proud of wanting to do something amazing, something important with my life."

"So what I'm doing—"

"That's not what I'm saying. And while we're on the subject—"

"What?" I said sharply.

"Don't you love Gerry?" asked Alex.

"We're not talking about me," I said.

"Maybe we should," said Alex.

"No, thanks," I said.

We sat quietly then, which was something I never did with

Gerry, feeling that we should be communicating at all times lest we become one of those couples who never speak. Frankly, it was a pleasure to be with my brother. I didn't have to worry about him falling out of love with me or loving me so much it could lead to misery. Alex was the only person who understood exactly how I felt, what it was like to grow up without parents.

We never even got our own room at Mort and Merilee's—the guest room (furnished with mahogany furniture and tasseled curtains) was where we'd sleep whenever we came back to Houston on school vacations. Alex and I never had a place that belonged to us, not after Ocean Avenue.

"Lauren," said Alex. "I just want you to know some things."

"Look at these stars," I said.

"The night of the murder—"

"What a night sky," I said.

"It's different this time. Lauren, if you look in the files—"

"Oh my God!" I cried, standing up. For years, my brother had been looking through the case files, trying to solve a mystery that, in my estimation, did not exist. I was so tired of Alex's attempts to rewrite fact.

"We both know what happened," I said, "and sometimes I feel like that's the only thing I *do* know. Mom was—"

"Lauren, please listen," said Alex desperately.

"Mom was so wonderful," I said. "Let me remember her the way I want to. I don't have a dad. I've made peace with that. I've gone on with my life."

"Your life," said Alex scornfully.

I thought about Gerry, our house, and our dog. I didn't want to look into the shadowy places—the night of the murder, the way love could turn on you. "How can I marry him?" I said. "We both know what can happen, Alex. How it can all just . . ." I opened my fingers as if releasing a bird, then dropped them to my lap. "How it can all just go wrong."

"You have to believe in something," said Alex.

"Why?"

Alex wouldn't meet my gaze. After a minute, he reached out and took my hand. I watched the campfire. We were high on a ridge, and somewhere beyond us was the sea.

"Okay," I said. "Okay. Say what you want to. Go ahead."

Alex swallowed. He squeezed my fingers too hard as he spoke, as though I would escape if given the chance. "In the case files," he said, speaking quickly, maybe afraid I'd interrupt him, "the detective wrote about household items that were found at the scene of the crime. In other words, they were found in Mom and Dad's room. I got him to send me a list of the items. One was an earring, a jade earring."

"Jesus Christ," I murmured.

"Lauren, please. I'm just asking you to hear me out."

"Sorry," I said. "A mysterious jade earring. Go on."

"Why do you have to be so difficult?" said Alex angrily. "I'm just wondering, Lauren. Why can't you shut up for once?"

I pulled my hand away, made fists in my lap. "It's just . . ." I said. "It's ridiculous, Alex! An earring? She could have borrowed earrings. Someone could have given them to her—a patient, a friend—who knows?"

Alex pressed his lips together. He breathed out through his nose, then spoke in a measured tone. "Lauren, I need you to listen. For me, okay?"

I nodded. "Okay."

"So I didn't remember Mom having any fancy things. I didn't want to get Dad's hopes up, so I didn't tell him anything, but I did ask him if Mom had any expensive jewelry, and he said no, just her engagement diamond. The earring was an antique. I got the police to send it to me, and then I traced its origins. It was bought at Harry Winston in 1968, then sent to a woman named Pauline Hall. They even had her address."

I felt a twinge of jealousy at the thought of Alex and our father chatting on the phone. It wasn't that I didn't *want* a father—I did. But I had loved him so fully, a girl's love, and he had betrayed us all. I felt a familiar rush of anger and need; they were bound together for me. So as not to be subsumed, I shoved the surging back. In my mind, I pictured a heavy metal door. I closed it with all my strength and tried to listen to Alex.

"I made a list of people named Pauline Hall," said Alex. "In New York and around New York. And I . . . I called them. I called them all."

"Oh, Alex," I said.

"Please *be quiet,*" he said. He stood, facing away from me.

"I'm sorry," I said.

Alex didn't say anything. "So that's it," he said. He turned back around, his eyes burning. He crossed his arms over his chest. "A dead end, okay? You were right. I just wanted you to know."

"Is that all?" I said.

"That's all," said Alex. Unburdened, he was my brother again: wistful and sad, with really good posture.

"What do you want me to do about all this?" I said.

"I just wanted you to hear me," said Alex. "I just wanted you to know."

That night I lay awake with the name Pauline Hall spinning in my head. My heart was beating too fast. I thought I could hold it together but was scared I could not. I climbed from the bunk and took three Tylenol PM tablets. In time, I fell asleep.

4

Alex's apartment, one half of a duplex, was right underneath Interstate 35. When he had parties, you could sit outside at his splintered picnic table and watch the lights of cars flying by overhead like spaceships. Alex played sad jazz music or heavy metal from his computer speakers and stood by his barbecue, poking meat with giant tongs, usually wearing his favorite yellow T-shirt, which read GOOD TIMES.

It was completely dark on the morning I picked up Alex to take him to the airport. Though it was early September, it was clammy and warm, with no hint of fall, which didn't arrive in Austin until late October. Around Halloween, the weather shifted abruptly from scorching to tepid, then in December to vaguely chilly. January held a few thirty-degree days during which people pulled out parkas and even fur hats, and by March it was hot again. Once every few years it snowed for twenty minutes to an hour, and people crashed their cars or stayed home from work and school to marvel. I had never seen a snowman in Austin.

"Hey," said Alex when he opened his front door.

"Hey," I said.

Alex picked up his duffel. It was a flowered bag; Alex had bought it for cheap from REI online. It said HANNAH on the side, and sometimes I wondered about the woman who had ordered it and then changed her mind. I saw her as a stewardess from Honolulu, a woman who had finally admitted a wheelie bag was more damn practical.

Alex seemed thin in his worn jeans and black cardigan sweater with a white button-down shirt underneath. He was good-looking in an unkempt way—you wouldn't guess he was a medical doctor in his Converse sneakers. He looked more like an out-of-work actor or a philosophy graduate student. But Alex stood with his shoulders back and had a loping gait that told the world he was someone important despite his scruffy getup.

I didn't turn down the radio; it was *Love Songs for the Lonely,* my favorite show. On the drive to Alex's apartment, the husband of an elderly woman had dedicated Whitney Houston's "I Will Always Love You" to his wife. "She's sitting right here with me now," he had told the DJ, "and she's as beautiful as the day I met her at the Dairy Queen on Hamilton Boulevard." The radio show was syndicated, but it didn't really matter in what city (or town) Hamilton Boulevard was located. At least not to me.

"I've got to say, I'm excited," said Alex, settling next to me.

"How nice," I said, putting the car in gear. Whitney Houston ran out of steam, and the DJ (her name was Mary Helen) began talking to a high school freshman who had been dumped by a baseball player. "My heart hurts for you," said Mary Helen, "but you have so much happy ahead, honey, and this is just God getting you ready for your real true love." Mary Helen cued up "Like a Virgin," which seemed an odd choice.

"What a load of crap," said Alex, snorting.

"I love this show," I said.

"I find that really strange."

"What?"

"You are the least romantic person in America," said Alex.

I felt a headache gathering behind my eyes. "That isn't true."

"Forget I said anything."

I didn't answer, but I knew Alex was wrong. I was filled with desire. I read romantic novels. I watched Lifetime television. I wanted love so badly it made me feel sick sometimes, scraped out. But I knew the cost.

The sky lightened as we drove south on Airport Boulevard. "I'll be honest with you," I said. "I feel like maybe you won't come home."

"Hey." Alex put his hand on my knee. "Shhh," he said, which was what he always said when he wanted me to calm down. *Shhh* also meant that he would protect me.

"Even if you marry a beautiful Iraqi," I said, "come home and tell me in person."

"I promise."

"Or a TV reporter. Christiane Amanpour. Is she married?"

"I don't know."

"I think she is. But to tell you the truth, Alex, I could see it. She's similarly dour."

"I am not dour!" He shook his head, smiling. He smelled so familiar—that dirty-sock funk had been the same since we'd shared the guest room at our grandparents' Houston house.

"Alex," I said, "what happened to all our stuff?"

"What stuff?"

"From the house on Ocean Avenue."

"It's in a storage locker. I guess if Dad ever gets out, he'll want some of it."

I ignored the bait about my father, who was never getting out, as we both knew. "Where?" I said. "Where's it in storage?"

"White Plains."

"How do you know this?" I said.

"I'm paying for it," said Alex.

"Are you kidding me?"

"Gramma and Pops told me to clear it out years ago," said Alex. "I didn't. I don't know why. I haven't been there. I just called and had them send the bill to me."

"I only have that one picture of her," I said.

He knew what I was talking about because he had the same photograph: our mother sitting on the living room couch, a toddler me on her lap, a boy-size Alex to her right. She was reading to us, a Richard Scarry book, *Busy, Busy Town.* Maybe that book was in a cardboard box, too, somewhere in White Plains.

"Where's the key?" I said.

"Don't go there without me," said Alex.

"Why not?"

"Why not? You'd freak out! And you were too young when everything was put in there. You won't know what's important and what can be tossed."

"When you come home," I said.

"Right," said Alex. "When I come home."

Austin-Bergstrom Airport was bustling with early-morning commuters. I turned in to the parking garage, and Alex said, "It's expensive to park. You can just drop me off," and I said, "Shhh."

I carried one strap of Alex's girlie duffel bag, and he carried the other. "Did you pack any books?" I asked.

"Blue Highways," said Alex.

"I loved that in college," I said. "This is the ultimate blue highway, I guess."

"I guess," said Alex.

"Or blue *air*way," I said.

"Hm," said Alex, unimpressed, or maybe not listening.

I stood with my hands on my hips as Alex checked in, showing his new passport to the woman behind the counter. I had gone with him to Kinko's for photographs, and had applied for my first passport as well, in case Alex wanted—or needed—me to visit. I didn't want to go to Iraq. I didn't want my brother to go to Iraq. My general feeling about Iraq was: leave them the hell alone.

We walked across shiny floors, past a Swatch shop, a Which Wich? sandwich shop, a Waldenbooks. I noticed a woman with a baby staring at us. Though it had been ten fucking years since the attacks, our coloring still earned us nervous glances at the airport. I wanted to meet the mother's gaze with defiance but turned away, peering into the window of the bookstore.

"What are you going to read on the plane?" I said. "Let me buy you another book."

Alex looked at his watch. "Okay," he said.

I scanned the best sellers, trying to figure out what might bring Alex comfort, or even better, a story that would make him think twice about leaving. What book, I wondered, would make him get off the plane, meet a nice woman who could be my friend and his wife, and encourage him to buy the 3/2 for sale down the street from us? I could even broker the deal and give him the commission for some new clothes.

"Lauren, I should go," said Alex.

"Wait—just one—" I grabbed *For Whom the Bell Tolls* off the shelf. "Hemingway," I said, moving to the register. "You can't go wrong with Hemingway!" I paid and brandished the plastic bag.

"Thanks," he said.

"Let me . . ." I said. I sat on an airport bench and rummaged in my purse for a pen. I found a ballpoint and wrote, *Dear Alex,* on the title page. Then I wrote *Love, Lauren.* I added the date. I stared at the blank inch I had left for something careful, something meaningful, some poetry.

"I'll come home for your wedding," said Alex.

"Shut up," I said.

"Seriously. He's going to stop trying eventually."

"What are you talking about?"

"You know what I'm talking about," said Alex.

I glared at him. Then I admitted, "You're right. I do."

"Say it to Gerry," said Alex, "not to me."

We were still for a moment. I looked back at the book but couldn't think of anything to write. "It's okay," Alex said finally. "I've really got to go."

I stared at my message: *Dear Alex, Love, Lauren, 9/08/10.* Starting to cry, I wrote, *Goodbye.*

Alex took the book and pulled me into his arms. We hugged for a minute, and then Alex broke free. "Here," he said. He took a small object from his pocket. "It's the earring. I don't want it anymore."

"What do I want with one damn earring?" I said.

"What do *I* want with one damn earring?" said Alex.

With that, he kissed me on the forehead and walked toward security. The earring was cold in my hand.

5

The listing was a 2/1 on Texas Avenue. White picket fence, yard that needed landscaping, minimal termite damage. My clients, a day-care worker and her musician boyfriend, were waiting for me, their Vespas parked side by side in the gravel drive. I waved gaily as I pulled to the curb.

"Hey, Lauren," said Mitch, touching the top of his hipster fedora.

"Hello, hello!" I said, smiling hard. Liz was slim with red hair. On her jeans she had small handprints in green and yellow paint.

"I like it," said Liz. "I like the window boxes."

"This is a great street," I said. "Close to campus, but more young families than students."

"Let's go in," said Mitch. "Lead the way, lady."

I smoothed my Ann Taylor pantsuit. I was too old to be called *lady* by some skinny drummer, but I knew when to keep my mouth shut. "Follow me," I said, heading up the cement walkway. I found the lockbox, entered my Realtor code, and removed the key.

"There's a big crack in the foundation," said Liz, pointing.

"Interesting," I said. "These old houses . . ." I couldn't really think of what to say, so I trailed off.

"These old houses *what*?" said Liz.

I cleared my throat. "Some have foundation problems. Some have charm. Some, Liz, have both. Foundations can be fixed."

"Oh, okay," said Liz, taking Mitch's hand and stepping across the threshold.

"The fireplace works," I said. "Nice light here in the living room." I consulted my cheat sheet. "Built in 1942. Kitchen renovated last year."

Mitch looked around, nodding. He was so thin it made me wince. Liz made her way through the house. It was empty and smelled a bit like mold. If the homeowners were my clients, I would have put a simmering pan of apple cider on the stove.

"Whoa!" said Liz. We followed her voice and found her in a top-of-the-line kitchen. Stainless-steel fixtures, Corian countertops, stained concrete floor. "This is amazing," she said. "Look, hon, if I'm washing dishes, I can see the trees!" She mimed scrubbing a pot, gazing at the large backyard. Mitch stood behind her and put his arms around her waist. She leaned in to him. "It's wonderful," she said.

Mitch kissed the top of her head.

Out of nowhere, I felt a panic attack coming on. "I'll be right back," I said. "I'll leave you two lovebirds." I walked quickly, finding a bathroom off the master and slipping in, shutting and locking the door. In the mirror, my face was very pale. I sat down and put my head between my knees. I concentrated on my breathing.

"Lauren?" said Mitch. He was knocking, hard.

"Okay," I said, standing and brushing dust off my pants. "I'm fine. There's an oversize tub. Chrome-plated faucets!"

"You've been in the bathroom for, like, a half hour," called Liz. "Um, I've got to get back to work."

"Right, right," I said. I unlocked the bathroom door and opened it. I smiled as brightly as I could. "So, looks like we've got some Kohler bathroom fixtures."

"Have you been crying?" said Mitch.

"No," I said. But when I touched my face, it was wet.

"Thanks for showing us the house," said Liz. She was holding Mitch's hand. "We'll, um, we'll be in touch."

"Great!" I said. "Awesome." I followed them out of the house and returned the key to the lockbox. I waved as they made their way down the street. Then I called Gerry.

"I am going crazy," I said when he answered.

"What?" said Gerry. "Where are you?"

"Texas Avenue and Liberty Street," I said. "I'm having a heart—or a panic—attack. Maybe both." But just being on the phone with Gerry made me feel calmer.

"It's okay, honey," said Gerry. "I love you. Do you want me to come get you?"

I lay down on the lawn underneath a coffee tree. "I'm sober, I swear," I said. "The sky is very bright."

"Good God," said Gerry, laughing.

"I'm scared, honey," I said.

After a while, I heard a car pull up. When I opened my eyes, Gerry was standing above me, his sweet face blocking the sun. "Get up from underneath that tree," he said.

"Or maybe you should join me," I said.

Gerry lay down. I rolled on my side and rested my head on his shoulder. "What happened?" he said.

"I don't know," I said. "I kind of blacked out."

"Are you all right now?"

"I guess," I said. "But I'd like to stay here awhile, if that's okay with you."

"It's a Wednesday afternoon," said Gerry. "I think this is the perfect place to be."

I lay back and he touched his head to mine. We watched the blue, blue sky.

"I'm going to therapy," I said. "I'll fix this. My brain, I mean."

"This is a very comfortable lawn," commented Gerry. His lips were close to my ear, and his words made me turn and kiss him.

"Do you think you'll still love me when I'm not crazy?" I said.

"Yes," said Gerry.

6

I went on the Blue Cross Blue Shield website and found a list of therapists in Austin. Because she was located down the street from Texas French Bread, which had great coffee, I called to make an appointment with Jane Stafford, MA, LPC. On her answering machine, Jane's voice was warm. She sounded like my college friend Amy's mother, who used to send packages of homemade chocolate-chip cookies. As I left a message, I remembered how Amy was always worried about her weight so gave the treats to me. I used to nibble while I studied, cookies and Diet Coke.

While I waited for Jane to call back, I Google-searched my symptoms. According to WebMD.com, it seemed I might have OCD, ADD, or generalized anxiety disorder. Perhaps it could be disassociation.

Jane called back, and I told her about my self-diagnosis. "Are you free next Wednesday, September twenty-fourth, four P.M.?" she asked.

"Um," I said, "yes, yes, sure."

"I look forward to meeting you, Lauren," she said.

"Me, too," I said. Then I hung up and wondered why I had said *Me, too,* and what Jane Stafford would make of that.

Gerry finished his latest podcast an hour later, and when he came inside, I told him about my appointment. He gave me a hug and then said, "Put on your flip-flops. Two-for-one kebab night at Fatoosh."

7

With Alex in Iraq, time passed slowly. Though he had been gone only two weeks by the time I first met Jane Stafford, it seemed much longer. I thought of him all the time and read his daily emails over and over. He was happy and tired, was the gist of them.

Iraq, wrote Alex, *is both boring and brutal. People are on edge, waiting for more bad news. But they're living their lives anyway—what else can they do? A boy came in today with a broken elbow, but his injury had nothing to do with war. He'd been playing soccer on pavement and had taken a dive to keep the ball out of the goal. His mother brought me a syrupy dessert thing to thank me for taking care of him. I told him about how we sign casts in the U.S., but I couldn't find a marker to show him. Maybe can you send one, and some stickers or something? And Double Stuf Oreos?*

Jane's office was in a house. Her own house? There was no way to know. There was a taxi parked on the street in front. Was a taxi driver in therapy? Did someone take a taxi *to* therapy? (A

DUI?) Again, there was no way to know. I parked behind the cab. I began to get a light-headed, hysterical feeling. *Keep it together,* I told myself.

On the front door was a printed sign reading NO SOLICITATIONS. I was glad of this, because a Jehovah's Witness knocking at the door while I confided my innermost feelings was something I did not need. What *did* I need?

I was wearing my work clothes. I wanted Jane Stafford to know that I was a professional. Coolly, I estimated her home office/home to be worth about 300K. It was a one-story ranch with ugly siding but a nice yard, room for a pool. I stopped before entering, noting that you could hear MoPac Highway. That would knock 10K off the price, give or take. Some people didn't care about highway noise, but some people did.

I opened the door. A sparse living room with a pale blue couch led to a hallway. I sat on the couch and picked up an old *Glamour.* I didn't open the magazine, just tried to look relaxed and waited. In fact, I did feel a bit relaxed. What could possibly happen to me here? I felt secure, if a bit loopy, in this 3/2 (I guessed) ranch with original hardwood flooring.

After a few moments, I heard a door open and the click of footsteps coming toward me. Hurriedly, I opened the *Glamour* and shifted my gaze, trying to seem engrossed. I appeared to be in the middle of an article about faux-fur shoes.

"Lauren?"

I looked up into the brown eyes of Jane Stafford, who, despite her WASPy name, was Asian. I stood.

"I'm Jane Stafford," she said, holding out her hand. She was wearing a cream-colored sweater and dark pants.

"I'm Lauren," I said stupidly.

"Please," said Jane, turning and walking back down the hallway. She opened the door to a small room with a sound machine whirring in the corner. She sat down in a chair and gestured to a couch. I sat on the couch, which seemed to be elongated; my feet dangled. I felt like Alice in Wonderland or Lily Tomlin in that big chair. I crossed my hands in my lap and swallowed.

Jane said nothing.

"So," I said. "I'm . . ."

Jane was silent, only raising her eyebrows. She had black hair cut in a swingy bob. She was quite a bit older than I was, maybe fifty.

"My father killed my mother when I was eight," I said. "But that's not why I'm here."

To her credit, Jane's face did not change. Her expression was kind and interested, like that of a good bartender. We sat quietly for a while, and then I continued. "I'm here because . . . my brother is in Iraq. He's not a soldier, he's a doctor. I can't sleep. I'm frightened, more frightened than I should be. Like I'll crash my car or get cancer or something. I feel out of it. Weird."

"Weird?" said Jane.

"I get this feeling like I'm about to pass out. I can hear my heartbeat but nothing else."

"That must be frightening," said Jane.

"Yes," I said. "It is frightening." I felt a wash of relief, as if my fear had finally been validated, as if someone cared. I remembered my mother putting her cool palm to my forehead to see whether I was sick. I knew, if I had a fever, she would take care of me.

"Were you there on the night your mother was killed?"

"Murdered," I said. "Yes. No. I was in the tree house out back. With my brother. Or I might have been inside. I don't know. I can't remember. But that's not why I'm here."

"I see," said Jane.

"It's not that I don't want to marry him," I said. "Gerry. I do want to marry him."

"You want to marry Gerry," said Jane, a solid statement.

I nodded miserably. "Sometimes," I said, "I wake up in the middle of the night and think, *I have got to get out of here. I have to go.*" I felt my heartbeat speed up, and I struggled for air. "I feel like I have to get out. But I don't know why or where I have to go. There's nowhere to go."

Jane nodded. "Tell me about Gerry."

"What?" I said.

"Where did you meet him?"

I had a whole story about this: any half of a couple does. Gerry fed me seaweed, was the story. I was a lonely college graduate taking real estate licensing exams and working at an upscale children's clothing store in Westlake. The store was called Caramel Apples. Every morning I woke in the run-down house I shared with four of my college friends, bought a giant cup of coffee at Quack's, drove out 2244, and opened Caramel Apples in time for the barrage of beautiful but bored mothers who arrived almost as soon as I turned on the lights. They settled their kids into carts and shopped, gathering cute T-shirts with dinosaurs and fruit appliqués. Some used the Germ Blockade, a fabric contraption that covered the cart seat, took about five minutes to set up, and cost $25.99; the Germ Blockade was our second biggest seller, after the Hooter Hider nursing apron.

The bookstore in the same shopping center had kids' story time, and the whole parking lot was jammed with minivans and SUVs from nine A.M. on. The women (and they were almost all women) had already worked out and taken a shower by the time they arrived. They pushed expensive strollers across the parking lot, calling to each other and air-kissing.

I didn't really know what to make of them. In New York, my

mother had dropped me at day care before dawn. My father worked on his poetry at home and picked me up around three or four. When I was in elementary school, he was often late and usually unshowered, sticking out like a sore thumb among the suburban mothers. He'd stand at the edge of the playground with his hands in some rumpled pants, his big tummy hanging over his belt. He had a goatee and John Lennon spectacles. My pride in him remained strong, even as the years went on and his scribblings seemed to amount to little. We would walk home, stopping at the Holt bakery for a snack. He bought me any cookie I wanted, asking only for a piece—the ear of a mouse or the wing of a bat—to dip in his afternoon espresso.

But even the most polished mothers in New York were nothing compared to the Texas crowd. I felt like an anthropologist watching them. I wanted to learn how to be normal, how to be a wife and mother. I didn't mind my life, but I hoped to transition to something else eventually. Maybe that was why I gravitated to real estate—I could observe people's homes with a scientist's detachment. If I could see what a house looked like when it was happily lived in, then maybe I could piece together what had gone wrong on Ocean Avenue.

After work some evenings, I would take in a movie or walk around Hyde Park and West Campus. One night, for a change, I took myself to dinner at a cheap spot called Now and Zen sushi. I was sitting at the counter, surveying all the ingredients, when a white man in a black button-down shirt came from the back room. His hair was a bit long and curly, and he had a spray of freckles across the bridge of his nose. He seemed genuinely glad to see me. "Welcome," he said.

"Hi," I said.

"What can I do for you?" said Gerry.

"Feed me," I said. And he did. After making me the California roll and miso soup I had requested (I had never been to another country; even miso soup was exotic to me), he asked if I'd be willing to taste-test some new creations on the house. Happy to have something to do besides watch *Buffy the Vampire Slayer* reruns in my room, I agreed. He made me a strong but sweet cocktail and fed me mussels marinated in Kaffir lime juice with fresh cilantro; tuna on a slice of apple with a bit of goat cheese; and sea urchin, which melted on my tongue like salty sea foam. He gave me a foil-wrapped square of chocolate for dessert.

When the chocolate was gone, I didn't want to depart. As I folded the foil in my fingers, Gerry told me he had grown up in Tokyo: his parents were both teachers at the International School. He was working as a sushi chef to put himself through a computer science degree at UT, and though Now and Zen catered mainly to students and college grads on a shoestring budget (like me), Gerry liked to play around with the fish, serving "specials" to customers who seemed interested. He kept his textbooks in the kitchen and studied when things were slow.

"Why computer science?" I asked him. "You don't seem like a . . . nerd." I slurped my cocktail. My face felt warm, and I was smiling too much.

"I thought about trying to work in food or entertainment," he said, leaning on the polished counter, "but I guess I never felt safe financially while I was growing up. I'm good at computer science. And I want to make a steady living, so I can eat well, travel, you know . . . wine and dine my wife."

"Wife?" I said. I made a sound between a choke and a giggle.

"I mean my *future* wife," said Gerry. There was a pause as we looked at each other. I felt my damn mouth curling up again. I reached for my glass of ice water. "Would you like to . . . do you want to . . . have lunch or brunch this weekend?" he asked.

"Yes," I said. I wrote my number on his hand and felt the inexplicable urge to press my lips against his palm. Thankfully, I refrained.

I walked home that night filled with a giddy happiness. I'd had boyfriends but had never felt so electric. Though he was from another part of the world, Gerry seemed just like me, someone burdened by unnecessary responsibility. There was something to be said for precaution, and I felt that Gerry understood this. For the first time in my life, I thought it might be possible for me to share my life, to feel that kind of exquisite joy. I was so happy, and so frightened.

8

"Lauren?" said Jane Stafford.

"Yes?" I said.

"Are you all right?" Jane tilted her head to the right, causing her glossy hair to fall across her cheekbone.

"We met at a sushi restaurant," I said, "Gerry and me. And I. Gerry and I."

She smiled, expectant. When I said nothing more, she commented, "That sounds nice."

"Yeah," I said.

"How long ago was this?" said Jane. She held a cheap Bic ballpoint, a pad in her lap. I felt alarmed, wondering what she would write down, how she would distill me into sentences.

"I don't know," I said. She peered at me questioningly. I stared at her large brown eyes, and the room grew hazy.

"I love him," I whispered, a familiar dread rising in my chest, making me feel feverish. "I'm really hot."

"You feel hot?"

"Yes," I said. Jane was intent, looking at me through what

seemed to be a room of smoke. I cleared my throat and tried to shake it off. "I'm very dizzy," I said.

"You're feeling anxious?"

"Yes," I said. "And I'm feeling really hot."

"Breathe," said Jane. "How else do you feel?"

I took a deep inhalation, but the woozy feeling remained. "What's wrong with me?" I said.

"Nothing is wrong with you," said Jane.

"I'm scared," I said.

"It's all right," said Jane. I don't know how long we sat in silence—a few minutes? Finally, the fog around the room dissipated, and it was just Jane and me again.

"I feel very small on this couch," I said.

Jane laughed. I was glad to have pleased her. She looked quickly at the digital clock on a table next to me. "Do you feel okay to leave?" she asked.

"I guess so," I said.

"That will be twenty dollars for the co-pay," said Jane.

I fumbled in my purse. Gerry and I had recently consolidated accounts, and he had ordered checks with the University of Texas football insignia. Burnt-orange-colored checks. They were hideous. I wrote one to Jane Stafford. "I'll see you next week," she said as I handed her the check.

"Okay," I said. I felt wobbly as I rose and walked down the hallway. I did not turn in to the kitchen. There was a brunette woman in the waiting room. She was paging through the same *Glamour.* I didn't speak to her, just pushed the door open and went into the warm September day. I walked slowly to my car and got inside. I turned my key in the ignition and waited to cool down.

I didn't want to drive away. I felt—bizarrely—as if I had left something, or someone, inside Jane Stafford's office, on her couch. A girl. A doll. I had left a part of myself or something similarly weird. I felt guilty about leaving, though I had to get to work—I was meeting a couple from Massachusetts tomorrow morning and had to plan a full day of showings. But it was hard to put the car in gear.

I rested my head against the hot steering wheel. "It's okay," I said out loud to myself. I waited for something to come: some memory? Was I going to lose my shit someday and remember that I saw my father kill my mother? *Come on,* I said to myself silently. *Just bring it on.* I tried to conjure a vision, my father swinging, the glint of crystal, blood, but nothing came. I punched on the radio, and good old Willie came on singing, *Whiskey River, take my mind.*

"You said it, Willie," I said. The taxi was still parked in front of my therapist's office. I put the car in drive and hit the gas, singing along: " 'Whiskey River, don't run dry, hi-hi-hi! You're all I got, take care of me.' "

On my drive home from work, I bought a bottle of Yellow Tail chardonnay at the Drive-Thru Liquor Barn. Later that night, after three mugs of wine, four Tylenol PMs, and a few hours of the *World Series of Poker,* I fell asleep.

At some point, Gerry came to bed. The way he curled around me was one of my favorite things about him. I felt his warm breath on the back of my neck, his slow, sleepy exhalations. It was too good to last, I knew. So I tried not to grow accustomed to being loved, to being held in the night. I tried not to believe he would always be there, so I wouldn't be too crushed when everything went wrong.

In the morning Gerry told me I had been snoring.

9

I met the Hendrixes outside the main terminal at the airport. A tanned couple wearing bright fleece vests, they were moving from New England to Texas, Betty Hendrix had said in her emails. They were *looking forward to warm weather!!!* I'd polished off a grande latte and was still so tired I felt stoned.

"Whew!" cried Betty Hendrix as I held open the passenger door of the Neon for her. She had short brown hair and a ruddy complexion, as if she spent time outdoors, cross-country skiing or chopping wood. "It is sweltering!" she said gaily. "Nothing like Boston." She spat out *Boston* as if saying *poison*.

"Can I help you with your bags?" I asked. I felt a headache beginning to bloom.

"Oh, Benny's got them," she said, dismissing her husband, a distinguished-looking man who had thick reddish hair, with a swipe of her hand. Amid the gaseous fumes from passing buses and idling cars, I could smell her fruity lotion.

Benjamin Hendrix slammed the trunk shut and joined us, holding out a pink hand. "Hello, hello," he said. "You must be

Lauren." He smiled kindly, and I wondered if he had children, and if they knew how lucky they were.

"I am," I said. "Nice to meet you, Mr. and Mrs. Hendrix."

"Ben, please. Ben and Betty."

"Okay, then," I said. "Please, climb in. Let's go find you two a house."

"Let's do," said Betty. She slid into the backseat, and surprising me, Ben settled himself into the front passenger seat. We pulled out of the airport and promptly got embroiled in traffic on 71. "Feels just like home," said Betty drily.

"Now, come on, dear," said Ben, gesturing to a topless club along the highway. "We don't have anything called the Landing Strip near Logan."

"Hmph," said Betty.

From my attaché case, I took the stack of stapled papers I had spent the previous afternoon preparing. "Take a look," I said. "I've selected some wonderful homes for you to preview. I think you'll be pleased." In fact, the Hendrixes' price range was well below the cost of fulfilling Betty's dream of acquiring "a big Victorian-style home with at least an acre of land, four or five bedrooms, and a few fireplaces, but in the city, no gated communities, please." For a half million, the Hendrixes were either going to be well into the 'burbs or giving up the land and the fireplaces; and they wouldn't be getting four bedrooms unless they went for the utility-closet-as-bedroom, which I doubted they would.

Ben slipped his glasses down his nose and peered at my printouts, frowning. "Where are these places?" he asked. "Steiner Ranch? Circle C? Are these the suburbs?"

"Not *officially,*" I said.

"I'm confused," said Ben. "I thought we were looking at condos. I want a downtown feel, an urban lifestyle."

"I told her close in," said Betty. "I told her, Benny. Oh, look at this one! Three fireplaces!"

Ben took the printout and squinted. "Where the hell is Round Rock?" he said.

"It's close," I murmured, "to many things."

"I can just feel a warm fire with Yo-Yo Ma—our cat—curled in my lap," said Betty.

"Mr. Hendrix," I said. "Ben. What are you looking for, exactly? I'll call my assistant and have him send some more listings immediately." I didn't have an assistant, but I knew Jonesey would help me out if the day was slow.

"Well," said Ben, putting his glasses back on and folding his hands in his lap, "I want to walk or, worst case, ride a bus to work. I've been driving for thirty years, and I'm sick of my car."

"Okay," I said. Betty had told me her husband worked in finance and that his new office was on Third and Congress.

"Furthermore," said Ben, "I'd like to try ethnic restaurants. I want to walk to various ethnic restaurants from my home."

"No problem," I said encouragingly. After all, the P. F. Chang's in the Arboretum mall was—technically—ethnic, and you couldn't throw a rock in Austin without hitting a burrito.

"I love the capitol building," added Betty. "I've seen pictures. Let's have a view of that, wouldn't it be neat? And I'd like to walk to a park."

"There's Zilker Park," I said. "Barton Springs is a great place to swim."

"Okay, let's be able to walk to the park, whatever," said Ben. "And maybe something sleek, something modern, you know?"

I thought of the folder in his hand, which was filled with photos of sprawling limestone homes decorated with cowhide furniture.

"And at least two fireplaces," said Betty. "A nice big garden, maybe a cozy extra bedroom for my sewing? A turret or a widow's walk would be over the top, I know, but a gal can dream, right?"

"Tell me about your home in Boston," I ventured.

"Big stuffy old place in Sudbury," said Ben. "Terrible commute. The house is full of the kids' crap."

"It's a charming Victorian," said Betty. "It has four bedrooms, but now that the children are gone, it does feel large. Then again, the boys come home for holidays." My palms grew sweaty with the realization that I was trapped on Highway 183 with a couple on the verge of divorce.

"We're looking for a change," said Ben. "That's why I took the transfer. A new leaf."

"I'm a little nervous," confessed Betty. "I've heard some Texans are . . . a bit gauche. Kind of nouveau riche. Big hair, right? But you're a nice girl. So that's a start!"

"I think I'm getting a better idea of what you're looking for," I said, deciding to show them homes way out of their budget so at least they could see the problem for themselves.

When I started out in real estate, I used to take people's budgets seriously, showing clients only homes they could comfortably afford. But as the years passed, I realized that people were leaving me for Realtors who showed them their dream homes and then either figured out the financing or let *them* decide they had to look at less expensive homes. Clients wanted to dream. They didn't seem to care if you respected their bank account.

"How about we start in Clarksville? That's a beautiful historic area adjacent to downtown," I said.

"Clarksville," mused Ben. "I think I've heard of that one."

"It has a nice ring to it," said Betty. "Very classy."

"Clarksville has a long, storied history," I said, "and yet is one of the sleeker, more hip places to live in the city."

Both Hendrixes leaned in, listening with rapt interest as I began talking about the former plantation of Governor Elisha M. Pease, historic Nau's drugstore with the working soda fountain, and Jeffrey's restaurant, which was rumored to be George W. Bush's favorite. I wondered which Hendrix had had the affair. While Ben seemed a likely candidate—the *sleek* stuff sounded like it was parroted from some youthful secretary's Facebook page—there was something squirrelly about Betty, all her talk of fireplaces and snuggling cats.

"Let's pop into a local breakfast spot," I suggested, thinking of Lucinda's, an Austin institution, which was scheduled to be demolished soon to make room for a Marriott. "You can get the feel of downtown Austin, and I can call my assistant for some more central listings."

"Okay," agreed Ben.

"That sounds perfect," said Betty. "I love it here already!" She reached forward and patted Ben's hand, then had a second thought, unbuckled her seat belt, lunged, and gave him a big kiss on the cheek. He looked both stunned and pleased.

By the time we had eaten (egg-white omelet for Betty; *migas* with extra cheese for Ben; egg, papas, and cheese taco for me), Jonesey had sent a list of addresses to my phone. They ranged in price from one to two million.

As the Hendrixes sipped their coffee, I called Jonesey from a bathroom stall. I explained Ben's sleek, modern desires and Betty's fireplace fixation. Jonesey, an elegant gay man in his sixties, sized the Hendrixes up at once. "Oh Lord," he said, "affair city."

"Right-o," I said. "So what do I show them?"

"The guy's posturing," said Jonesey. "Show them the condo

first. It's so modern that everyone on the hike-and-bike trail can watch you brushing your teeth. Floor-to-ceiling windows. An aquarium built into the kitchen, plasma screen in the bathroom."

"Sounds awesome," I said, thinking of my cluttered apartment, my fat TV with rabbit ears.

"Then hit the five-bedroom in Clarksville. It's too ye olde colonial for its own good. Three fireplaces, needs work, but it's a million, and she'll go low. Lady's desperate, wants to retire. Window units, for God's sake."

"Is she moving to Lakeway?" I asked, naming the town near Austin where many Texans moved after their children left home. Lakeway had golf courses and houses with fishing docks.

"Oh, no, honey," said Jonesey. "She's moving to the W downtown."

"Glamorous," I said.

"Haul them out to Lakeway before rush hour. Show them a few of the waterfront listings. Then drive back around four-thirty, five. That will give them an understanding of what they're paying for, living central."

"Right, Lakeway," I said.

"What's your take?" said Jonesey.

"Hmm?"

"What do you think they'll buy?"

"My guess is a nice two-, three-bedroom close in. Traditional. He says he's looking for something new and different, but I don't know . . ."

"Okay. Drive through Tarrytown next, east of Exposition. The houses are smaller there, a bit cheaper, but still dripping with charm. Then bring them to my place."

"What?" Jonesey was a notorious homebody who loved cooking every night for his husband, Gil. Gil came from big money, and they shared an amazing colonial in Pemberton Heights.

"Gil's out of town. What the hell. Invite Gerry, too. We'll have a little cocktail party. Seven sound good?"

It did. I put on some lipstick and straightened my blazer. I let myself imagine how fantastic a sale would feel. I hadn't sold anything substantial in a while, just some student crumboxes. If I got a big commission, we could move, or at least buy a new couch. Maybe I could convince Alex to meet me and Gerry somewhere thrilling for a vacation.

I smiled at myself in the mirror and went back to the Hendrixes. We had a big day ahead. I approached the table and felt it immediately: there had been a fight. Ben was red-faced and bristling, and Betty looked gray and deflated. "Ready to go look at some homes?" I asked brightly.

Betty crossed her arms. Ben said, "I think we'll go back to the hotel for a bit, if that's okay with you."

"Of course," I said. They were staying at the Quality Inn all the way back near the airport, but I wasn't going to hold them captive.

"Honey," said Betty, not to me.

"There is a condo right on this block," I fudged. "Quite modern, if you'd like to check it out before we drive back."

"Let's do," said Betty.

"Fine," said Ben.

"Brunch is my treat!" I said. I left cash on the table, and we walked outside. Surreptitiously, I scanned my listings. There was indeed a condo on the block, but it was a studio, and I had no idea whether or not it was modern. I strode purposefully along Congress, the Hendrixes lagging behind and hissing at each other. The listing had a note: *Call before showing.* I punched in the phone number, and a man who sounded sleepy answered.

"Hello," I said, "this is Lauren Mahdian from Sunshine City Realty. I'm hoping to—"

"Lauren?" said the man.

"Yes," I said. "I was wondering—"

"That's a great name," said the man. "Underrated."

"Uh," I said, "I was wondering if I could show your condo now?"

"Oh, okay," said the man. "Give me a sec to get dressed."

"Great," I said, cutting the call. I whirled around to face the Hendrixes. "Isn't this a vibrant street?" I said, feeling like Vanna White. I waved my arm, almost hitting a bearded wino with my purse. "Watch it," he said.

"I'm sorry," I said.

"Glorious!" said Betty with some desperation.

"Is it much farther?" asked Ben, eyeing what appeared to be an antiwar rally heading our way.

"Here we are," I said, pushing open a glass door. A chilly blast of air that smelled like Band-Aids greeted us. Behind an onyx-colored desk, a black man with platinum hair smiled. "Welcome to Le Dome," he said. "What can I do to please you?"

I quickly checked the address: we were not in some sort of brothel but a new high-rise. "Hi there," I said. "We're visiting Unit 302, taking a look."

"Bien sur," said the concierge. "The elevator is on your left, past the lovebird cage."

Betty looked charmed and Ben, nervous, as we boarded the elevator. "This unit does have a fireplace," I said, and Betty said, "Do tell." Ben studied his shoes.

When we reached the third floor, an attractive, balding man about my age was leaving Unit 302, a computer tucked under his arm. "Enjoy," he said, brushing past us. Before he stepped into the elevator, he turned back and caught my eye. "I'm Arthur," he said. Flustered, I did not answer.

We went inside the condo, and Betty said, "Whoa!" It was blindingly bright: a wall of windows showcased Congress all the way to the capitol. A kitchen filled with stainless steel ran against one wall, and a spiral wrought-iron staircase led to the second floor.

"Everyone can see me," said Ben.

"Many of the more modern condominiums feature large windows or walls of glass," I agreed. I felt myself morphing into enthused-Realtor mode. It was strange how this happened to me—I went from my normal low-key self to a sales dynamo. In a way, I liked this showy, confident side; it was heady to be a loudmouth instead of my usual shy self. And then I could finish with the Hendrixes and go home and put my feet up.

"Good thing we don't have toddlers anymore," said Betty, testing the staircase with her navy heel.

"Who cleans the windows?" asked Ben.

"Cleaning services are included in the monthly fees," I said, reading from the listing. "As well as use of the pool, the entertainment pavilion, and the Armadillo Spa."

"Armadillo Spa?" said Betty.

"The armadillo is the state animal of Texas," I said dopily.

"Oh," said Betty with an expression of distaste.

"The state mammal is the Mexican free-tailed bat," I noted. "And the state reptile is the Texas horned lizard."

"Aren't you a fount of information," said Betty, curling her lip in annoyance. I told myself to dial it back as she climbed the staircase gingerly. At the top, she exclaimed, "This is gorgeous! Benny, get up here this very minute!"

Ben dug his hands deeper into his pockets. His bluff, it

seemed, had been called. He cleared his throat, then marched toward the staircase and tromped up slowly.

"I'll be down here," I said. "Take your time!"

The living room was furnished elegantly, with a soft gray couch and reclaimed-wood table. On the kitchen counter was an antique typewriter. I peered at the page, which read: *Nobody could tell. Still, he felt he knew her, could see her heart through her silk blouse. Her heart, her ribs, her nipples.*

My face grew flushed. From upstairs, I heard a laugh, then Betty saying warmly, "You old fuddy-duddy, you!"

When the Hendrixes came down, I went over a few more listings with them and relayed Jonesey's cocktail invitation. The Hendrixes accepted. By the time we walked past the blond doorman again, something had warmed between them: they seemed to be enjoying themselves.

That night, after dropping the tipsy Hendrixes at their hotel, Gerry and I took Lamar Boulevard home. I drove, and Gerry rested his hand on my knee. I wondered if we would ever be as ill at ease around each other as the Hendrixes. I did feel often far away from Gerry, but I assumed this was normal. It was what I wanted. I had found a good man who wanted a simple sort of joy. Wasn't this love?

10

"What do you remember about your mother?" said Jane Stafford at our next Wednesday meeting. I was settled in, my raincoat balled up next to me, rubber boots sticking out from the couch awkwardly. Jane sat in a high-backed leather chair, her slim legs crossed.

"She's dead," I said. "I believe I mentioned that."

Jane folded her hands in her lap and tilted her head. "Are you feeling angry?" she asked.

"No," I said.

The sound machine purred as if someone invisible were whispering, "Shhhh."

"A little angry, I guess," I amended. "I miss Alex."

"He's still in Iraq?"

"What is he doing there? You know? He's a fucking doctor. I'm sorry. He's a medical student. He's almost done with his residency. I didn't mean to swear."

Jane nodded but did not speak.

"You know one thing," I said, "is that you need some new

magazines in your waiting room. I've pretty much finished with that *Glamour.*"

"Do you think you use humor," said Jane kindly, "as a way of avoiding troubling emotions?"

I took a breath, then let it out. "It's as if . . ." I said. Jane waited, silent. "It's as if Alex feels like he should atone for something," I went on. "Volunteering to go to Iraq."

"You said *atone for something.* What do you mean by that?"

"I don't know. Like he couldn't save our mother, so he needs to save some Iraqis. It doesn't make sense. As if I don't need him!"

"What could Alex have done?" said Jane. "How could he have saved your mother?"

I sighed. "Alex doesn't think my father did it."

Jane nodded. Her brow creased. "Alex thinks your father is innocent."

"Right."

"What do you think?" said Jane.

"I don't know," I said. "I mean, I do know. My father killed her. He was the only one there. If he didn't do it, who did?"

Jane had no answer for that one.

"And there were times . . ." I put my hands over my eyes.

"Are you feeling dizzy?" asked Jane.

"No," I said.

"What are you feeling?"

"I remember this framed picture . . . of my parents. My mom kept it on the kitchen counter."

"Go on."

"It was a snapshot of the two of them in Egypt," I said. Though I hadn't held the photograph since I was a child, I could see the image clearly in my mind: my parents holding hands. While my father looked hot and annoyed, my mother was beaming. In the photo, my father wore an ankle-length *gallibaya* shirt; my mother was young, in cotton shorts and a University of Texas T-shirt, her blond hair in a ponytail. "It was my mom's first visit to Cairo," I said.

"Go on," said Jane.

I shook my head and began to tell Jane my mother's story, which had always troubled me.

The whole city of Cairo was beyond her comprehension. There was always something happening: a donkey defecating, a child screaming, men's laughter, shisha *smoke, car exhaust, blinding sunlight, the call to prayer blasting from the minarets. Izaan's parents' apartment was filled with mirrors and fringe, and every possible object was ornamented: the Kleenex box had a gold tasseled cover, the toilet seat glittered, and Izaan's brother had suspended CDs on strings from the ceiling of his car, lending the interior of his Honda Accord a dizzying disco feel.*

Izaan's family had been polite to my mother, though it was clear they weren't thrilled about the upcoming wedding. Izaan had called off an arranged marriage to the daughter of a prominent Egyptian family at the last minute, after meeting my mother, who they thought was entirely unsuitable.

My mother preferred the company of the men, who sprawled on cushions, smoked, and spoke raucously, laughing often. The women served fragrant dishes of ground beef and rice. In the kitchen, they gossiped in low tones. My mother didn't know any of the people they talked about, even when they tried to translate, and she knew even less about the European designers Izaan's sisters revered. The women were very physical with each other, and my mother tried not to shrink away when they hugged her impulsively or kissed her cheeks.

She hadn't known how wealthy Izaan's family was, by Egyptian standards, until they'd arrived. It helped explain his arrogance. Izaan took my mother boating on the Nile with his friends. They motored past weary women washing clothes and naked children bathing near the muddy banks. My mother asked one of Izaan's friends if he felt uncomfortable in the fancy boat, blaring music from the stereo, but the man shrugged, smiling under his sunglasses. "In shalla," he said. He told my mother this meant it was God's wish. She found out later that it actually meant if God wills it so.

On their last day in Cairo, Izaan finally acquiesced to my mother's pleas and took her to Khan el-Khalili, the giant market, which sold glassware, spices, mother-of-pearl backgammon boards, sandals, clothes, leather goods, and water pipes. Izaan's brother dropped them off, snapping the photo that would end up in our house on Ocean Avenue, and then they walked into the teeming marketplace.

My mother loved the dim stalls, the smell of incense. When she walked by other tourists, she felt superior, with gorgeous Izaan at her side. She bought a chess set for her father, Mort, and a leather bag for her mother, Merilee. Izaan wanted to barter, telling my mother the vendors didn't respect someone who didn't haggle, but she shook her head and paid the first price. Izaan told her she was a softie.

At one stall, knives were laid out in a row, glinting. "These are beautiful," said my mother, putting her hand near them but not daring to touch. The vendor came from shadows, speaking in Arabic to Izaan. Switching to English, he said, "These are the best knives in the world. Very special. A special price for you."

"How much?" said my mother. She looked at Izaan, who shook his head. The man named a price, and she reached for her wallet.

"No," said Izaan. "These knives do not belong in our kitchen."

"Our kitchen?" my mother said playfully. Though they were engaged, they did not yet share an apartment in New York. Grabbing her hand, Izaan tugged my mother out of the stall and down a *passageway. It seemed they were going toward the center of the market; the stalls were less tidy, darker. Inexplicably, my mother felt scared. "Izaan," she said, "I want to go back."*

My mother's face would change as she told the rest of the story. It would take on a faraway look, as if she had forgotten she was speaking to me. She seemed to be trying to make sense of the story herself.

"Your father told me to follow him," she'd say. "And so I did."

Izaan led her to a ruined building. Inside a crumbling doorway, my mother heard the chanting of prayer. "I have made mistakes, some very big mistakes, but that time is over," he said. He kissed her—

She would shake her head. "Anyway, that's the story of the knives. He told me he would buy me the best knives in the world when it was time," she said. As my mother took out her chef's knife, she always said, "See? Your father was right after all."

My father had been true to his word—after he had sold his first poem to the literary journal *The Cottonwood Review,* he had gone to the Stamford mall and bought my mother the most expensive Wüsthofs. *The Cottonwood Review* paid Izaan thirty dollars and five free copies of the magazine; the set of knives had cost four hundred fifty dollars. But it was the thought that counted—Izaan had arrived and could buy his wife the best.

I always felt that she was leaving something out. What "big mistakes" had my father made? When I asked, my mother said that it had taken my father a while to figure out who he wanted to be.

"What do you suppose she meant by that?" asked Jane.

"I don't know," I said. "I guess that's why I remembered the story. It never really made sense."

"Did anyone else ever talk about your father making big mistakes?"

"I don't . . . No," I said. As I spoke, the room grew hazy. I knew there wasn't really any smoke, so I tried to stay calm. But what if the building *were* on fire? I felt my lungs, too large, in my rib cage. I wheezed, trying to get enough oxygen.

"Lauren? Our session is almost over. Are you feeling all right?"

I sat up straight, the smoke dissipating. "I'm fine," I said. "I just . . . I can't think of what to say next."

"You don't have to say anything. You can use this space to be with your thoughts, if you like."

I shuddered. With my thoughts was the last place I wanted to be.

"What do you mean by that?" said Jane.

"What?" I said.

"Being with your thoughts, you said. You said it was the last place you wanted to be. What did you mean by that?"

"Oh, jeez," I said. "My thoughts! They're so . . ."

Jane cocked her head, giving me the interested-sparrow look.

"They're so . . . They hurt," I said.

"Your thoughts hurt you?" said Jane.

"I think if I let myself feel it all," I said, "I'd be in so much . . . It would hurt so much. Too much. So I just . . . I go on. I make plans and watch TV."

Jane looked down. She seemed sad. She looked back up and said, "Are you feeling all right to leave?"

"Yes, sure," I said. "I'm fine."

11

That night, after work, I headed to the Elephant Room to meet Gerry and listen to some jazz. I found a spot outside Manuel's, and as I locked the car, I peered into the dim restaurant, watching a man lift a nacho to his mouth. Up Congress Avenue, the capitol building was illuminated, glowing against the evening sky.

I crossed the street and opened the door to a staircase. I could hear horns as I descended, and I breathed in the smells of whiskey and floor wax. Sitting in front of the stage, sipping a drink, was Gerry. He wore jeans and the blue sweater I'd bought him for his birthday. He leaned across a candle toward a very pretty woman. The woman told a joke, wrapping wheat-colored curls around her finger, and Gerry laughed. He looked happier than he'd looked in some time.

"Hey," I said, approaching the table.

"Lauren," said Gerry, standing, "this is Rose."

"Nice to meet you," said Rose.

"Likewise," I said. "What are you guys drinking?"

"Scotch," they said in unison. I ordered a beer. Rose, it

turned out, was a jazz singer. When the set began, she sat on the edge of a wooden stool, leaning toward the microphone. Her voice was low and sultry.

"Maybe you'd be happier with someone like Rose," I said to Gerry after I'd had a few beers.

Gerry put his arm around me, but said, "Maybe."

That night, when I thought he was asleep, I whispered, "Gerry, why do you stay with me?"

He tightened his hold on me and whispered back, "You make life more interesting. And you love me."

I was silent, letting his kindness settle over me like a blanket.

12

There is a deep blue place between wakefulness and sleep. I have always been afraid of that place—it's where bad memories reside, I believe, or thoughts that have no purpose. Lusty desires for old boyfriends. Things I'm mad at myself about. Fears, worries about bombs and gunshots and what happened to Jack Nicholson in *The Shining* happening to me, leaving me in a creepy mansion with a maze garden jabbing away at an old-fashioned typewriter. Images of all my teeth falling out, or all my hair, or my fingernails.

What I love about sleeping pills is that they let you avoid that place. You go from wide awake to zonked in one fell swoop. I had almost forgotten about the deep blue. And then, around the middle of October, the pills stopped working.

I began walking Handsome to the Capitol Building and back, which took up much of the night. I picked up breakfast tacos on the way home and warmed them up for Gerry, who said he'd rather have me in bed than a bacon, egg, and cheese with salsa.

Nonetheless, he took the tacos, and I climbed under the sheets for an hour or so.

I was unmoored without my brother. It was as if a bandage of some kind had been removed, and I was raw and exposed. When I met with my therapist, I told her I was afraid of the deep blue. "Instead of sleeping," I said, "I lie there remembering things."

"What sort of things?" Jane asked.

"Things from when I was little," I said. "But I don't want to think about that stuff."

"What do you remember?" said Jane.

"Oh, jeez, like my walk to kindergarten."

"Tell me," she said.

I couldn't see what the point was, but I told her about strolling through Holt's small downtown. There was a crossing guard in front of the library, a heavy man with a ruddy face. He wore a bright blue uniform complete with a hat. I could see him as I spoke to Jane Stafford: the brass buttons, the shiny black shoes. He held an octagonal sign, flashed it straight when he wanted us to halt at the corner of Oak Street.

"I haven't thought about Holt in years," I said. "Why would all this come back to me now?"

"Sometimes your mind waits until you're ready," said Jane.

"I can't seem to turn it off," I said. "I remember the whole freaking town."

"Go on," said Jane.

I told her about the apartment building where divorced families ended up, puzzles with missing pieces. I was taught that living there was somehow disgraceful. *Real* families—families like ours—lived in houses with yards. "My father must have been the one who gave me that idea," I said. "I think he wanted us to know that we were better than other people, even though he was unemployed. Well, he said he was an artist, but . . . there he was, an Egyptian man in the white-bread suburbs. It must have been . . . hard for him."

"Why do you think it was hard for him?"

The room started filling with smoke again, and Jane was looking at me. "I feel like the room is filling with smoke," I said.

"Smoke?"

"Yes," I said. "It's like . . . I can't see."

"Take a deep breath, Lauren."

"I don't know what's happening," I said weakly.

"Lauren," said Jane. "You're fine. You're safe."

"I don't know about that," I said. "I'm really not feeling very well."

"Tell me," said Jane.

"It's still all smoky. I can't breathe in here," I said. "I'm so hot."

"You feel warm?"

"This isn't working for me," I said.

Jane was silent.

I sat up straight. "This couch, it's so big. You know what I mean?"

She furrowed her brow.

"I don't mean to hurt your feelings," I said. "But I think this couch is just too big. And all this talking, it's just making me feel kind of nauseated."

"I see," said Jane Stafford.

"I think I'm going to take a break," I said. "From all this . . ." I waved my hands around, trying to clear the smoke. "The more I dredge up all this old . . . I appreciate all you've done for me. Honestly, this isn't your fault."

"Lauren—" said Jane, but I was already halfway to the exit.

"I'll mail you the co-pay," I said, and then I walked quickly to the kitchen, which was also smoky, wheeled around, and found the correct door, which let me out.

13

As I drove away from my therapist, I felt terrible. A black hole seemed to be yawning open in me, something I knew I needed to seal again, and fast. "Black hole?" I said to myself in the rearview mirror. "What are you, Mr. Spock? What is this, the starship *Enterprise*? Redirect to starbase!" I laughed, and the sound was high-pitched and hysterical.

I needed to pull myself together. I didn't want to feel whatever was coursing through me—I just wanted it to stop. I thought about booze and how it helped to transport you, even as you sat still on the bar stool. Drinking did for me what old age seemed to do for Gramma: it made me less present in a world I wasn't so crazy about anymore. I could be elsewhere, numb.

I drove to the Elks Lodge off Barton Springs Road, which was one of the last places in Austin where you could actually smoke cigarettes indoors, so my vision problem would not be as pronounced. I had sold a ramshackle 1/1 to the bartender, so when I pressed the intercom and said, "I'm here for Jerzy," the Elk-in-Charge let me in.

"Well, well, well," said Jerzy as I entered. He was in his mid-sixties, a muscular Vietnam vet. I had shown him apartments and carriage houses for six years before he went for his Zilker fixer-upper. "It's Lauren the Realtor! What can I do for you, honey?"

"How about a drink?" I said.

He slapped the top of the bar. "That's my girl," he said. He lit a cigarette and offered me one. I accepted, and the unfiltered Marlboro almost made me gag. An elderly man at the bar said, "You know what *BPOE* stands for, sweetheart?"

"Best people on earth," I exclaimed, the nicotine making me feel both giddy and ill. Jerzy had asked me this every time I took him house-hunting.

"Damn right," said the man. "I'll have a Jim Beam," he added.

"Make it two," I said. "And maybe a cheeseburger with onion rings?"

"Burger and a Beam," said Jerzy. "Coming right up."

After a few drinks and half a cheeseburger, I went back to my car. The good thing about a Dodge Neon with tinted windows is that you can lie down in the backseat, if you're so inclined, which I was.

When I closed my eyes, I saw my mother the day before she died, sunbathing next to the tree house, shiny with baby oil. Her body was tan in an aqua bikini, and her hair was held back in a rubber band. She was squinting, resting a large square of cardboard covered in aluminum foil underneath her chin. I saw my own girlhood toes, painted purple. I remembered the way I had once felt: safe, bored, sunburned. These were the waning minutes of the life I'd thought would always be mine.

14

Again I lay awake past midnight. Gerry slept with his arms around me. When I sneaked from Gerry's embrace, Handsome rose from his dog bed, expectant. I climbed from bed and went into the living room to find Handsome's leash. My head hurt, so I swallowed a half dozen Advil.

The moon was dazzling. Handsome trotted happily as we made our way south toward downtown. The air felt like a warm swimming pool. I walked along my street, noticing the fresh paint on the bike messengers' house and the way a couple down the street had strung lights and placed folding chairs in their small front yard: preparations for—or remnants of—a party. Though I had once loved being home with Gerry, now I was more comfortable out of my house, on the move.

I crossed under I-35, giving the people who lived beneath the bridge a wide berth, and made my way to Congress Avenue. Turning left, I had a clear view of the Capitol Building. It was two A.M., which was ten A.M. in Baghdad; I wished my cell phone could call Iraq. Then I thought, *Well, why not try?*

I sat down at the bus stop at Congress and Tenth. I rummaged in my wallet until I found the phone number of Ibn Sina Hospital. Under the bright sky, I dialed. This was going to cost a fortune, I knew. But I suddenly had to talk to Alex. He was the only one in the world who would understand what I was feeling—this soupy fear and dread. Without Alex, I was carrying the heavy memories alone.

I waited, pressing the phone to my ear. But I had mixed up the digits, it seemed. I couldn't get the string of numerals on the scrap of paper to connect to anyone, just annoying beeps and a recorded statement: "We're sorry. The number you are trying to reach is disconnected or no longer in service." The message was in English, so I figured I must have the access code wrong. I called the Verizon operator, but she put me on hold. I listened to a recording of Barry Manilow singing "Can't Smile Without You" and "Mandy." Finally, I cut the line.

Handsome was yanking at his retractable leash, ready to move on. We had made it down Congress almost to the river when I remembered the guy who lived in Le Dome, Unit 302. I was feeling reckless. I walked to Le Dome and looked up. There was a window lit on the third floor. His name came to me, unbidden: Arthur.

I stood there for a while. *Why not just go inside?* I thought. *Why not have a drink with a handsome balding man? Why not a rollicking night of sex?* I deserved some joy!

Before Gerry, I'd had lovers—short-lived physical relationships with guys who were messed up in one way or another. Heavy drinkers, manic wackos, the kind of men who told me they loved me after a night and never called again. I felt strangely safe with people who were broken. I knew what to expect from them.

Loving Gerry was different. I found myself counting on him, believing in him, dreaming about babies and wedding rings. It was unnerving and dangerous and very, very stupid.

I whispered a message to Arthur, who was likely typing in his boxer shorts. Did he have a gut? I couldn't remember. And honestly, who cared? *Come to the window,* I thought. *All you have to do is come to the window and you can have me.*

Nobody came to the window. As I was about to murmur another message, the light on the third floor went out. I looked at Handsome, who was confused. I realized it was time to go home.

When I let myself in the door of my purple-and-yellow house, a bag of warm tacos in my hand, I saw a message light blinking on our old answering machine.

I pressed the button and heard my brother's voice. "Hey there," he said. "I'm thinking of you guys. I'm sorry to call so late. I just happened to be near a phone, so. Well, anyway. It's . . . it's getting hard here. It's very disheartening. I'm doing my best, but Jesus . . . Lauren, I miss you. I love you. Bye."

I played the message three times, and then I lay down on the floor and cried.

15

It might have happened right then, while I was on my carpeted floor, sobbing and then falling—finally—into a dreamless sleep. It could have been while Gerry carried me to bed, gave me a back scratch, and sang "It Had to Be You." Maybe it was while he showered and I lay in the sunlight, smelling Irish Spring soap and feeling Handsome's heavy head on my tummy. I lay on my expensive mattress, and two Iraqi men drove to either side of Ibn Sina Hospital and detonated cars full of explosives, demolishing the building and everything inside.

The news came the way I'd always feared: a phone call that showed up on my caller ID as RESTRICTED. It was late afternoon, and I was watching *First Time Home Flippers.* I answered the phone tentatively.

"Miss Lauren Mahdian?" said a man's voice in an accent I couldn't place, maybe French.

I said, "Yes?"

"This is Laurent Janssen with Médecins Sans Frontières. I am calling about your brother, Dr. Alexander Mahdian."

I hit mute on the television. The man was talking about my brother and two suicide bombers and an explosion.

"An explosion?" I said.

"It is a terrible tragedy, a terrible mess," said the man.

"A mess?" I said.

"At present, we are tending to the bodies. We believe that most inhabitants of the hospital did not survive."

"What are you telling me?" I asked. I rose, screaming into the phone, *"What are you telling me?"*

"We have not identified your brother at this time," said the man. "We will keep you informed of any developments. You have my deepest sympathies."

"It was a bombing?" I said.

"It was a bombing, yes," said the man.

"They bombed Alex's hospital?" I said.

"They bombed the hospital, yes," said the man.

After I had hung up, I fell back onto the couch and tried to feel something—some communication—from my brother. Was he dead? Did it hurt? I felt that I should know. But I did not know.

It had been only hours since his phone call. I had been planning to call him back at nine A.M. his time, which was midnight my time. I'd already emailed, telling him to be near the phone. His message was still on the machine! Alex could not be dead.

I tried to call Gerry, who was out doing research. But after I dialed, I heard the ring tone ("Folsom Prison Blues") in the kitchen, where Gerry had left his phone charging in the wall socket next to the blender.

Who could I call? What should I do? I thought about trying to reach my dad. They had phones in jail, after all. I could just telephone information and ask for the number of Attica Correctional Facility. I could say it was an emergency. In fact, it was an emergency. But I washed down four Tylenol PMs with a tumbler of Sprite and lay on my bed.

I heard the phone ring a few hours later. After the beep on the machine, a man cleared his throat. "Lauren," the man said. I knew at once who it was, and I stood up, holding the sheet around my body. I walked toward the voice.

"Lauren," the man—my father—said. "I've gotten the news about your brother. About Alex. I'm calling to tell you I love you. I love you. I'm so . . ." He began to falter, but after a moment, he continued. "I hope you can . . . can find it in you, in your heart, to call me. Or write. I want you to know I'm here. You're not alone." I heard a shuffling, and then he cleared his throat. "I'll call again soon," he said. "I love you, Little One."

When he had hung up, I waited for the tape to rewind. I realized with a blunt pain in my gut that Izaan had recorded over Alex's voice. "No!" I cried, pulling the tape from the machine. A piece of the ribbon caught and tore. "No!" I said, desperate. My father. My father! He ruined everything, everything, everything.

Book Two

1

Sylvia Hall pressed her fingers to the hot glass as the city bus lurched from Rubey Park. The driver, a compact woman with a ponytail, wound her way through streets Sylvia knew by heart, and she silently bade them farewell. *Goodbye, Silver Circle; goodbye, Little Nell; goodbye, my Ajax Mountain.* From Glenwood Springs, Sylvia would catch a Greyhound to New York City, where she would become the person she had always meant to be. Brittle sunlight caught a small crack in her window and blinded Sylvia for a moment, but then her vision cleared.

Sylvia was forty-one years old and five months pregnant. When the bartender at the Snowmass Club said, "No offense, Sylvie, but maybe you need less cheese and more elliptical," Sylvia realized it was time to put her getaway plan into action. She had packed a bag after Ray had fallen asleep, had lain on the couch all night, wide awake, as if plugged in to an electric socket. Instead of going to work, she had walked into town, bought a last bear claw and a coffee at Main Street bakery, and caught the Roaring Fork. She read a discarded *Aspen Daily News* as she waited for the bus to arrive: *Aspen Club not energy-efficient today, but it could be. Elk and bighorn sheep give birth in proposed wilderness area.*

Sylvia sighed and pulled her knees to her chest. Maybe she could fall asleep, despite the coffee. Goodbye, J-Bar; goodbye, sunburned men reading the condensed *New York Times* in the Black Saddle Bar & Grille; goodbye, Ray, who was never going to sober up, who was never going to be a great painter, who was—in the end—a jerk with a dwindling trust fund who'd made Sylvia get two abortions and a navel ring.

In other words, Ray Junior was out of the question, namewise.

Sylvia figured she would tell the baby that Ray had died. In a car chase. A Denver cop who died in a car chase. That would be a good father to have, she thought. And as soon as that whopper was out of the way, Sylvia would be honest. She was going to use her college degree, wear cashmere. She would read Proust, the whole thing, whilst eating madeleines.

Reflected in the bus window, Sylvia's dirty-blond hair was the same as when she'd been a teenager, but the skin around her light blue eyes and generous smile was puckered. One afternoon Sylvia had seen a leather change purse in the Junior League thrift shop and thought, *That change purse looks like my face.*

Life was short, as it turned out. Sylvia picked at her chapped lip. Maybe you got one chance to reinvent yourself, maybe two. She had been lazing along for so long, assuming there was always more time to begin her *actual* life, her adulthood. But the child inside her had changed Sylvia already: she was stronger, brave enough to climb out of the sluggish quicksand of her days with Ray. She couldn't say he had been mean, or even distant. He loved her the best he could, and the truth was, she loved him, too. The way his hair stuck up at the crown of his head—who would smooth it down now?

Sylvia opened her window, and cold mountain air filled her nostrils. The bus accelerated, and Sylvia told herself it was done: there was no turning back now.

2

In Denver, Sylvia disembarked. The late-afternoon light was murkier, less crisp than in Aspen; Sylvia felt as if she were wearing smudged glasses. Though she didn't wear glasses except for the red-framed sunglasses she'd taken from the lost and found at the club. As the driver hauled bags from underneath the bus, Sylvia stared at a discarded bouquet of flowers.

"What's it look like?" said the bus driver.

"Sorry?" said Sylvia. An image sprang to mind from one of the pregnancy websites—a five-month-old fetus complete with finger nubs and alien eyes.

"Your *bag,*" said the driver wearily. "What's it look like?"

"Oh, I've got my bag," said Sylvia, gesturing to her navy duffel. "I'm just . . . enjoying the sunshine."

The driver smiled, and the friendliness in her face surprised Sylvia. The woman angled her face to the sky and took a deep breath, her hands on her hips. "It's a nice one," she murmured, and then she shut the cargo door with one smooth motion and climbed back onto the bus. She gave the horn a light tap as she pulled away.

The Denver bus station was large and sterile. Like a hospital, thought Sylvia, or the veterinary clinic where she had brought her cat, Dickens, when he'd been hit by an asshole in a rented Hummer. (Dickens died that night, though Sylvia had resolved to pay for whatever it took to keep him alive—heart transplant, traction for his little broken leg, one of those wheelie carts, anything.)

It was cool inside the bus station, and most of the benches were occupied. Sylvia seemed to be in the minority: she was white, female, and not wearing headphones. She felt distinctly dowdy in her jeans (held together at the top with a rubber band—a trick she'd gleaned from a mom-to-be website) and floral shirt. Her boots clonked against the linoleum floor as she approached the café.

Sylvia had two hours before the next bus, bound for Chicago. She wolfed down a cheeseburger, fries, and a chocolate milk shake. Spotting a pay phone, Sylvia thought she'd better call her best friend, Victoria. Maybe Victoria would make a WELCOME, SYLVIA! banner and hang it in the foyer outside her apartment. Maybe but probably not.

Sylvia had left her cell phone on the kitchen table of the house she shared with Ray. (This was part of her plan—she knew cell phones could be traced, and if Ray found her, she might be persuaded to go back. She was weak and needy, but at least she *knew* she was weak and needy.) He was probably waking up from his afternoon siesta by now, wondering where Sylvia was and whether she'd bought a pizza from Taster's on the way home. She was never buying a pizza from Taster's on the way home again! Ray could take his large Buffalo chicken (extra jalapeños) and he could shove it. From now on Sylvia would pick up Perrier and macadamia nuts. She'd watch *Masterpiece Theatre* in a small but tasteful apartment, maybe on the Upper West Side.

Sylvia punched Victoria's number into the keypad. She savored the feel of the 2, the 1, the 2. Sylvia felt glamorous dialing Manhattan even as she stood next to a dented bathroom door.

Uli, Victoria's husband, answered the phone, barking, "Yessus?" He was Greek and did something related to importing. Or maybe it was exporting. Uli was a bald barrel of a man who loved liquor and strong European cigarettes. He and Victoria had spent years living it up, but the birth of Sunny, their first daughter, had cramped their style. Uli seemed to have adjusted to parenthood better than Victoria, who was, to put it kindly, a bit self-involved.

Sylvia smiled, hearing Uli's voice. When Victoria and Uli had last visited, staying at the St. Regis even though Sylvia and Ray had a spare room and a pullout couch, Uli had bought a leopard-print ski suit, wearing it all week, to his daughters' delight. He'd performed an amiable bump-and-grind in the middle of the Snowmass mall, causing Sunny and her younger sister, Georgia, to collapse in giggles.

"Uli? Uli, it's Sylvia."

"Sylvia! Hello, Sylvia. Have you talked to her?"

"No, not in a few weeks. Is she home?"

"Oh, no," said Uli. "Oh, no, Sylvia. There is only bad news in this house."

Sylvia's stomach turned. "Can I talk to Victoria, please?"

"She is not living here, Sylvia," said Uli. "She's gone home to her mother."

"What?"

Uli laughed, but it was a mournful sound. "You call her yourself. She's going to need you."

"I was calling to tell her I needed her," said Sylvia. The words just slipped out.

"You need her!" said Uli, laughing again. "You can have her."

"Uli, what's going on?"

"Goodbye, Sylvia. I think it's best if we don't talk for a while."

"Uli!" cried Sylvia, but he had cut the line.

Slowly, Sylvia replaced the receiver. She felt in her pocket for change but found only a penny. Impatiently, Sylvia dialed the operator and told her to call collect. She knew the number of Victoria's childhood apartment by heart.

In some ways, though not officially, Victoria's parents had adopted Sylvia after her mother died. Sylvia moved into the Brights' apartment for her senior year of high school. It felt so good to have adults in charge—Sylvia's mother had never cared if she'd had enough dinner (she could forage in the fridge or order something) or needed clean socks (what was Pauline, a laundress?).

When Sylvia went to college, she stored her belongings with the Brights. Victoria went to live in Europe for the summer after high school graduation, then never returned to the U.S. She was attending *the college of the world,* she wrote.

Sylvia and Victoria exchanged letters during those years. In some ways, the physical distance helped keep their connection intact. Sylvia didn't have to watch Victoria on drugs—the way she'd get languid, lean in to people, in to *men*—she didn't have to be Victoria's babysitter, as she'd been toward the end of high school. Victoria wrote about the way winter in Venice was *as gray as heartbreak.* She wrote that she loved pistachio gelato so much she wished she could mail Sylvia a package full. She said she'd seen someone with the same color hair as Sylvia in Paris:

I almost ran after her. I would have been so happy if she had been you, and we could have sat on a bench in Luxembourg Gardens and talked all afternoon! Wouldn't that have been amazing, if you'd just surprised me like that? (Why not, Sylvie? This place would be heaven if I weren't lonely. Can't you see it? You and me in gay Paree?)

But Sylvia never visited. She didn't have the money, but she also dreaded the way things could get dark around Victoria. Sylvia felt secure communicating through letters. From across the ocean, Sylvia could have the good parts of Victoria—her loyalty, her adventurous spirit—and avoid the messy late nights and regretful mornings. Though, of course, Sylvia had regrets of her own.

During school vacations, Sylvia claimed the second twin bed in Victoria's room. The Brights welcomed her with open arms, even driving up to Cambridge when Sylvia played Sarah Brown in *Guys and Dolls.* After college, Sylvia worked in the accounting department at the Museum of Natural History and rented a windowless apartment a few blocks north of the Brights, visiting often and spending every single holiday seated at Mae's giant mahogany table, the linen napkins rolled just so and slipped into silver rings. During those years, Sylvia still wrote to Victoria regularly, but she stopped writing back. Every few weeks, Victoria would call instead, and her messages were slurred and frightening. She began to make threats—"I don't know what I'll do if you don't call me back, Sylvia."

Sylvia always called back. In her terry-cloth robe, flipping through channels with her television volume on low, she listened to Victoria's complaints (they were rants, really, fueled by booze and anger and who knew what else). Victoria was often betrayed, abandoned, bereft. It seemed that no one could handle her impossibly high standards, her volatility. No one else understood; no one else was honest, always there for Victoria; no one else was a true friend who always called back.

Only Sylvia.

When Victoria eloped with Uli, they settled down in Greece, and for a time, the late-night calls stopped. Sylvia was relieved, but she found she missed Victoria, too. Sylvia felt less important somehow—she didn't matter as much to anyone else. Life with Victoria was scary, but it was fierce and hot. Sylvia was lonely, her days a little colorless without her best friend in the background.

One March, Sylvia had taken a spring ski trip to Aspen with some colleagues. Sipping a glass of wine in the Caribou Club, she met Ray. Sylvia had never found a calling (being an assistant to an accountant suited her fine—she had no desire to go to accounting school) or a boyfriend; when Ray asked her (after four passionate days) to move in to his house on West Hopkins Avenue, she accepted. It turned out that Sylvia was scared of skiing; she was the only person in Aspen who would rather just read.

As the years went by, Sylvia and Victoria gradually lost touch. When Victoria's father, Preston—a tall, regal man with a distracted but loving demeanor—died, Sylvia sent an enormous bouquet. It had taken her a while to decide what flowers best honored the man. Calla lilies, she had decided: elegant, assured, a little snobby.

Sylvia's heart beat fast at the thought of being near Victoria and her family again. Life was so luxurious and exciting around the Brights. In the end, Victoria, despite her flaws, had been a loyal friend.

Sylvia waited for a ring, then two, and finally, Mae answered the phone sleepily and accepted the charges.

"Mae?" said Sylvia.

"Sylvia, dear? Is that you?"

"It's me! I'm coming home. I mean to New York. Which will be home from now on. Again. Anyway, is . . . is Victoria there?"

"No." Mae sighed, and in a tone Sylvia wasn't sure how to translate, she said, "No, Victoria is most certainly *not here.*"

"What's going on?" said Sylvia nervously. She had always counted on Victoria if she ever got the courage to run.

"It's a long story," said Mae. "I'll leave her a note to call you. Did you say you're at home?"

"I'm . . ." said Sylvia. She stared at her feet and swallowed. "Do you know when she'll be back?"

"No, dear," said Mae. "I have no earthly idea."

"Does she have her cell phone?"

"Yes! Why, yes, she does. I'm glad you thought of it. Let me get the number for you right now. I keep it on a pad in the kitchen."

"Thank you," said Sylvia.

"How are things in Aspen?" said Mae.

"I'm . . . Well, like I said, I'm thinking of moving back to New York," said Sylvia. Idly, she wondered if Ray had even noticed she was gone. She could still, she supposed, change her mind. She hadn't quit her job or anything. She could tell her boss in membership relations that she'd had the flu. She'd had the flu and been too sick to call.

"Back to New York! Well, well," said Mae.

"Do you think I should?" said Sylvia. "Do you think I should come back?" She twisted the phone cord around her finger until it hurt.

"I'm sure I don't know," said Mae. "Where would you live, dear?"

Sylvia had figured she'd live with Mae. She'd imagined staying in Victoria's sumptuous childhood bedroom, the way she had as a girl. There was plenty of room! Sylvia bit the inside of her cheek, suddenly exhausted. Her getaway plan was a flimsy fantasy, it seemed, though it had gotten her out of the valley.

"I guess . . ." Sylvia couldn't bring herself to say it. "I have some money saved up," she said instead.

"Here's Victoria's phone," said Mae, listing the digits slowly.

Sylvia fumbled in her bag, found a ballpoint pen. She wrote the number on her hand.

"Goodbye, sweetheart," said Mae distractedly. "You know you're like a daughter to me." She had always said that, from the time Sylvia's mother died.

"Thank you," said Sylvia. But she didn't feel like Mae's daughter, not at all. She felt like no one's daughter, abandoned. Sylvia got change for a dollar, then called Victoria's cell, but there was no answer.

Sylvia and Victoria hadn't been close in years. But just the imagined safety net of the Brights had brought Sylvia comfort. Where else would she go? Sylvia had certainly helped Victoria—she could only hope Victoria would be there for her now.

From a vending machine, she bought a pack of gum and a can of Cherry Coke. She found an empty bench and sat down. The Coke was cold and sweet in her mouth. A bus pulled in to the station, but it was not her bus. A few people filed in, looking disoriented and sleepy. Sylvia wished she had an iPod filled with dance music. She wished she had a book to read. Now would be a good time to slip into a fictional world—Queen Victoria's castle or Jane and Rochester's giant house.

There was a newsstand next to the café, and Sylvia stood in front of the bright paperbacks, looking for a book that would transport her. She didn't need a bodice ripper (*Taming the Ty-*

coon), and she didn't want to be worried about a mutant disease (*Ebola and YOU*) or a deepening economic depression (*The End of the American Dream*) or terrorism (*Bombs in the 'Burbs*).

For a time, Sylvia had taken Paxil to calm her anxiety, but then she had realized that she really *was* living the wrong life. She was sick of having to mingle with rich people in the hope that they'd buy one of Ray's elk paintings; disgusted with Ray, who slept all day on the couch in their overheated house; bored to tears of conversations that revolved around snow accumulation and kind bud. So she'd jettisoned the Paxil and started saving.

Sylvia had closed her account at First Colorado National Bank the day before, removing her paltry life savings: almost two thousand dollars. Now here she was in Denver. She grabbed a book called *Sisters on the Shore.* The Adirondack chairs on the cover looked so appealing, as did the two pairs of sexy shoes nestled into the sand.

Back on her bench, Sylvia opened the book. It was a balmy day in Martha's Vineyard, and a fight over a man was taking place poolside. One MacFarlane sister slapped another, and amid the drama, Sylvia fell asleep.

When she woke, sitting up quickly and making sure she still had her bag, the bus to Chicago was already boarding. Pregnancy was an amazing thing: when the baby needed your strength, the tiny thing knocked you out, just sapped every last ounce. Even after an hour-long rest, Sylvia was spent and slightly nauseated.

On the bus, she balled up her sweater for a pillow but could not fall back to sleep. By now Ray would surely be looking for her. She supposed he could even put out an APB, or whatever they called it. He was very possessive: he hacked into her email regularly and sometimes showed up at her office without warning, saying he was "just passing through," though there was nothing past Snowmass but Basalt.

In her bag, Sylvia found a package of peanut butter crackers and ate them all. She opened the window a few inches, enjoying the breeze across her face.

She thought of Victoria then, about how, when they were teenagers, they would ride the Staten Island Ferry and sit at the very front, feeling the wind blow their hair straight back, the safety bar cold as ice in their fists. Riding the ferry was one of the things they did on the days they skipped school.

When she met Victoria, Sylvia had been a mouse of a girl, cowering in the shadow of her glamorous and fucked-up mother. Pauline had been single, desperate for love and security—Sylvia understood that now. But when Sylvia was a child, Pauline had seemed all-powerful, impossible to fathom or impress. Who could blame Sylvia for what had happened—for doing anything to escape Pauline?

Sylvia lifted her chin. The past was done and gone, she told herself and her baby. She opened her book. But still—and always—Sylvia's mind wandered backward, as if there were something to figure out, a mystery hidden in her tangled memories.

3

When Sylvia was six, her father had written a large check to her mother. The money was to be used for Sylvia's schooling. Sylvia's father explained to Pauline that the money should cover school tuition, uniforms, supplies, and incidentals. For the next thirteen years. Until she went to college. He told Pauline he felt that with this check, he had fulfilled his responsibilities. He was, he pointed out, a good man. But he had never wanted a child with Pauline, she knew it as well as he did, and he was moving on with his life.

By the time Pauline returned home, she was hysterical, crying, holding out the check with a shaking hand, saying, "A good man! A good man!" and sort of laughing, too, and Sylvia turned off the cartoons her mother had left to babysit her. She helped Pauline into bed, then stared at the check, finally knowing her father's full name, anyway.

Pauline enrolled Sylvia at the exclusive Lark Academy for Girls. On the first morning of school, Sylvia's alarm clock went off at five. Her mother curled her hair with a curling iron, gave her a charm bracelet from her large jewelry box, and even let her have a touch of Chanel No. 5 on each wrist and behind each knee.

They rode the subway into midtown together. At Grand Central, Pauline disembarked, giving Sylvia a tight squeeze and saying, "This is the first day of the rest of your life."

Sylvia knew it was unusual for a six-year-old to ride the subway alone, but Pauline didn't seem to worry the way other mothers did. Sylvia kept her head down, so as not to attract notice.

At Eighty-sixth Street, Sylvia stepped off the car, as her mother had instructed. Even the air smelled cleaner on the Upper East Side. Sylvia saw herself in a store window: velvet headband, wool coat with brass buttons. At P.S. 94, she had worn jeans, a parka, and thrift-store sneakers. Her new penny loafers were stiff and hurt her feet.

A row of Lincoln Town Cars idled in front of Lark Academy. Sylvia stared at the building. She just needed to walk in and go to the Grade I classroom. (They used Roman numerals at Lark Academy, Pauline had noted, impressed, as she flipped through the school catalog. Sylvia wondered what was wrong with the regular numbers used at her public school.)

Everything would be fine if Sylvia could just find the place she was supposed to be, a chair where she could sit quietly. But she couldn't do it; she was nailed to the sidewalk. It was a beautiful fall day, the sun glinting coldly in the trees. Sylvia felt tears behind her eyes. *Go inside,* she told herself, *just step forward.* But she was motionless.

"Honey?" A black woman in a pink cardigan sweater had spotted Sylvia. "Honey?" she said again.

Run away, said a voice in Sylvia's brain. It was her own voice, interestingly. But Sylvia was, if nothing else, obedient. "Yes?" she said.

"Come here, sweetheart," said the woman. Her name, Sylvia would learn later, was Mrs. Horning. She was the school guidance counselor and could spot a lost girl a mile away.

"Okay," said Sylvia. She walked toward the woman.

"Are you a new Lark?" asked Mrs. Horning, peering through glasses that could use some cleaning.

"I am a new Lark," said Sylvia.

"Well, then, come on in," said Mrs. Horning. Still Sylvia could not move. She fidgeted on the sidewalk, literally paralyzed with fear, until Mrs. Horning came and took her arm. And then, in the dorkiest manner possible, she walked into her new school.

They passed through the Upper School on their way to the Lower. Sylvia felt as if she were dreaming: an entire hallway of long-haired girls much older than Sylvia stretched before her, talking frenetically, tossing expensive handbags into lockers. The girls were thinner, angrier, more lovely than any Sylvia had seen in her previous life on the Lower East Side. (The school itself was spotless; Sylvia's shoes—the wrong shoes, of course, though they were expensive loafers from Saks Fifth Avenue—made an awful whining sound.) A ferocious floral smell filled the hallway. The scent, Sylvia thought, of money. Later, she discovered it was simply perfume: Opium by Yves Saint Laurent.

In the Lower School, girls Sylvia's age swarmed, creating a terrifying din. They shrieked each other's names, embraced, whispered secrets, cupping their hands to hide their words. Sylvia thought about the twister in *The Wizard of Oz,* the way it sucked houses and Dorothy into its merciless path of destruction.

"What's your name, dear?" asked Mrs. Horning.

"Um, Sylvia," she said.

"Sylvia what?"

"Sylvia Hall," she said in a whisper.

Mrs. Horning clapped her hands. The hallway noise lessened considerably, and Mrs. Horning announced, "Girls, you have a *new classmate*!" The girls turned toward Sylvia with adult expressions, surveying her like a sandwich they might choose to purchase or discard.

"Are you French?" a sarcastic voice yelled.

Wordlessly, Sylvia shook her head.

"Come with me," said Mrs. Horning.

As Sylvia followed, head down, another girl yelled, "Are you from Dorky Town?" When this comment was met with catcalls and hysterical laughter, Sylvia knew she was doomed.

The next three weeks were arguably the most stressful of her life. Besides the sad weirdness of her mother, there were the early-morning subway rides, days filled with fear and loneliness, then afternoons by herself in the apartment.

The Lark girls weren't mean to Sylvia, exactly, just dismissive and quietly cruel. Sylvia learned she was the only new student in Grade I. Everyone seemed to know she was weak, of no real importance. They peppered her with oblique questions about her old school, her address, her mother's job at Tiffany & Co. She answered, as her mother had instructed, that she lived in the Eldorado on Ninetieth and Central Park West. Her mother's job was "for fun." She lay awake at night planning out her strategy, what she could say, wear, or do to make someone like her.

Lunchtime was the worst. There seemed to be unspoken rules about who sat where and with whom, and Sylvia couldn't fathom where she belonged. The popular girls had lunch boxes filled with deli-meat sandwiches and packages of cookies or chips. Pauline didn't have time to pack a damn lunch, she said, and she told Sylvia that if she wanted to wrap up dinner leftovers, she should feel free, but Pauline wasn't putting overpriced turkey slices on the shopping list.

Sylvia stood with her paper bag (she'd made a butter sandwich and rehearsed a story about food allergies), blinking fast to keep from crying, not knowing where to walk, terrified to sit down. The first week she put her bag in the trash can without eating at all, then hid in the bathroom, holding her feet up off the floor so no one would see her. She was hungry, but hunger could be managed.

One day a popular girl named Victoria walked up to Sylvia, stopped, and folded her arms over her rib cage. Sylvia's stomach ached, anticipating a new humiliation. But Victoria smiled, and Sylvia nervously smiled back. "Do you want to come over?" Victoria asked.

"What?" said Sylvia.

"I have a bed with a top on it," said Victoria. "And I have a fish named Kennebunkport."

"Oh," said Sylvia. Hope shot through her, as painful as needles. "I don't have a fish."

"You can come feed my fish," said Victoria.

"I live in the Eldorado," said Sylvia.

"I don't know what that is. Do you want to come over?"

Sylvia nodded. "Yes," she whispered.

"Okay, your mom can write a note to my mom," said Victoria. "You can be my new best friend." As she spoke, she looked over her shoulder at Chelsea Davenport, her former best friend, who watched with naked sorrow, biting one of her pigtails.

Why had Victoria chosen Sylvia? Maybe she was bored. Maybe she smelled Sylvia's longing and wanted someone to control. Maybe it was the lucky penny Sylvia had found that morning on the subway and put in her pocket, squishing her eyes closed and praying, *Please let someone help me.*

Underneath the Lark Academy cafeteria table, Victoria would take hold of Sylvia's hand. Sometimes she rested her head on Sylvia's shoulder, and Sylvia tilted her head slightly to fit the curve of Victoria's head into the hollow of her cheek. Victoria smelled of expensive shampoo, a strong, synthetic scent of flowers and cheese.

Sylvia loved Victoria's laugh, her dismissive snort, the way she peered up at Sylvia when someone said something stupid, something they could make fun of later, when they were alone. Victoria's gaze caught Sylvia's and sent her the same message always: *We are better than everyone else.*

As soon as they could write, they began passing each other notes. They had so much to say to each other, it never ended, a river of scrawled words, hearts, exclamation points. They made up jokes, mean names for their classmates, calling Cynthia "Sin City" and Penelope "Penny Pincher."

One afternoon Sylvia unfolded a sheet of notepaper that read, *Truth or Dare??? Check one.*

Sylvia checked the box next to *Truth.* Victoria's dares were always terrifying—*Steal something from Miss Hovland's desk* or *Don't wear any underwear tomorrow.*

Victoria raised her eyebrows at the answer, then wrote quickly. While Miss Hovland, their teacher, taught them a song about apples in the apple tree, Sylvia unfolded the paper again: *Where do you really live?*

Sylvia felt her face grow red. Victoria had asked about Sylvia's parents, but she had hoped murmured responses would put off the inevitable. Sylvia looked at Victoria, who mouthed, *Tell me.*

Sylvia wrote, *306 East 11th.*

Victoria responded, *Take me.*

After school, they stood close on the subway platform. Sylvia was scared of what Victoria would think, but she had begun to realize that Victoria was attracted to dark things, dangerous things. And in the late seventies, Sylvia's street was seedy, frequented by drug addicts and homeless people. There was a junkie sleeping on the ground a block away from Sylvia's apartment. Victoria stopped to stare.

Unlike Victoria's entranceway, manned by a staff of uniformed doormen, Sylvia's lobby was dirty and empty, lined with rusty mailboxes. On the steps to her floor, as they passed Mr. Roberts sitting in a bathrobe in the hallway having a cigarette, when the warbling voice of a drag queen practicing her show rang through the stairwell, when Sylvia paused outside her own badly painted doorway, Victoria was silent.

Sylvia unlocked the three locks and shoved the door open. She saw her tiny apartment through Victoria's point of view: the dining room filled with clothes, the cheap blinds on the windows, the light the color of dishwater even after Sylvia turned on all three lamps. A phone began to ring shrilly, and Victoria said, "Do you need to get that?"

Sylvia shook her head, too embarrassed to inform her friend that it was the phone next door, audible through the thin walls. "Where's your mom?" said Victoria.

"She's at work," said Sylvia.

"Do you have any graham crackers?"

Sylvia nodded and led Victoria into the kitchen. She found a box of stale crackers and pulled milk from the refrigerator. She opened the carton and smelled that the milk had turned—

Pauline and Sylvia could never finish the milk in time. "Where's your room?" said Victoria.

Sylvia opened the closet and pulled the string to turn on the light. Victoria paused for a moment. Then she said, "Come on."

She crawled on top of Sylvia's bedding, crossed her legs Indian-style. "We can have a graham-cracker picnic," said Victoria. Sylvia sat next to her friend, feeling exposed as Victoria looked at the maps and pictures of glamorous places that Sylvia had taped to the wall.

"Don't be ashamed," said Victoria, meeting Sylvia's gaze and putting her hand on Sylvia's bare knee. "It's not your fault you have to live like this."

4

In Chicago, Sylvia had a forty-five-minute layover. She found a pay phone inside a McDonald's and dialed Victoria's cell again, breathing in the smell of french fries and ammonia. A large man in a cowboy hat ate a salad in the booth next to the phone. He sipped an extra-large soda through a straw. The mouth sounds nauseated Sylvia.

Victoria answered on the first ring. "Sylvie!"

"Hey," said Sylvia, her whole body relaxing at the sound of her friend's voice.

"Sylvie," said Victoria. "What's shakin', bacon?"

"I'm coming to New York," blurted Sylvia.

"What?" said Victoria.

Sylvia said nervously, "I left Ray. I finally did it. I'm coming to New York." She giggled, a girl's laughter. "Can you believe it?"

"Wow," said Victoria. "Yes, left on Fourteenth. Sorry, Sylvie, I'm in a taxi."

"Victoria?" said Sylvia.

"This is a bad time for me. I have a lot going on right now."

"Victoria," said Sylvia. "You always said—"

"I know, I totally know," said Victoria. "You are the *best* friend. You're so, *so* good to me. You came when I was at Hazelden, and Betty Ford, too."

"And Passages," said Sylvia, who had been trying to help Victoria get sober for years. "And I took care of your girls . . ."

"You're so awesome," said Victoria.

"I watched your daughters for ten days while you and Uli went to France," Sylvia soldiered on. "Well, now I need you. It's a long story. But I'm actually on my way. I was hoping I could maybe, just until I get on my feet, you know . . . I could maybe . . ." She pressed her lips together. It appeared that Victoria was going to make her grovel. "Vee," she said, "I'm in a bad spot. I'm going to need somewhere to stay."

"Shit, sorry. Here! Pastis!" said Victoria to the cabbie. "Let me call you tomorrow, Sylvie. I'm late for an appointment. A doctor's appointment."

"At Pastis?" said Sylvia angrily, recognizing the name of a hip restaurant. She had read the *New York Times* in the club library for years, idiotically making note of eateries she wanted to try and off-Broadway shows she wanted to see. In a leather chair, she would circle all the things she wanted to do in Manhattan, and then she would hang the newspaper back up on the wooden rod so some dot-com millionaire could page through it while enjoying an après-ski drink.

"Love you!" cried Victoria, hanging up.

Sylvia held the pay phone for a while, knowing that when she set down the heavy receiver, she would have to reevaluate her flimsy plans.

She turned around, and the man in the cowboy hat was staring. "What?" she asked.

"Not a thing," said the man. "I'm just eating my Southwest Salad."

"Hmm," said Sylvia. "I'm going for the Quarter Pounder with cheese myself."

"I don't blame you, miss," said the man. "Can't say I blame you a-tall."

When Sylvia reboarded, the bus was completely full. She squeezed next to a heavyset woman. The woman began playing ballads so loudly on her iPod that the whole bus could hear. Sylvia found herself soaking in the profundity of Bonnie Raitt's wisdom: *I can't make you love me if you don't.*

What could Sylvia have done differently along the way to have ended up somewhere else—somewhere like Paris, maybe, or Omaha, Nebraska? On HGTV the week before, she had watched a young couple shop for their first home in Charleston, South Carolina. That seemed like a good place, with a simple yet mellifluous name: Charleston.

Sylvia wanted to be loved.

She and Ray had started out strong. He was much older, and she'd admired his tweedy jackets, which had circular suede patches on the elbows. He wore his graying hair combed back, a lion's mane. He had authority, and he smelled like tangerines. He was an elegant skier, and everyone in town knew him and spoke admiringly of his animal portraits. For months Sylvia thought he had actually read some of the leather-bound books in his house. (In his defense, when she asked, he freely admitted that he had bought the whole collection from an antique store to "make things look distinguished.")

Your whole life could change in an instant, Sylvia mused. Certainly, she had never guessed that the time she'd rolled over and said, "Okay, but make it quick, hon" (half asleep while Ray yanked at her nightgown) would be the moment she'd become a mother. Who knew? She hadn't even had an orgasm.

The first time Ray had asked her to get rid of a baby, Sylvia had been thirty. When she saw the lines on the pregnancy test from the 7-Eleven, she wasn't sure how she felt. She told Ray over dinner at Campo de Fiori, and he poured her a glass of Chianti and said, "I think I've told you how I feel about babies, Sylvia."

"I know," she'd said. "Right. So I guess that means—"

"Yes," said Ray. "I'll make an appointment. It doesn't hurt, but you should take a few days off. You'll get pretty worked up and cry a lot."

"You talk like you've been through this before," said Sylvia.

Ray leaned over the table to kiss her on the forehead. "I'm twelve years older than you," he said without further explanation.

The second time she was thirty-seven and tried to argue Ray out of the abortion. "This might be my last chance to be a mother," she'd said.

"I think you'd better decide whether you want me or a baby," said Ray. "I'm trying to be impartial, dear, though I hope you'll choose me." Sylvia had chosen Ray and another horrible visit to the Aspen Valley Hospital, followed by a home-cooked meal. (He'd made the same meal as the time before! Meat loaf and garlic mashed potatoes.)

Four years later, Sylvia had stopped taking the pill. When she began to feel her breasts swell and her sense of smell sharpen—she'd yelled at one of the personal trainers for making microwave popcorn that made the membership office stink for days—she bought a test and took it at work in the ladies' locker room. Listening to a group of women chatter in the hot tub, Sylvia saw that she was pregnant. This time, without hesitation, she chose the baby.

Sylvia watched the oncoming cars as the bus barreled along. She leaned back in her seat and listened to her seatmate's next selection, Fleetwood Mac's "Landslide." Despite the brush-off, Sylvia knew they had been friends for too long for Victoria to refuse her. They were bound, like sisters.

5

When they were nine, Sylvia and Victoria spent the night in Central Park. Earlier that day, Victoria had handed Sylvia a note as they parted ways after school. On the subway, Sylvia had unfolded it.

Belvedere Castle, midnight tonight, under the dragon. I dare you.

Ever since they had studied the history of Central Park, the public expanse of land that ran from Fifty-ninth Street to 110th Street and between Fifth Avenue and Central Park West, spanning over eight hundred acres, Sylvia had been obsessed with Belvedere Castle. Built in 1865, the castle now served as a weather station. When you climbed to the turret, the highest point in the park, you gained a panoramic view in every direction. The first time Pauline took Sylvia up, Sylvia stood in the afternoon sunlight—shading her eyes to see the Delacorte Theater, the Great Lawn, Turtle Pond—and felt an unfamiliar but thrilling sentiment: power.

Power was something Sylvia had very little of. Pauline controlled Sylvia's every move outside of school, and Victoria basically told Sylvia what to wear and whom to speak to during the day. Maybe it was to get some measure of strength that Sylvia had begun leaving bugs and even a dead bird in Victoria's locker. When Victoria ran to Sylvia, almost in tears over the latest disgusting discovery, Sylvia held her friend, savoring the feeling of comforting someone, taking care. In idle moments, Sylvia tried to figure out what sort of shock might lead Victoria to need her even more.

When their class had taken a trip to Central Park, Sylvia had led Victoria away from the group. "Please," she'd begged. "I want to go to Belvedere Castle." The chaperoning teacher was distracted, and the girls easily broke away. They held hands as they followed a paper map, eventually reaching the stone building. Above the castle entry was a giant dragon made of metal: an eagle's face, a serpent's tail, the wings of a giant bat. "That's freaky," said Victoria.

"I love it," said Sylvia.

It was clammy inside the castle. Sylvia reached out to touch the stone wall, and it was rough and cold. The air smelled of grass and something darker, like rust. The bright afternoon disappeared, replaced by a murky light. Sylvia could still taste her peanut-butter-and-honey sandwich in her mouth.

The girls ignored the tourists peering at skeletons and telescopes (the castle also served as a nature observatory and museum) and climbed to the turret. Their footsteps were heavy and loud in the enclosed space, but the observation tower was flooded with light. As Sylvia stood next to her friend, taking in the view, she wondered—just for an instant—how it would feel to push Victoria off the edge and watch her fall.

The night of Victoria's dare, Pauline went to bed late, leaving the television on in her bedroom. Sylvia had packed a backpack with a blanket, bread, and one of Pauline's Coca-Colas. She shouldered the pack and quietly let herself out of the apartment. Her hallway was empty, but she could hear someone shouting on the second floor. Sylvia waited for the shouting to stop, and then she ran downstairs, pushing open the door to East Eleventh Street, which was alive with music and neon lights. No one—not the druggies sitting on the sidewalk, not the man at the newspaper kiosk, not the guitar strummer at the entrance to the subway station—no one noticed Sylvia or asked her what on earth a nine-year-old was doing out of her apartment in the middle of the night. She walked to Greenwich Village, slipped a token into the turnstile.

Sylvia was nervous as she waited for a train in the deserted subway station. Her eyes darted to every shadow, worried that someone would hurt her, push her down. She was ready to fight back: they had learned from a self-defense video in gym class to grab for an assailant's ear or try to break his or her nose. A group of loud kids in nylon jackets walked by Sylvia, yelling and punching one another, but they did not pay her any mind.

Finally, her train appeared on the track, its lights blazing. Sylvia stepped back as the train halted, the smell of the brakes burning in her nose. There was a man slumped into the corner of the car—asleep? drugged?—but Sylvia sat down far away from him, watching the empty stations as they passed. She got off at Seventy-ninth Street.

It was quieter uptown, and smelled as if a heavy rain had cleansed the pavement while Sylvia was underground. As Sylvia entered the park, her backpack heavy on her shoulders, she heard a woman crying on a bench but ignored her.

It was a spring evening, and the air tasted of asphalt. Jutting out from Vista Rock, the castle loomed large and dark. Sylvia moved toward it quickly, trying not to think about who could grab her, about the stories of murder and rape that Pauline read aloud every day from the newspaper, saying, "Sylvia, listen to this! *This* is why you come straight home after school . . ."

She reached the doorway of the castle and squinted, but Victoria was nowhere to be seen. Sylvia was exhausted, the small thrill of a midnight liaison completely faded. She figured she'd wait for a few minutes—and then what? She'd get back on the subway. But the thought of the Union Square station in the dead of night made her stomach heavy.

"Sylvia!" Victoria's voice came from a shadowed area to the right of the castle.

Sylvia narrowed her eyes but saw nothing. "Vee?" she hissed.

"Over here," said Victoria.

Sylvia crept toward the sound, hoping her vision would adjust and she could find her way. After a few steps, she saw a shadowy light, and behind a tree, she found Victoria. Somehow, Victoria had smuggled her expensive pink bedspread out of her apartment and spread it out on the ground. She held a lit candle. "You came," said Victoria, her smile dazzling. "I knew you would. Look!" She lifted a cardboard bakery box. "Chocolate cake!"

All Sylvia's fears dissipated as she sank down next to her friend. They ate the rich fudge cake with their fingers and drank Pauline's soda. Then they snuggled under the bedspread, and Victoria blew out the candle. The sky above them was a velvet cape embroidered with diamonds, and Sylvia was filled with an unfamiliar sense of peace. It was so nice to be sleeping outside, not in her stuffy closet space. Victoria took a length of Sylvia's blond hair and braided it together with her own. She said something softly, and Sylvia said, "Mmmm?"

"I love you," said Victoria.

Happiness washed over Sylvia. She fell into a deep sleep, perhaps the most complete sleep of her life.

That year for her birthday, Victoria gave Sylvia a silver bracelet with a single charm: a winged dragon. "I got one, too," said Victoria, latching it around Sylvia's wrist. "You can never take it off, no matter what. Promise?"

"I promise," said Sylvia.

6

Victoria and Sylvia began solving mysteries in Grade IV. Mae bought Victoria anything she wanted, so when she showed a bit of interest in Nancy Drew, all thirty-two books were individually wrapped underneath the Bright family Christmas tree. Victoria and Sylvia read them in order and voraciously, relishing Nancy's thrilling life, titian hair, and handsome boyfriend, Ned.

The first of their own mysteries they tackled was the Case of the Break Room. At lunchtime they ate under the supervision of Lark Academy aides; Victoria and Sylvia were curious about where the teachers went during these twenty-five minutes. What exactly happened behind the heavy oak door marked STAFF ONLY?

They made a plan. Sylvia would pretend to be ill (stomach poisoning, they decided), and while she distracted the aides with her moaning and eventual collapse, Victoria would run to the break room, twist the heavy knob, yell about Sylvia's sickness, and gather evidence. Victoria had packed her supply kit inside one of Mae's larger Coach purses: a magnifying glass, flashlight,

French-English dictionary, apple, and a change of clothes, including underwear. (Nancy Drew was always getting dirty inside old castles and attics.)

Victoria gave Sylvia the wink just after they opened their lunches. "Oh!" Sylvia said loudly. "Oh, my stomach!" Jeanine Barrack, sitting next to her, raised an eyebrow.

"She's really sick!" cried Victoria, running out of the cafeteria, her supply kit banging into her hip.

"Oooooh," moaned Sylvia. "Oh, my stomach! I feel shooting pains and impending nausea!"

One of the aides, a young blond woman, came over to help. Sylvia recited all the symptoms she had memorized after consulting *Where There Is No Doctor* in the library, and she was sent to the nurse's office. Lying on a cot, her face pressed against a pillow that smelled like mint, she began to actually feel sick. By the time Pauline arrived, her hair frizzed out, her cheeks pink from a rushed trip between Tiffany and Lark Academy, Sylvia felt downright awful. Pauline splurged on a taxi and said, "Poor baby," but shrank back when Sylvia tried to lean in to her. Pauline did not like to be touched, at least by Sylvia.

At home, Pauline heated up a can of chicken noodle soup and made toast. Sylvia lay in her mother's queen-size bed, guilt and gratitude swelling in her stomach like bread. Pauline served Sylvia on a tray, and then the phone rang. Sylvia heard Pauline laugh throatily and then say, "An unexpected gift from Sylvia, yes, exactly! Yes, yes, a half hour." Pauline went into the bathroom and Sylvia heard the water running. Pauline emerged in a towel and changed into a lacy slip and a cotton dress with heels.

"Where are you going?"

"Oh, I've got to go back to work, honey," said Pauline. Before leaving, she sat next to Sylvia and brushed her hair back from her forehead. "You don't have a fever," said Pauline kindly. "Don't wait up," she added.

Victoria met Sylvia by the Lark Academy entranceway the next morning. "Read this and then destroy it," she said, looking both ways before handing her a sheet of notebook paper.

> THE CASE OF THE SO-CALLED BREAK ROOM
> Entered Room at 11:21 A.M.
> Ms. Neumann was smoking a cigarette! Drinking something from a mug.
> Room filled with all the teachers.
> Mrs. Drake was reading a book with a man with no shirt on the cover.
> Mr. Henry was talking to Mrs. Moray—LOVE CONNECTION???
> Gathered all evidence: matchbook from BUD'S BISTRO, Ms. Neumann's mug, French worksheets in garbage can, man's cardigan sweater that smells like BO.
> DESTROY AFTER READING!!!!

During homeroom, Victoria kept trying to catch Sylvia's eye, but Sylvia had lost interest in the game. She kept thinking about her mother and the lace slip. Her mother's eager face made Sylvia feel hot with embarrassment and anger. She had wanted her mother to stay with her, feed her more soup and then ginger ale, even though Sylvia had been faking the illness.

After school, in her fancy room, Victoria lay out all the stolen items, and Sylvia pretended she cared. When Victoria said huffily, "What's the problem?" Sylvia just shook her head. She couldn't think of where to begin, how to explain what was wrong. When Victoria sat next to Sylvia and put her arms around her, Sylvia let her head fall into her friend's shoulder. Victoria held her like a child, stroked her back the way Pauline had not.

Sometimes Sylvia was overwhelmed by envy. If there was a God, why did He give Victoria a rich family and parents who cared about her? Why did he give Sylvia only Pauline? Sylvia wanted to *be* Victoria, not just her friend. When Victoria suggested they solve the mystery of where Sylvia's father was, it seemed like a good idea.

There were nights when Sylvia let herself believe that if she found her father, he would make everything okay. There was some explanation for his abandonment. Perhaps Pauline had hidden Sylvia from him, or maybe she had refused to let him contact Sylvia. Pauline's story about Sylvia's father was perfectly logical, but Sylvia couldn't help dreaming that if her father met her and his wife died or something—a car accident? a fall from a building? someone mugging her? she could even be murdered, like the chauffeur in the movie of *The Hidden Staircase*—then Sylvia's father would marry Pauline, and Sylvia would have a real family, like Victoria. Sylvia could bring lunch for the two of them sometimes, or ask Victoria to come and lie on Sylvia's big canopied bed and eat homemade cookies.

The Case of the Missing Father began one night when Sylvia was sleeping over at Victoria's apartment. Her parents were out, and unlike Pauline, they didn't believe that nine-year-olds could be left alone without a babysitter. Victoria's favorite babysitter was Casey, who lived in her building. Casey was in Grade X at Lark Academy, and she brought a bag of popcorn in her backpack and usually let them watch TV until they got headaches.

Over Mello Yello soda and takeout Maria's pizza, Victoria asked Casey to help solve a mystery. "Sure, Vee," she said. "What's the deal?"

Casey loved talking about boys, so they had made a plan that they hoped would entice her to help but not alarm her enough to mention the mystery to any adults. "I met a boy this summer," Victoria began. "At Popover's. He was with his dad. Um, he likes strawberry butter, too."

Casey put her chin in her hand, leaning toward Victoria. "Go on," she said.

"Well, I just thought . . . I want to write this boy a letter," said Victoria.

"Did you kiss him?" asked Casey. "You're a little young for kissing," she said, furrows appearing on her brow.

"Oh my God! No!" said Sylvia, exploding into giggles.

Victoria glared at her. "I know his father's name," she said. Sylvia felt a shock just hearing the name spoken aloud. "So how do I find this guy?"

"How do you know his father's name?" asked Casey suspiciously.

"Um, Victoria looked at his credit card, when he paid . . . for the popovers," Sylvia said.

"Right, right," said Victoria.

"Have you tried the phone book?" suggested Casey.

Of course they had tried the phone book. Victoria's shoulders slumped. "Can you think of anything else?" she asked.

"Maybe he doesn't live in the city," said Casey, taking another slice from the pizza box. "Maybe he's B&T."

B&T meant *bridge and tunnel.* It was what they called kids who came into the city from the suburbs to shop at Antique Boutique or see *Cats.* Victoria's eyes lit up. "How do we find someone in the suburbs?" she asked.

"There's some phone number where you can search the whole state," said Casey. "Nine-one-one? No, that's emergency. It's four-one-one, I think. You can search the whole country with four-one-one."

Victoria had a big-button phone on the wall of her room. Casey had a pen with a feather on top. Sylvia was sitting on the rug, toes in the deep white shag, when Victoria said, "Write it down! I've got him." She recited the address, hung up the phone, and hugged Sylvia too tightly.

That weekend, Sylvia and Victoria traveled incognito to Holt, New York. They wore disguises—ski hats and sunglasses from Victoria's hall closet. Victoria had packed her father's Nikon camera, and they bought Twix bars and magazines at Grand Central. It was early spring, so the stares they attracted might have been about their wool hats and long coats, but they imagined spies along the shadowy halls, bad guys intent on thwarting their mission crouched at the edge of staircases.

Victoria told the man at the ticket booth that they were sisters and their mother was getting a cup of tea to drink on the train. The man put his forearms on the counter in front of him and stared at them distrustfully. "What about *her* ticket?" he asked.

"She has a pass. Like, you know, a bus pass or whatever," said Victoria.

"A commuter monthly?" said the man.

"Definitely, yes," said Victoria. "A commuter monthly. For

sure." She looked at Sylvia, nodding way too enthusiastically. "Right, sis?"

"Right," Sylvia said.

"You girls need a round-trip?" said the man.

"No," said Victoria. "I mean yes."

"Peak or off-peak?"

Victoria licked her lips. "Um," she said, "how about off-peak. Definitely off-peak, for sure."

"Off-peak, definitely," Sylvia said. They had no idea what peak was all about—they had never left the city unaccompanied.

"Track nine," said the man, taking Victoria's cash and handing them tickets.

"That was a close call," said Victoria as they walked across the giant lobby.

"Don't talk so *loud,*" said Sylvia.

"Right, right," said Victoria. She scratched her head. "My hair is hot."

Sylvia laughed, and Victoria grabbed her hand and squeezed it. They walked down the stairs to the lower level and made their way to track nine. The steel-toned light in the train car was made even darker by their sunglasses; Sylvia smelled oil and sweat. She tripped and fell, and Victoria helped her up. They slid into an empty seat. Sylvia's hands were red and a bit skinned. She was upset, close to crying.

"Maybe this isn't—" she began, but Victoria was rummaging in her supply kit. She drew out a tube of first-aid ointment, and as the train pulled from the station, she began applying it to Sylvia's scrapes. Sylvia kept her sunglasses on so nobody could see her tears.

It already felt like summer in Holt. As they stood on the platform with a bunch of babysitters and maids, Sylvia said, "I've got to take the hat off," and Victoria nodded.

"Taxi," she said, pointing at two cabs idling in the parking lot. She walked purposefully, and Sylvia hesitated. She knew in her heart of hearts that this was not a mystery. Her blood father lived with his real wife and family and wanted nothing to do with Sylvia. Seeing his house wouldn't change anything. Most likely, it would make things worse. But there was no stopping this mission. Once Victoria decided on something, that was that.

"Come on!" said Victoria, who had already climbed into the taxi and confidently given the driver the address.

The driver nodded and began to drive. They whizzed along under a railroad bridge and past some shops and then some big houses and then some really big houses. Victoria rolled down the window, and Sylvia could smell salt water.

"Nice town," said Victoria. "You could live here."

"Right," Sylvia said sarcastically.

Still, she couldn't help but wonder: what would it be like to leave the East Village, her grimy street? To wake up every day and smell the ocean, instead of the urine-stench of East Eleventh? To know where her mother would be every night—at home, safe. Sylvia wished this for her mother and for herself—some safety, some affection, a street that smelled like grass and the sea. Sylvia hadn't shut off her gaping desires yet; she hadn't given up, and hope was as painful as a knife.

They turned onto Ocean Avenue. The houses were neat, lovely, with shutters next to the windows and bright green lawns.

"Here we are, girls," said the driver.

"Just hold on a sec," said Victoria. She pulled out the Nikon, and the driver slowed in front of number twelve.

"Don't go in the driveway," Sylvia said. She was ice-cold, despite the high temperatures, despite the sun.

"Whatever you like," said the driver.

Victoria began to snap, taking picture after picture. The house was white, with a picket fence surrounding it. "I'm getting out," Sylvia said.

"Don't get out," said Victoria, but for once, Sylvia defied her. She pulled the wool hat on and pressed the sunglasses to her face. She opened the car door and walked to the edge of the fence. The front door was black, with a brass knob in the middle. There was a mailbox on a metal pole, and feeling calm, as if she were dreaming, Sylvia opened it. There was a bill from the phone company inside, and a copy of *The Economist*. Sylvia looked at the name, and it was her father's name, and this was his house.

The yard was perfect. Sylvia went down the driveway and peeked into the back. There was so much grass, you could play soccer on that grass, or just lie in it and look at the sky. There was an oak tree in the corner that would be perfect—if somebody had a father to build one, who loved her enough to build one—for a tree house.

As they drove back to the station, Sylvia looked out the back window. Before they turned the corner off Ocean Avenue and onto Purchase Place, Sylvia thought, *I wish I lived in a house like that.*

And then she said it aloud.

"Maybe there's a way," said Victoria.

Sometimes Sylvia loved Victoria's bullheadedness—the way she saw the world in black and white, the sense she held that anything was possible. But in this case, it made her furious. "There's no *way,* Victoria," she said bitterly. "Don't be stupid."

"There's always a way," said Victoria.

Sylvia snorted, staring out the taxi window. But a seed had been planted in her, and hope took root.

7

In Grade VIII, Sylvia met a boy in her building, Robert, and they began dating. Sylvia was crazy about her new boyfriend, but Victoria seemed skeptical, making comments about Sylvia's "thug" and her "ghetto boy." One night when Pauline was out, Victoria came over to watch *Girls Just Want to Have Fun* on the VHS player she'd given Sylvia for her birthday. As they ate ice cream after the movie was over, Victoria said, "You should break into Robert's apartment while he's sleeping."

"What?" said Sylvia, crossing her Tretorn sneakers and holding her spoon midair. "Why would I do that?"

"To watch him," said Victoria.

"That's just bizarre."

"Do you dare me to do it?" asked Victoria, finishing the Chunky Monkey and tossing the container into the trash.

"And get you arrested by his dad, *the cop*?" said Sylvia, hoping to laugh it off.

"Dare me," said Victoria. "I'll even get something to prove I was there."

"No," said Sylvia.

Victoria's eyes blazed. She didn't like it when Sylvia resisted her, but a dare was one thing, and breaking and entering was another. Besides, Sylvia thought she was in love with Robert. She was considering third base, having thoroughly enjoyed exploring first and second during the afternoons she spent entwined with Robert on Pauline's couch, watching soap operas and *Donahue.*

"Vee, you're being kind of a weirdo."

"Word," said Victoria, rolling her eyes. She got up and slung her bag over one shoulder. She had cut her hair to shoulder length and tied neon-colored netting in it to look like Madonna.

"Do you want to sleep over?"

"In the *closet*?" said Victoria dismissively, though they'd slept there countless times together.

"Bye," said Sylvia. Victoria let herself out and clomped down the stairs. Sylvia watched part of *St. Elmo's Fire* by herself and, humming the theme song, brushed her teeth. She wanted to call Robert but did not, afraid she'd wake his parents. She lay in bed thinking of him. He played football for P.S. 94. He wanted to be a guitarist, like Slash. His hair was brown, and his eyes were blue. He made fun of Sylvia for being a bookworm. Sylvia fell asleep wondering if she'd marry Robert and what she and her bridesmaids would wear.

At school the next day, Victoria passed Sylvia a note: *He's even cute when he sleeps.* Sylvia stared at the paper. She was filled with both fury and fear. She did not write back and wouldn't meet Victoria's gaze.

After class, Sylvia cornered Victoria next to her locker. "You went into his apartment?" she yelled. "Jeez, Vee! That's messed up!"

"I just climbed in from the fire escape and watched him sleep for a while," said Victoria. "No biggie."

Sylvia glared at her friend. She had the urge to strike her, to smack the self-assurance from Victoria's face. She wanted to wound Victoria, make her feel as small as Sylvia herself felt.

"These were under his bed," said Victoria, rummaging in her knapsack. She pulled out a blue pair of boxer shorts and handed them to Sylvia.

Sylvia raised her hand. How long had Victoria sat on the shag carpet, smelling the private smells of Robert's sheets, his socks, his sleeping breath?

"Oh, you're going to hit me?" said Victoria.

"If you go near Robert again, I'll kill you," said Sylvia in a low and serious voice.

"Yeah, right," said Victoria, and her dismissive laughter boiled in Sylvia's gut like poison. "You're so funny, Sylvie," said Victoria.

8

Pauline died of cancer when Sylvia was seventeen. Sylvia could still smell the apartment: beef broth and soap. She held her mother's hand until the end. It was warm for a long time, and then it grew cold and Sylvia let go.

She took a bath with her mother's Jean Naté bubbles. It felt like something had been torn down—the wall between Sylvia and death. Words ran through her head: *You are next in line*. After her bath, Sylvia went back into the living room. The sun was still hours away, and most of the apartment windows surrounding her were dark. The nurse would arrive at seven A.M.

She knew it was time to call the nursing service and have Pauline taken to the funeral home. Once Sylvia dialed, everything would run smoothly. But she went back to Pauline and took her hand again. "Bye, Mom," Sylvia said.

After the doctor had signed the papers and Pauline's body had been carried away, Sylvia closed the door to the building and was alone in the lobby. The few neighbors who had been roused by the ambulance had gone back inside their apartments. Sylvia glanced at the row of mailboxes as she walked toward the stairwell, then stopped. There was a postcard pinned to their mailbox, an outgoing missive. It had three stamps and was addressed in Pauline's wobbly script. Pauline must have given the card to a visitor and asked him or her to mail it, thought Sylvia.

She pulled the faded card and stared at it. It pictured a dining room in a restaurant called Gene's: wicker chairs, tables covered with white cloths. GENE'S FRENCH-ITALIAN FOOD, a swirling font said. DISTINCTION. LUNCHEON, DINNER, COCKTAILS. Pauline had written nothing except a name and an address in Holt, New York. Sylvia stared at the name: her father's name.

Then she put the card back where it had been.

Sylvia dressed carefully for the funeral a week later. She wore a Fendi gray skirt and matching jacket. She'd been around the Brights long enough to know the power of wealth. Before leaving the apartment, she looked coldly at herself in the mirror. Her skin was unblemished, her makeup light. She pinned her blond hair back with combs, fastened her mother's gold buttons on her ears, looped a matching necklace around her neck. If her father did come to the funeral, she wanted him to be proud of her, to think she was beautiful. She wanted him to feel sorry for what he had lost.

During the funeral service, Sylvia saw a portly man in an expensive wool coat move quietly into the church. His expression was polite. He looked sad and honest. But in his deep-set eyes and high forehead, Sylvia saw a resemblance to her own face. He had her nose, too, a bit wide. She wanted to run to him, to hold him, to punch him.

While the priest droned on, the man kept his gaze on the prayer book. Pauline's old colleagues from Tiffany lined up to peer into the open casket (Pauline's vain request), but the man remained in his pew. When the service concluded, Sylvia saw him preparing to leave. He checked his watch, gathered his coat from beside him. Sylvia knew she didn't have much time. Darting past well-wishers, she walked straight toward him. He looked up with a distant but pleasant expression.

Sylvia reached the man. She was blinking back tears already. His hair was trimmed neatly around his ears, which were Sylvia's ears, the lobe attached and fleshy. "Hello?" he said.

"I know who you are," Sylvia said. She smiled up at him, and what had she expected? An embrace after all this time? Did she think he would adopt her, take care of her? In a way, in a small part of her heart, she did.

His eyes darted upward, the only evidence of his deception. And then, without missing a beat, he met Sylvia's hopeful gaze. "Who am I?" he asked.

"You're my father," she said. "I'm Sylvia."

The corners of his mouth lifted, and he looked for all the world like a good man. But he said, "No, Sylvia. No. I can't be your father." He cupped her shoulder and turned to go. "I am very sorry about your mother," he said. And then, before walking away and letting strangers take his place, he kissed her on the cheek.

Sylvia's shoulders fell forward, but she wouldn't rush after the man, wouldn't ask for help or love, like Pauline. She tried to make a mask of her face. She had to turn around, to go back to the scraps of her life.

In a corner of the church, she saw Victoria and her mother. Mae stood with her arms crossed, her black hair neatly curling at the padded shoulders of her suit.

Victoria was watching Sylvia's father, staring daggers at his back. She was fiercely loyal, like a pit bull. Mae was looking at Sylvia. She lifted her chin and walked over briskly.

"Come on," she said, reaching out to Sylvia. "You're done with all of this, sweetheart. Come with me. You're a Bright girl now."

A few weeks later, Victoria took Sylvia to the party on the beach.

9

The Cleveland Greyhound station was located on Chester Avenue, which sounded quaint but was not. From a grimy booth (why—really, *why,* did people feel compelled to stick their used chewing gum on pay phones?), Sylvia decided to call her own cell and check for messages. If she dialed the number and hit the pound key and her password, she could hear the messages without making the phone ring on the kitchen counter. What was Ray doing now, she wondered—had he gone to the club to look for her? Most likely, he was fixing a drink, settling into his La-Z-Boy recliner and flipping through the channels, resting his drink on top of his large belly. It was disgusting—revolting! A stomach big enough to rest a cocktail on!

As she dialed, Sylvia watched a throng of people smoking. They were confined to a glass-walled smokers' area but seemed genial enough, lighting each other's cigarettes and smiling. Sylvia smoked sometimes after a few glasses of wine. But that was over, too: the smoking and the wine both, for a while. There was a woman with a baby in the smokers' area. The woman held the baby with her free arm. It was wearing a blue outfit, so perhaps it was a boy. If Sylvia had a girl, she'd let the girl wear blue, too, whatever she wanted. But the child would have to eat healthily. And not too much TV, for sure. Books, lots of books. Sylvia smiled at the thought of a plump child in her lap, pointing to pictures of animals in a book.

As promised, Victoria had called back, full of apologies and empty promises ("a girls' weekend" probably wasn't what she needed, Sylvia thought). Sylvia's boss had checked in, wondering if she had swine flu.

Sylvia erased both messages. She decided she was hungry for a midnight snack. There was a Bob's Big Boy adjacent to the station, with a plaque reading PLEASE SEAT YOURSELF. When a sleepy waitress with lots of mascara came over, Sylvia said, "I'll have the Brawny Lad burger with onion rings. And just some lemonade. No, you know, make it the Super Big Boy. I'm really hungry, because I'm with child."

"Are you, now?" said the woman.

"Yes," said Sylvia. "Is that how you say it? 'With child'?"

"I don't think so," said the waitress. "But I don't know, I guess you can say it however you want."

"You're the first person I've told," said Sylvia.

"Okay," said the waitress.

"I don't know if it's a boy or a girl," said Sylvia.

"I'd say boy," said the waitress.

"Really? How can you tell?"

"I'm just guessing," said the waitress.

"A boy," said Sylvia. Wonder ran like water from her scalp to her toes. "A boy," she said, more quietly.

"I'm going to give you a slice of pie on the house," said the waitress. "As long as nobody sees me take it."

"Thank you," said Sylvia. "That's really nice of you."

"I can just say I dropped it on the floor and threw it out," said the waitress. "It's no big deal."

"I appreciate it," said Sylvia.

"There's this thing you can do with a wedding ring on a string," said the waitress. "It'll tell you boy or girl for sure. But I guess neither one of us has a ring at the moment."

"Right," said Sylvia. "That's true."

"I was married once," said the waitress. "But anyway."

Sylvia couldn't think of anything to say to that, so she looked down at her place mat.

"I'll put your order in," said the waitress.

"Thanks," said Sylvia. She looked out at the rain and thought about a boy. *Charles,* she thought. *Benjamin. Scott. Jennings.* She had never been so happy in her life.

When she was so full she could barely speak, Sylvia went back to the station and boarded the next bus, for the last leg of the journey. Thankfully, there was a row she could claim for herself, and she stretched out, yawning.

She daydreamed about her mother. Pauline would come home from work at Tiffany and put on her bathrobe. If Sylvia rubbed her feet, Pauline would stay still and talk to Sylvia. In the overheated bus, seven hours from Manhattan, Sylvia remembered her mother's favorite story. "I was so young, so full of hope," Pauline would begin.

Pauline bought the green dress during her lunch hour, eating her ham and cheese sandwich as she walked back to work. She had stored the sandwich in her handbag; the slice of American cheese and the butter were soft. After she finished, she shook the waxed paper and folded it, slipping it into her bag to use the next day. Then Pauline thought about Izaan Mahdian and what she had to tell him, and she threw away the waxed paper, letting it fall to the sidewalk, thinking that perhaps she'd never have to pack a sandwich again.

Some of the girls were standing outside as Pauline approached the store, and red-haired Carole said, "Well, la-di-da! Who's shopping at Saks?"

"Special occasion," Pauline said, giving them what she hoped was a mysterious smile and slipping into the building. All afternoon, as girls like her (or not like her—girls like she wanted to be, girls who'd never been to Brooklyn or Queens, never even been south of the Empire State Building) chose engagement rings, and men like Izaan bought cuff links and gold watches, she allowed herself to dream of being on the other side of the glass counter.

Izaan was meeting her at the Carlyle Hotel at six. She had told him it was very important, and he had raised his eyebrows and said couldn't she tell him important things right there, in his bed? He was brash, proud of his body, unashamed of sex, though he was betrothed to a woman in Egypt—an arranged marriage—one that would unite two powerful families.

Pauline and Izaan had met when Izaan had bought the girl—her name was Dalia—a diamond solitaire and had it sent to Cairo, Egypt, insured for the full value, nestled in a midnight-colored velvet box. Now that Pauline had triumphed, she felt sorry for Dalia. And she wanted to deliver the news to Izaan over cocktails at Bemelmans bar, her collarbones exposed in a green silk dress.

There was no time to return home to Brooklyn; Pauline waited nervously for everyone to leave so she could change her clothes in the employee bathroom. Usually, she left as soon as her shift was over, and a few girls glanced at her curiously as she read The Waves *in the corner of the smoker, uncomfortable in a folding chair. Her heart was racing and she could barely concentrate on the words before her:*
"I love," said Susan, "and I hate. I desire one thing only. My eyes are hard."

Carole was the last to depart. "What are you doing here, Pauline?" she said rudely, her hand on a cocked hip. She had put on a new outfit, too: a miniskirt and a tight poorboy sweater.

"I'm reading," said Pauline, staring at the page. Izaan was probably finishing up his last call of the day, stacking his papers, rising and taking his hat from the coat tree in his office. Was he thinking of her, anticipating their kiss?

"Bookworm," said Carole jovially. "Want to join me for a drink at P. J. Clarke's? Me and some of the girls."

"No, thank you," said Pauline. "I'd better get home." She turned the page. "I just want to finish this chapter." She thought of Izaan putting on his overcoat, wrapping a scarf around his neck. He was tall, with wiry brown hair. He dipped his comb in lotion in the mornings, slicking his hair back, pressing it into place with his palm. Like Pauline, he was a product of the fifties. He wasn't growing a mustache or wearing bell-bottom pants. He wanted a wife in a bra, a wife who would happily stay home and cook for him. He'd complained about Dalia. "She wants to go to university, but what the hell for?" he'd said. Pauline had nodded mightily, sipping her root beer.

"Well," said Carole at last, "see you."

"Yes," said Pauline, "see you." But in her rib cage she held the hope, warm and fragile as a new-hatched bird, that this would be the last time she ever saw Carole, that after tonight she would move into Izaan's apartment and he would not allow her to set foot in Tiffany & Co. again. He would buy her jewelry from somewhere else—Cartier, maybe, or Bulgari. (And what would her mother do without Pauline to care for her? She'd have to make the best of it, Pauline decided definitively, grimly.)

In the small employee bathroom, which reeked of hair spray and Bon Ami, Pauline took off her panty girdle and sensible shoes. The Saks bag was filled with tissue paper; it rustled as Pauline drew the silk from its trappings. The dress slid over her skin as it had in the store, settling perfectly into place. It was sleeveless, with a jewel neckline and a small bow at the center. The skirt flared out from her still-small waist, and there were two slanted pockets covered with fabric buttons. It had cost a month's salary—an expensive bet, and the first real gamble of her life. Pauline reached behind to grasp the metal zipper. She tugged, but could get it only to her shoulder blades. "Damn it to hell!" she whispered, yanking, but the zipper did not rise.

In her stocking feet, Pauline pushed open the bathroom door a few inches. Maybe someone still remained, someone who could keep a secret. It would be a relief to confide in one of the girls, to have a friend. An only child, Pauline had always held her thoughts—and her suburban fantasies—secret. The world she read about in books, a sunlit world, clear, full of loving glances, fresh-cut flowers, and new appliances, seemed more real to her than her mother snoring a paper-thin wall away, the clank of their ancient heater, the musty blankets on her bed.

But the smoker was empty. Pauline gathered her things and jammed them in her locker. She put on her coat and opened the box that held the emerald shoes she'd bought to match the dress. She took a last look in the mirror (she wore hardly any makeup; Izaan had told her he liked "a fresh girl") and shut her eyes, saying goodbye to the Pauline who stood barefoot on dilapidated tile, her beautiful future in front of her, a shining road to the Upper East Side or even Westchester.

The door banged open, and Pauline screamed. "Jesus!" said one of the cleaning crew, a heavyset man with wide brown eyes. He held a mop in one hand; the other he put to his chest. "You scared me," he said.

"I'm so sorry," said Pauline. She bit her lip.

The man nodded warily. "I'll come back," he said.

"Is there any way . . ." said Pauline, taking her coat off. "I can't zip this."

"I don't think so, miss," said the man.

"Please." Pauline grabbed his upper arm; it was firm and strong. He smelled of toothpaste. "Please," she said. "I'm late. It's very important. Please, just zip me up!" She let go and whirled around. She could hear him exhale, and she felt the cool touch of his fingers. Carefully—tenderly, even—he raised the zipper, then latched the clasp at the top. For a moment there was silence. Pauline could not bring herself to face him. "Thank you," she said quietly.

"You're welcome," said the man, not moving.

For the first time since the moment when the doctor first told her, his brow creased, his gray eyes both worried and sad, Pauline felt ashamed.

"There she is!" cried Izaan in his elegant accent, standing up but not relinquishing his drink. Pauline walked toward him, hoping she looked radiant. He embraced her, then set down his glass and put his cigarette in his mouth to help her remove her coat, which he handed to a passing waiter. "Let me look at you," he said.

Pauline tilted her head as she had practiced in her childhood bedroom, peering at him sideways, letting her hair fall forward, a glossy curtain. "You're beautiful," said Izaan.

Still silent, she sat down, moving her shoulders back, exposing the hollow of her throat. A waiter appeared, and Izaan ordered a Dubonnet on the rocks for Pauline and another Manhattan for himself. Then he sat back in his seat. "So what's the big occasion?" he said.

"Do you like my dress?" said Pauline.

"I already said," said Izaan, lighting another Gauloises Brunes with a match, "you look beautiful."

Pauline glanced around the bar, pierced with a sudden terror. It was too late, the doctor had told her, and she would have to go through with it, whatever happened.

"See the ceiling?" said Izaan. Pauline looked up. "Twenty-four-karat gold," he said, exhaling smoke. "Can you believe it?"

Pauline nodded amiably. She was immune to gold, sick of the luxe and shiny. She just wanted to put her feet up and relax. Around the bar, Ludwig Bemelmans had painted playful scenes—bunnies smoking cigars, giraffes in Central Park, even a few portraits of his most famous creation (and Pauline's favorite character), the impish Madeline.

Izaan followed her gaze to the row of Parisian schoolgirls painted on the wall. "They say he did all this to pay for his hotel tab."

"I wish I were talented," said Pauline.

"You are, honey," said Izaan, but he did not elaborate.

The waiter brought their drinks, and Pauline took a small sip. "I bought this dress at Saks Fifth Avenue," she said.

"Did you, now?" said Izaan.

She looked at him, his clean jawline, features sharp and distinct, unlike the melted features of her mother and their neighbors. At first his dark coloring had seemed dangerous to her, but now she thought he was perfect. "Something has happened," she said. She took another mouthful of the Dubonnet, fortification. "Something wonderful," she added.

"Hmm?" said Izaan, though Pauline was sure he had heard her. From the Café Carlyle, on the other side of the hotel, she could faintly hear Bobby Short playing Cole Porter songs on the piano. "Hmm?" repeated Izaan.

"I'm going to have a baby," said Pauline. She tried to infuse the words with joy, and gripped his hand tightly. She heard the faint notes of "In the Still of the Night."

Izaan stared at her. He stubbed out his cigarette. He appeared to gather his thoughts, and then he said in a honeyed tone, "No, Pauline. No, you're not."

"I am," said Pauline, her voice quavering.

"It's okay," said Izaan soothingly. "Just stay calm. We can work this out, don't worry. I'll take care of it. Of you. I'll take care of you."

Pauline felt the bird in her chest begin to stir. "Really?" she said. "Really, Izaan?"

"It's a medical procedure," said Izaan. "It's very safe."

At first, Pauline thought the sound in her ears was a drum, pounding out a beat. She looked around to find its location as it thudded too loud, causing her head to hurt, an impending migraine. But then she realized it was just her own slow heart.

"It's too late," said Pauline. "We're having a baby."

Izaan stood. "You're having a baby," he said. He patted her on the shoulder, turned his gaze from one side of the room to the other, coughed. "I'll give you money," he said quietly. "I'm a good man. But that's all I can do."

Pauline watched him as he walked to the bartender, handed him a fold of bills. She felt drugged, immobile, her head pounding. By the time the bartender turned back to give Izaan his change, he was gone.

Pauline stood up and ran to the hotel lobby. Through the glass windows, she saw Izaan hail a taxi. "Izaan, wait!" she cried, pushing open the heavy door.

The taxi was still for a moment, and Pauline thought that he would get back out, turn to her.

"I thought he would break off the engagement with Dalia," Pauline would whisper. Sylvia's mother stared into the Eleventh Street living room, but Sylvia knew she was seeing Madison Avenue as the cab pulled away.

Pauline watched until Izaan was out of sight, she told her daughter. "It was then," she'd say to Sylvia sadly, "that I understood how it would be."

Sylvia's father had sent the antique jade earrings from Harry Winston the following week, along with a check. Pauline showed Sylvia the yellowed card: I wish I could be the kind of man you deserve, lovely Pauline. These are to match your green dress. Best wishes, Izaan.

The bus veered to the edge of the road, and the loud sound of the rumble strip woke Sylvia. She sat up, blinking. The bus headlights illuminated the Pennsylvania welcome station, but the driver did not stop. Sylvia put her hand on her stomach. As her baby grew, there was less and less room inside Sylvia for secrets.

Book Three

1

It was October 29, ten days since I'd gotten the call about Alex. Though I spoke with Laurent Janssen every day (he was Dutch, it turned out, the head of the operational arm of Médecins Sans Frontières in the Netherlands), he had no news for me.

There were at least a hundred burned bodies from the blast, said Laurent. They were "simply overwhelmed" trying to identify who was who in all the rubble. The disorder reminded me of September 11, when people had made posters of their loved ones and Scotch-taped them all over New York. I even thought about printing posters myself, flying with them to Baghdad. *Have you seen my brother?*

I was disheartened by how chaotic things were in Iraq. Though Mr. Janssen assured me that the Red Cross was in charge, and I received daily emails from the State Department, it was seeming increasingly possible that I would *never* know what had happened to Alex. After all, there were new bombings every week. Laurent Janssen told me wearily that sometimes bodies were "just blown to pieces" by a blast and were not identified at all. "Time, it will tell you," said Laurent, meaning, I suppose, that after long enough, they'd stop trying to sift through the debris and would just assume Alex was dead. This thought was unbearable.

When I pressed a State Department employee, he admitted that Alex had *already* been classified as "missing, presumed dead." Maybe they weren't even looking for him anymore. But I had not given up hope. Until they showed me his body—with the mole on his shoulder and the stupid tattoo of the word *love* in Arabic on his right wrist—until I kissed his cold face, as far as I was concerned, he was alive.

What do you do while you wait to find out if your brother is dead? Nothing seemed like the right thing to do. I couldn't bring myself to show houses. It felt impossible to get out of my chair to walk Handsome. Even hitting the South Austin trailer park for fried avocado tacos was unbearable: the sun too hot, the lemonade too weak, those fat pigeons who wouldn't leave me alone. If I thought about anything other than Alex, if I shifted my attention for a second, I feared I would lose him. It was exhausting to believe with all my might that he was okay.

I sat in front of my computer every morning, closing my eyes as the browser window opened, trying to see a message from Alex in my mind's eye. The subject line would be FLED TO PARIS! or *Amnesia—can you believe it?*

There was no email from Alex. There were no phone calls. He had not appeared in the middle of the night, tapping on my window. He had not surprised me at Central Market, his hair damp and curling along his forehead. Still, I waited for him to arrive, and to explain where he had been.

I didn't know what I would do with Alex's body. We had been brought up without religion, but our mother was buried in Beth

Israel Cemetery in Houston, so I figured that was where Alex would be buried, too.

A drive to Houston seemed as good a thing to do as any, so I made an appointment at the funeral home. A rabbi named Rabbi Goldman met me in a maroon waiting room. The room reminded me of the Paramount Theater in downtown Austin, what with all the tasseled curtains.

As Rabbi Goldman led me to his office, I thought about the time Alex and I went to see *Casablanca* during the Paramount summer movie series. It had been a rainy summer night, hot as hell. This was during Alex's Vespa phase, and he'd told me to wear a raincoat and "take it like a man." I muttered insults as I climbed on his sopping-wet ride, but the air smelled like basil as we whizzed by the community gardens, and the drops on my face felt cool and wonderful. We drove downtown as the sun broke through, and I watched my city light up—dazzling—and I held on to my brother.

I looked around the waiting room in the funeral parlor. *This is a place for dead bodies,* I told myself, *but Alex is not here.*

Rabbi Goldman cupped his hand around my shoulder as I looked at caskets with holes bored into them, "to let the worms in," as the rabbi said. "The body will return to the earth," said Rabbi Goldman. He said lots more, but I wasn't really listening. We went to the graveyard, and I stared at my mother's gravestone. *Alex's body will not return to the earth,* I told myself. *Not yet. Not if it is up to me.*

Of course—heartbreakingly—it wasn't up to me.

I had not attended my mother's funeral, but a year afterward, my grandparents brought us to her stone setting. Alex and I stood in the muggy Houston afternoon, surrounded by our grandparents' friends. I'd wanted to bring hydrangeas, my mother's favorite flower, but my grandmother told us that flowers counted as ostentation, and I could bring a rock instead to place on the gravestone. I didn't want to bring a rock. I held my right hand as if carrying a bunch of invisible hydrangeas, and I bent down and placed the secret flowers on the grave. I knew my mom would understand what I was doing.

That night Merilee told us we could no longer mourn our mother. She stood in front of the television and spoke in her important voice, her hands on her hips. Alex and I poked each other in the ribs as Merilee explained that the stone setting was all about closure. We were not to move back, we were to *go forward*. "The stone is now set," she said grandly, and then she went to wash the supper dishes.

Alex whispered to me about our father getting out of jail, even on the day of our mother's funeral. Our father would "come to claim us," Alex told me—he would "take us away from all this," Alex said, waggling his fingers at our grandparents' matching furniture, the sound of Gramma crying softly in the kitchen. Alex and I had already started down different paths—while he thought our days in Houston were temporary, I knew we were never going back to Ocean Avenue. I wanted to believe his promises, but even at age eight, I was pragmatic, logical—and without hope.

After saying goodbye to Rabbi Goldman, I drove to Cypress Grove Retirement Village. I found my grandmother in the hallway, looking at a purple orchid. "Hi, Gramma," I said. She glanced up, her eyes clear, but she did not speak. "So, Alex might be dead," I said.

"Alex might be dead?" said Gramma, finally turning to me. "It was Izaan," she said, nodding.

"No," I said. "It was an Iraqi suicide bomber. It was two Iraqi suicide bombers, actually."

She shook her head. "That doesn't make any sense."

"I hear you," I said.

"He killed my girl," she said. "He killed my baby."

"Gramma," I said, leaning in so close that I could smell her baby powder, "how do you know?"

Merilee shook her head, the prim certainty in her features softening in befuddlement. "I don't know."

I felt very cold. "What do you mean?"

"He's a bad man," she said. But all I saw on her face was uncertainty.

I stood up, dizzy. Gramma was senile, but was it possible she had never been sure what had happened on the night of my mother's murder? If my father hadn't killed my mother, then there was no explanation for her death, no lesson, no story. If this—my one truth—was not constant, then there was no ground underneath me.

2

Alex's landlord called and told me it was time to clean out his apartment. His lease ran only through the end of the month, she said, and if he wasn't going to renew, she would have to find a new tenant. Gerry looked at our finances and said we could try to pay Alex's rent for a few months if I was willing to eat cornflakes for breakfast and noodles for dinner. (We could forage the neighborhood park for berries and wild mushrooms, he noted.) But when I called Alex's landlord back, she said she had already found someone who would pay more and move in ASAP. The deal was done—signed, sealed, delivered. This struck me as brutally unkind.

When I refused Gerry's offer to help me take Alex's things to storage, he sighed and said, "Lauren, I need to talk with you. A serious talk."

"Oh, really?" I said. "A serious talk? Because what I need is a client looking to pay too much for a duplex. And another drink."

"I know you're going through hell," said Gerry. "But you

need to stop drinking, and I want you to go back to your therapist."

"I told you what I need," I said. "Are you pouring, or are you not?"

"I'm not," said Gerry. He folded his arms over his broad chest. "This is not an ultimatum, but I can't watch you . . . sink. I'm here, Lauren, but I'm not going down with you."

I was in pin-striped pajamas, though it was a workday, around noon. I got back in bed and pulled the covers over my head. The pills I had taken let me fall asleep in the middle of anything. "I don't need *help*," I said from under the covers. "I need a snack."

When I woke up, there was a plate with a sliced apple on the bedside table, and a little bowl filled with peanut butter.

The next day I went to clean out Alex's apartment. Alex had been a meticulous filer. His apartment had two bedrooms, and one ("the office") was lined with three enormous cabinets. I opened a drawer at random—it was Alex's papers, grades one through nine. I am not joking—he'd saved it all: progress reports, watercolor paintings, essays ("Abraham Lincoln: An American Hero," "What Democracy Means to Me," "A Visit to My Father"). I pulled out the last and scanned it. Alex hadn't gotten over our mother's murder, to be sure, but he had learned how to mine the situation for good personal-essay material. I knew he'd written about visiting Izaan in jail to gain entrance to Exeter and later, Harvard. Unwilling to pimp our family tragedy, I'd written about releasing turtles on South Padre Island ("Holding a Warm Shell at the Edge of the Sea") and had been rejected by both institutions and a long list of others.

I closed that drawer, then poked through a few more. There were his physical fitness certificates, graduation photographs, tax records, and med school diplomas. There was a thick file about possible vacations, organized under *alone, with L,* or *wife.* My stack was fairly dull: cheese tasting in Vermont, honky-tonk motel in Port Aransas. By himself, Alex had wanted to hit India and climb mountains in Tanzania. With his imaginary wife, the destinations had been quieter: a bed-and-breakfast in Wimberley, "romantic *gites* in the French countryside."

Surrounded by photographs of faraway locales, I felt a wave of sadness. I went into the kitchen and got a Hefty bag from under the sink. Then I went back into the spare bedroom and began shoving brochures into the bag. "I don't want to go cheese tasting!" I cried out, crumpling the image of a farmer milking a placid cow. "Why the fuck would you think I wanted to go cheese tasting?" I yelled. "And look at this stupid run-down shack!" I tossed the *wife* file, the *alone* file, the drawers documenting Alex's academic tribulations. "Arrogant asshole," I said.

I left the tax info, because who knew. But I emptied all the rest until I stood shaking in the middle of the room. Then I hauled the Hefty bag to the trash can and dumped it in, wheeled the can to the front of the house for pickup, and kicked it for good measure.

The woman who lived next door was sitting on her front porch in a lavender bathrobe, sipping a Lone Star. She regarded me without emotion. I went back inside Alex's apartment and into the spare bedroom. It looked the same—there was little evidence of all my hard work. The clock on Alex's desk read 3:02. The desk had been our father's; Alex had driven all the way to New York with a U-Haul to get it out of storage. I remembered sitting on my father's lap while he wrote longhand, the smell of his tobacco. My father had kept scraps of ideas for poems in the desk: *Lauren's hair* or *ocean at morning.*

On impulse, I went to the drawer. I reached out and touched the metal pull. I yanked, but it would not open. There was a keyhole, but I had never known the drawer could be locked. Certainly, my father had never locked it—who would want to steal his ephemera?

I peered around the room, looking for a key. Though I had ten days to clean out the apartment, I felt frantic. What was in the damn drawer? Probably naked pictures of some old lover of Alex's or *Playboy* magazines. Something racy, something private. I tugged at the drawer again, but it was shut tight. Then I ran into Alex's bedroom (that sweaty smell of him—I loved him so much) and looked in his bedside table, his closet. I opened his underwear drawer, pulling out socks, boxers, a strip of condoms, some smooth stones. And then I saw it glinting at the back: a brass key.

I knew I had to get out of Alex's apartment. I was freaking out, this was clear. But first: the drawer. Leaving Alex's belongings all over the bedroom floor (what the hell did it matter now?), I rushed into the office and inserted the key. I felt dizzy and could hear my heartbeat in my ears. The lock turned; I slid the drawer open.

Inside, there was an accordion folder packed with papers and photos. It was labeled simply, horrifyingly, MOM. I picked up the mess of papers and shoved it into my bag. Then I drove home, walked to The Studio, and handed the folder to Gerry.

"From Alex's desk," I said.

He took the papers and regarded me soberly. He turned off

his webcam and gestured to the beanbags in the corner of the shed where he'd told me he could "take meetings."

I sat down in the blue beanbag, rested my elbows on my knees. He sank into the red beanbag as I said, "I don't want to know the details. Can you just look through this file and see if there's anything important?"

"I can," said Gerry. He was well trained in this regard, having thrown away letters from Izaan for years. I wasn't sure he agreed with the way I had cut my father out of my life, but he knew it was complicated, and he respected me enough to let it be.

"I'm sure it can wait until tomorrow," I said. "If he's dead, there's no real hurry."

Gerry bit his lip and did not speak. For this, I loved him.

The next morning I got up and drank coffee, took a shower and went to work. "Well, well," said Jonesey when he saw me sitting at my desk, checking the new listings. "What have we here?"

"It's me," I said.

He touched the top of my head. "I'm so glad."

At lunch, I went to the New World Deli, where I had a tuna melt, a Diet Coke, and only one Advil. I spent the afternoon visiting houses, taking notes, almost even enjoying my walks through others' empty rooms and abandoned gardens.

That evening I felt something in me unwind as I parked in the driveway of my home. Two large trees flanked the house: a Texas ash and a Mexican plum. In February the plum tree would explode in fragrant white flowers. I had made a special cocktail the night the first bud had appeared—I'd called it the Texas Blizzard after adding a bit of Baileys Irish cream to a vanilla milk shake.

I paused on the pathway, trying to decide where I could plant geraniums come spring, and Handsome stood on the front porch and barked, happy beyond reason at my return.

Prompted by Handsome's bark, Gerry came to the door. "Welcome home," he said. I smiled and walked to him, pulling him close. Gerry had made a pitcher of sun tea, and as I sat on a folding chair, he poured me a glass. "Thanks," I said.

"For dinner, paella," said Gerry.

"Whoa," I said. I could smell garlic from the porch.

"I laid it all out in my office," said Gerry. "Let me know when you want to see."

I sighed and sipped the sweet drink. I wanted to add some whiskey, but I decided not to. "So?" I asked.

"Shhh," said Gerry, sitting in the chair next to me, tucking my hair behind my ear.

I breathed in the warm Texas night. The cicadas were out full force, and the air smelled like a river, though we were miles from the Colorado. "Okay," I said.

"Okay, time to make out?"

I laughed and kissed him. We went inside our house, not turning to go toward the shed. We ate the spicy seafood, and then bowls of coconut ice cream.

I climbed into Gerry's lap, and he kissed my forehead, then my neck. He unbuttoned my blouse and kissed my breasts. I started to cry, and he carried me into the bedroom. He undressed me, and his lips were soft on my stomach and my thighs. I stopped crying, swept up by the feel of Gerry's tongue, his lips. My brain shut off and I was only skin. Gerry entered me and I was wet and hot, liquid. I felt like I was about to drown. I let go, I went under. When the waves receded, I was lying next to my boyfriend in our bed, looking out the window at the evening light on the leaves.

"I love you," I said. But Gerry was asleep.

I got out of bed, put his T-shirt on, and went into the shed. I turned on the overhead light. Moths and mosquitoes filled the room—Gerry needed a screen door.

He had marked a place in the folder with a pink Post-it note. I turned there and found lined sheets with Alex's notes scrawled across them:

6/16

NY Visit

—Meeting with Detective Brendan Crosby (Holt police).

—Doors and windows yielded no useful fingerprints due to rain.

—One set of handprints found on Glenfiddich bottle—DID NOT match family or neighbors.

—"Household items" found at crime scene, did not lead to any suspects.

—Crosby will find items in storage.

6/18

—Called Brendan Crosby, left message.

6/20

—Visit with Dad. Dad says he did not serve any hard liquor at party, just wine and beer. But someone could have come inside and poured a glass; he wasn't paying attention.

—Dad's lawyer saw household items, none seemed relevant.

—Called Brendan Crosby, left message.

6/22
—Called Brendan Crosby, left message.

6/23
—Call from Brendan Crosby, found household items taken from house. Will fax photos.

There were no faxes, but a last sheet was stapled to the folder. It read:

7/31
—POSITIVE MATCH with Harry Winston earring. Limited edition, number 1800942, sent to PAULINE HALL, c/o Tiffany & Co., Fifth Avenue and Fifty-seventh Street, NY, NY.
EARRING = MURDERER
EARRING = PAULINE HALL
EARRING = FREEDOM for DAD

8/20
—Called all listings for Pauline Hall. (List attached—*S* for *Spoke with, LM* for *Left message, CB* for *Call back.*)

8/23
—See updated list.
—Spoke to all but one Pauline Hall.
—Left another message for last Pauline Hall.

8/24
—See updated list.
—Reached every Pauline Hall and none know about earring.

—Called Tiffany on Fifth Avenue. Pauline Hall worked there until February 1985. No further records.

—*Dead end?*

—Detective Crosby has case files in NY—go see them?

Alex had gotten on a plane to Iraq the following month.

I stood at the door of the shed and looked at the sky. Why had Alex decided to follow up with this clue now, after all this time? I wondered if he had known what would happen to him in Iraq. I narrowed my eyes at the stars. Was my brother up there? Was he anywhere? I clenched my fists, hoping without quite believing that my mom was floating above me, watching me, urging me on toward . . . what?

All I had wanted was to move forward, as Gramma had instructed, to have a happy life, and yet here was the past, pulling me back again like a fucking tar pit. I could hear my father's voice in my ear: "You're a smart girl, Lauren. Figure it out."

My brother had written *Dead end*. But he had followed it with a question mark. Footsteps rang out behind me, and I turned around. "Do you want me to come with you?" said Gerry.

"What?" I said.

"New York." He came to me and took me in his arms. He whispered in my ear, "I already found you a cheap ticket."

3

On the plane to La Guardia, after the flight attendant had passed out peanuts and I'd ordered a six-dollar can of Budweiser, I took Alex's folder from my bag. I put it on the tray table, next to my beer. I gazed out the window of the plane, seeing nothing but white, then cerulean, as we emerged above the clouds. It was amazing, the way we could graze the heavens inside metal birds. I had never been afraid of flying, not even after September 11. I always felt a rush of anticipation, thinking of the gleaming buildings of Manhattan, the sheer excitement of the city. I hadn't been there since I was a child.

I flipped through the SkyMall catalog, pausing to read about a scalp massager guaranteed to grow hair. I checked out the home hot-dog cooker and the life-size replica of King Tut's sarcophagus, which could open to reveal fourteen storage shelves ($895). I returned the catalog to the seat back.

I ordered a Coke when the stewardess came back around and, with a sigh, opened Alex's folder. I had never wanted to see all these papers, but if it was something I could do for Alex—and I could not think of one other damn thing I could do—I would read every word. There was the old crime-scene report, and there were the testimonies that sent my father to jail.

HOLT COUNTY SHERIFF'S DEPARTMENT

Incident Report
Investigating Officer: Det. Brendan Crosby
Incident Reported: 8/27/1986
Incident Address: 12 Ocean Avenue
Victim's name: Jordan Mahdian
Age: 46
Suspects: Izaan Mahdian (husband of deceased)

DESCRIPTION OF INCIDENT

Dispatch received a phone call from Izaan Mahdian, 12 Ocean Avenue, Holt, at 7:52 A.M. Mr. Mahdian had entered his bedroom to find his wife, Jordan Mahdian, on the floor. She was unresponsive with apparent head wound and "her heart not beating." EMT was dispatched to 12 Ocean Avenue but was unable to revive victim. Officer Campbell McGuinness was on patrol at the time and reported to 12 Ocean Avenue. Mr. Mahdian led Officer McGuinness to the bedroom, located on the second floor of residence. McGuinness radioed for backup and secured the scene. I arrived at the scene at 8:30 A.M. I was notified that the victim's children, Lauren and Alex Mahdian, were at a neighbor's house. We notified next of kin (Morton and Merilee Wegman, Houston, TX).

After photographing the scene, we canvassed for fingerprints and gathered all household items that could pertain to the crime. Forensics Officer Tyler Berman took all evidence to the lab.

The victim was lying on her side at the entrance to her bedroom, wearing a white cotton nightgown. There was a visible contusion above victim's right ear and a pool of blood underneath her head. The victim's mouth was open and her eyes were closed. The coroner examined the victim's degree of acute rigor and decomposition and estimated that she had been dead for several hours.

Shards of glass were found surrounding the victim. There was no further evidence of a struggle, and there was no sign of forced entry into the residence. The husband of the victim was extremely agitated and was taken to the station for further questioning.

INVESTIGATION

I interviewed Mr. Mahdian, who said he discovered the body when he went into his bedroom to get his bathing suit. Mr. Mahdian was distraught. He said he and his wife had had a dinner party the night before. (Interviews with all guests to the Mahdian home attached.)

Mr. and Mrs. Mahdian had sexual intercourse at approximately midnight. Afterward, he went downstairs and watched television briefly, then slept in the living room located at the northwest corner of residence. The Mahdians' two children spent the night in their tree house, located behind the home. Lauren Mahdian (8) said she had "very scary" dreams. When pressed to describe her dreams, she said she could not remember anything. Interview was halted when Lauren Mahdian said she felt dizzy and needed to lie down.

Mr. Mahdian could not think of anyone who would want to harm his wife. A cursory investigation showed that nothing of value was missing from the residence. Several times during the course of the interview, Mr. Mahdian asked, "Are you sure she is really dead?"

I put my head in my hands. Then I straightened and flipped through newspaper clippings: MURDER ON THE BEACH, THE END OF IDYLL, THE DECANTER OF DEATH. An enterprising journalist had even interviewed all the jury members after they had sent my father to jail. Alex had kept the transcripts.

Jocelyn Clement, thirty-six-year-old administrative assistant
No, I did not. I did not have a doubt in my mind. For one thing, no one else had been in the house. Nothing was stolen. There was simply no forensic evidence that anyone else had been inside—I saw the crime-lab report! A small fingerprint, but that could have been Jordan's—I mean Mrs. Mahdian's—own. Mr. Mahdian's semen, his fingerprints everywhere. I mean, really, the defense argument was patently absurd: some stranger broke into the house, left no clues, smashed Jordan Mahdian's skull, and left? It doesn't make sense. But a jealous husband? Now, that I understand. That makes sense to me.

That neighbor had given Mrs. Mahdian a present, and Mr. Mahdian went nuts. Adam Schwickrath. He gave her a pair of high-heeled shoes right in front of everyone. Were they having an affair? Who knows, but I'm sure Mr. Mahdian thought they were—why else would he have killed his wife?

There was the hospital report from the time he'd slapped her around before. The testimony about Halloween, how he was trick-or-treating after taking some stomach medication and it made him crazy, yelling at some poor kids, scaring them half to death. He had it in him, is what I'm saying. I'm not saying he was all bad, but some people have it in them and some do not.

We read his poems, for Lord's sake—you can read them, too. All about knives and women and war and sex. He wrote a poem about whipping someone—whipping! That's not something we talk about in this country. He was a troubled man, and he did not belong in Holt, New York, but that's beside the point.

I watched his face during the trial. He was often angry, indignant. He thought that he was better than us. He wasn't sad—he was furious. He scares me. I feel very confident in my decision. I hope he stays locked up there in Attica for the rest of his life.

Dizzy, I unlatched my seat belt and went to the tiny airplane bathroom. I splashed cold water on my face. Then I settled into my seat, feeling a dull fear in my gut when the pilot announced, "Welcome to New York!"

4

After taking a taxi from the airport to the hotel Gerry had chosen for me, I showered and tried to lie down. Too distraught to sleep, I called the Holt police station and made an appointment to take the train out and go through my mother's files in the morning. Brendan Crosby was saddened to hear about the explosion in Baghdad. "I'd wondered why Alex wasn't calling me every week," said the detective. "Jesus Christ, I'm sorry," he added.

"It's possible he's not dead," I said.

"Oh," said Brendan Crosby. "Right, of course."

"They haven't found him," I said. "They've found plenty of bodies, but not Alex's."

"That's great," said Brendan Crosby. "That's certainly good news."

I got dressed and went for a walk. I had no idea where I was in the city, and it was very cold. Things were smoky again without the benefit of Jane Stafford's soothing voice. I felt woozy as I stumbled along, my sneakers slapping the pavement. A vendor on the corner was selling handbags and scarves, and I stopped to buy a red scarf with matching mittens.

As the man counted my bills, I saw a beautiful building over his shoulder. I jaywalked across the street and went inside. It was the Park East Synagogue.

Round lights on brass poles surrounded an elaborate blue altar. When I sat down, I began to feel calmer, and the smoke dissipated. I wondered if my mother had been inside this synagogue. It was possible, wasn't it? I closed my eyes, trying to feel her.

Trying to feel anything.

After my mother's stone setting, I had been told to stop mourning. So I did stop—I was a good girl. But if you don't let yourself feel sadness, you don't feel any other emotions, either: hunger, happiness, love. Sitting in a synagogue pew, I missed the softness of my mother's hair, her quick, sweet kisses. I missed Alex, and I missed being someone's sister. And for the first time, I yearned for my father. But perhaps I had wanted him all along.

Without thinking hard about what I was doing, I walked back outside and looked for a bookstore. Before too long, I saw one. It was a dim shop located down a small stairway. The awning read: USED, RARE, COLLECTIBLE. A man with a cat in his lap looked up as I came inside, but he did not smile.

I found the poetry section and scanned the titles, my pulse fast. I made myself breathe deeply, as Jane Stafford had advised. *You're all right, Lauren,* I told myself in my head, with her voice, *you're fine.*

Then I said it aloud, "You're fine, Lauren, you're fine," as I saw my father's name. I took the book, one of his poetry collections, called *Incarceration,* from the shelf. It was a hardcover published in 1996, when I had been eighteen years old, a freshman at the

University of Texas. In a neat hand, someone had written in pencil, *First edition, $75.*

I turned the pages, which felt fragile and were a bit yellowed. The book's dedication page read, *In memory of my beloved wife, Jordan Wegman Mahdian.* I touched my mother's name, and everything went smoky again. I sank to the floor. I wasn't scared. My mother's name in black type was clear on the page, but everything else was blurred. I stared at the words: *my beloved wife.*

I thought about the night in the tree house. I remembered going to sleep next to Alex, but then there had always been a blank space, as if what happened next had been blacked out, wiped away with an inky marker. But now, as if I were remembering the day I'd met Gerry or the plane ride to New York, the memory of the night my mother died was there:

I had awakened and climbed down the ladder. It was raining—the slats of the ladder were slippery and wet. Inside the house, it was dry. I went upstairs to snuggle in between my parents, where it would be warm. I heard strange sounds and stopped at the doorway to their room. There was motion in the bed, a cry from my mother that made me think my father was hurting her. He moved above her in the dark, and his face scared me. His naked body, her cries—it seemed violent and wrong. Then they stopped what they were doing, and it was still raining, and the light from the streetlamp made it look like my mother was crying. Why was she crying? Had he hurt her? They were so still.

Then my mother murmured something, maybe "My love."

"Mmmm," said my father, and I watched them, and they were complete without me. I was terrified, alone. My mother stirred and looked toward the doorway. She said, "Lauren?" but I was gone, running back outside into the rain. In the tree house, deep in my sleeping bag, I closed my eyes tightly. What had I seen? It was smoky, so scary I lay awake, and when I heard another cry, I did not move.

I did not help her. And so she died.

"Miss?" I looked up, the smoke clearing. The man—the cat in his arms now—stood above me. "I have his novel, too," he said.

"Oh," I said.

"Please buy the book before reading it," said the man, scolding me.

"I'm sorry," I said.

At the register, I bought my father's poems. "Do you want the novel?" said the man, and I said, "Okay."

I signed the credit card slip. Back in my hotel room, I opened my father's giant tome, *The Noose,* and turned to the dedication page. *The Noose* had been published two years before. My father had written:

To Lauren and Alex,
In the hopes of holding you again.

Tabib el-jarayeh goum el-hagg
W'hatly el-dawa elli yowafig
Feih nas kateer bata'raf el-hagg
W'lagl el-daroora towafig

Doctor who treats wounds, help, hurry:
Get me the medicine that works.
There are many people who know the truth,
But who go along out of necessity.

—The Sira

5

Back in my hotel room, I took five Tylenol PMs, but I didn't fall asleep. I had searched *diphenhydramine* on Google, back when I cared about my health, and someone had mentioned it could lead to ringing in the ears, and someone else had mentioned that it would stop working after a while.

My phone woke me out of a blank sleep. I had a crushing headache. I figured it was Gerry, so I didn't answer. The only person I wanted to talk to was my brother, and one of these days I would have to admit that my brother was dead.

At the hotel's front desk, I arranged a rental car. I could take a commuter train to Holt, but then I would be stuck there, and with a car, I would be in charge. I asked for a sedan with a GPS unit, and I paid full price. I checked out of the hotel, and when the car arrived, I put my bags in the back. I sat in the driver's seat, started the engine, breathed deeply to get rid of the smoke that I knew I was imagining.

I drove out of the city on the Henry Hudson Parkway, wondering what it would be like to be a real estate agent in New York. Pretty lucrative, I figured. Nonetheless, there was something I didn't like about the light here. It was cold, brittle. It made me sad. I considered driving to the airport and flying home to Texas, but I kept on. My brother had started something, and I was going to finish it.

Holt was a nice town that could have been a movie set. A Steve Martin movie, one of his genial later ones, like *Father of the Bride.* As I drove along Main Street, I saw a barbershop called Snips with a spinning blue-and-white pole. There was a charming little toy store and a store that sold cookie bouquets. I saw two women in quilted vests holding Starbucks lattes and leaning again identical Lexus wagons, chatting. If my mother had lived, she might have become one of these ladies. If she had lived, *I* might have become one of these ladies.

The way I saw it, I could go to my old house on Ocean Avenue, the storage facility in White Plains, the Holt police station, or home to Maplewood Avenue in French Place, Austin, Texas, where my goddamn life waited for me.

"Okay, okay," I said to my brother, wherever he was.

The Holt police station was a stone building next to the post office. As I parked next to a cruiser, I looked at the post office entrance and remembered waiting in line with my mom to mail packages. If I was good and didn't wiggle too much, she would buy me stamps featuring reindeer or figure skaters. After the post office, we'd go across the street to the A&P for groceries. It all came back to me: the shopping cart, a chocolate doughnut from the box, my mother placing mayonnaise and raisin bread on the conveyor belt.

My third-grade class had gone on a tour of the jail, but I had been sick that day—chicken pox. I remembered staring at my face in my parents' bathroom mirror, picking at a scab on my forehead. "You'll have a scar forever if you scratch that off," my mother warned, folding laundry in her room. I pulled the skin anyway.

In the rearview mirror of my rental car, I could still see the faint indentation above my left eyebrow.

Inside the station, I approached a middle-aged woman sitting behind a pane of glass. "I have an appointment with Detective Brendan Crosby?" I said. She nodded and said, "Have a seat, sweetheart."

I wondered if she knew who I was. Holt was a small town. For all I knew, there hadn't been a murder since my mother's, just a bunch of parking tickets and kids stealing beer or skateboarding. I went to sit down in a folding chair next to a soda machine. The machine made a humming sound. It was kind of soothing, maybe because it reminded me of Jane Stafford's noise machine. The woman's phone rang, and she answered it.

At the end of the hallway, I saw a wiry man, about sixty. He had white hair cut short and a bristly mustache. "Hello, Lauren," he said, walking toward me. "I'm Detective Crosby. Brendan." He shook my hand and led me down the hall to a small office. "Please," he said, waving me inside. "Can I get you something to drink? Coffee? Water?"

"I'm fine," I said.

"Great," said Detective Crosby. "Please sit down. By the way," he said. "I'm so sorry about your brother."

"Well," I said, "me, too. But you know—"

"He might be alive," said Detective Crosby.

"It's not likely," I said. "But you never . . ." My voice trailed off. Trying not to cry, I whispered, "You never know."

Detective Crosby cleared his throat. He stood behind his desk. "I have all your mother's files here, if you . . ."

I looked up, and what I saw in the detective's eyes was pity. "You interviewed my dad?" I said.

Detective Crosby nodded. "I interviewed you, too," he said, sinking to his chair. "You were just a kid."

I looked at the floor, which was linoleum. "I don't think my dad is guilty," I said. "I always thought he was. But now . . . I don't know . . . something's changed."

"I've followed up on every lead," said Detective Crosby. "I assure you. I pulled all the files for you, though. If you'd like to . . ."

He slid a stack of papers across his desk. I opened them and flipped through perfunctorily. There was nothing new. After a while, I closed the folder and sighed. "What do you think about the earring?" I said.

"What?"

"The earring, found with my mom? It wasn't hers. Alex traced it—it belonged to a woman named Pauline Hall. Did you try to find her?"

Detective Crosby shook his head. "Your mother could have bought it secondhand, someone could have given it to her, she might have borrowed it . . . there's no evidence of a break-in."

"So you never followed that lead," I said.

"Lauren," said Detective Crosby, "Alex's fixation on the various items found in your mother's bedroom made him very unhappy. I'll answer any questions you might have, but there are no leads left to follow. There was no sign of a forced entry into the house, there were no footprints."

"You're telling me to give up?" I said.

"That's not my decision to make," said Detective Crosby.

On his desk was a photograph. "Is that your family?" I said.

"Yes." There was the detective, on Holt Beach. A woman his age sat beside him, and there were three grown children and two babies and even a goddamn dog.

"Is that Holt Beach?" I asked.

He nodded. "I was born and raised here," he said. "Never lived anywhere else."

"I didn't want to leave, either," I said.

"Yes, you did," said the detective.

"Sorry?" I said.

"You told me. You wanted to be a ballerina. And you were going to live in Egypt, where your dad's from."

"I said that?"

He nodded. "You told me all about it," he said. "The big market or something, camels. . . ." He smiled. "You told me Egypt was the birthplace of civilization. I remember it well. You were a confident young girl, with a lot of dreams."

"Why was I talking about Egypt when my mother was dead?" I said. "That's just crazy."

"It happens," said Detective Crosby. "Sometimes kids process things differently."

"Why would my dad kill my mom?" I asked. "He loved her."

"I can't answer that for you," said Detective Crosby.

"How does love turn into"—I picked up my mother's file—"into this?"

"Lauren," said Detective Crosby. I could tell he was ready for me to leave. He was antsy, but too polite to ask me to go.

"Have you ever pushed your wife?"

"No, I have not," said Detective Crosby.

"Really?" I said.

"Really," said Detective Crosby.

"I'm sorry," I said, standing. "Thank you for your time."

"I'll keep in touch," he said.

"That's okay," I said.

As I walked out, Detective Crosby said, "Lauren?"

I turned around.

"That isn't love," he said. "I promise you. Love is something else entirely."

I drove away from the police station, not sure where to go next. I saw Harry's pizzeria on my left and remembered going there with my parents, trying to convince them to let me order Mountain Dew with my cheese slice, though my mom always shook her head and told me my options were milk or water. I parked and went inside. The smell—a buttery, spicy scent, completely distinct and nothing like the doughy fragrance of the pizzerias in Austin—was wonderful. I could already taste the toasty crust in the back of my mouth.

Images exploded like flashbulbs in my mind: my father, sliding open the refrigerated case, slipping me a soda; Alex, after a game, wearing his green soccer jersey and cleats, folding a slice with his index finger to fit more in his mouth; my parents, their backs to me as they ordered, my dad's hand flat on my mom's back.

"You want something to eat?" said the man behind the counter. It was Vinny, his name was Vinny, though he didn't seem to recognize me. I pretended to look at the white menu board, the small red letters spelling CHICKEN PARMIGIANA PIZZA and BAKED SHELLS and HOT WEDGES.

"A cheese slice," I said.

"For here or to go?"

"Here," I said. "It's for here."

I took the thin paper plate to a table. My mom had used napkins from the metal dispenser to sop up the oil before eating, but my dad and Alex always made fun of her. "Mom, that's gross!" Alex would say, pointing to her pile of greasy napkins.

"Hush," she'd say, taking a bite.

I finished my pizza and went to the car. I didn't need directions, but I typed my childhood address into the computer: 12 Ocean Avenue, Holt, New York. The GPS woman's dulcet tones gave me simple instructions, and I obeyed them.

It took only about ten minutes. *The library, pajama story night,* Bedknobs and Broomsticks, *the crosswalk, my school, the Hallmark store, wrapping paper, pine needles along the road, the lapping waves of Long Island Sound . . .*

I turned on Ocean Avenue. It was a blustery afternoon. I reached the house and pulled over. There it was. I sat in the car for a while, just looking. Twelve Ocean Avenue was a 3/2, unless it had been renovated. Half an acre, give or take. The views of the Sound would bring up the price, as would the excellent Holt school system. "A million dollars," I murmured. "Maybe one-two-five."

I almost expected my father to open the door and light a Gauloises Brunes. I stepped out of the car and pulled on my red mittens. The house was freshly painted. Someone had put poinsettias on the front porch, nestled into festive green pots. A wreath had been hung on the door.

Thanksgiving—it was a few weeks away. I had forgotten spending Thanksgiving in this house. My mom used to make Merilee's sweet potatoes with marshmallows on top. My father, who had been raised without Thanksgiving, loved preparing the traditional turkey with stuffing and canned cranberries. He used the Wüsthof knives to carve, standing proudly at the end of our dining room table.

My mother always invited neighbors, whoever had no family in town, or was estranged. She dressed up, wearing silk blouses and slim wool pants, putting on cheap holiday earrings or light-up pins. She drank red wine (I could hear her say, "Pass that Beaujolais!") and got flushed and silly. She blew kisses to my father across the table. "What are you thankful for?" she'd ask us teasingly.

"For you, Mom," Alex would always say. She made him wear holiday vests over button-down shirts. For me, there was a new velvet dress each year, with a matching headband.

"What a wonderful surprise!" my mother would answer.

"Me, too," I'd say, kicking Alex under the table.

"And I am thankful for my beautiful family," my mom would say, growing teary and hugging us, pinching my father's bottom.

We were so happy. We were, we were.

I decided to walk around to the back of the house, and see the yard. It was late afternoon, and though the owners were surely home, I inched through the hedges on the south side of the property. Branches scratched my cheek, but I pressed on.

I just wanted to see the oak, the tree house my father had built for us. For some reason, it seemed important to see something he had made. I reached the back and stopped. The yard was taken up by a giant pool, covered for the winter with a dark blue canvas. Wind whipped my hair. It smelled like seawater. The tree house was gone.

"Hello?" called a woman's voice. I turned, panicked, and began to run. Breaking free of the hedges, I heard the woman call, "Hello! Can I help you?"

Back in the car, I found directions to La Guardia and began to drive. I ached to be with Gerry, if he still wanted me. I was done here—I'd followed almost every clue. What was left, going to Tiffany and trying to find somebody who remembered a woman named Pauline Hall? I yearned for Texas, where people watched football on Thanksgiving, and ate barbecue with pickles and sliced bread.

On the Hutchinson River Parkway, I daydreamed about my father. I remembered a summer afternoon at the movies. My father was taking me to see *Dumbo,* and he bought a bucket of popcorn. I sat next to my father, the taste of butter and salt, I said something, and my father—so young!—laughed out loud. "My funny girl," he said. He looked at me in his way, as if I were so special, the most wonderful person in the world.

Seeing my childhood home had changed me, reminded me what was at stake. I had forgotten how my father used to gaze at me, as if my face were the source of his greatest pleasure. Everything I said to Izaan was brilliant and astute. Now that I had taken a step down the road that might lead me to him, it seemed, I could no longer stop. Hope flamed inside me like one of those trick birthday candles that can't be blown out.

I turned around and drove back into Manhattan.

6

Two men wearing black overcoats and robin's-egg-blue scarves flanked the glass doors that led into Tiffany & Co. on Fifth Avenue. I paused, and one of them opened the door, ushering me inside with a sweep of his arm.

As I approached one of the glass cases, a young man with a pronounced chin smiled at me invitingly. I looked down and saw a beautiful ruby ringed with diamonds. "A lovely piece," murmured the man, taking the ring from the case and laying it on a strip of velvet. "Would you like to try it on?"

"I don't think so," I said, though I felt a strange desire rising in my throat. I lifted my left hand, saying, "No, thank you, I don't think."

The man opened his palm, and I placed my fingers inside. He held my wrist and, with his other hand, slid the band onto my ring finger. When it was in place, he met my eyes.

The first time Gerry asked me to marry him, we were hiking along the Barton Creek Greenbelt. Gerry had packed a picnic lunch, and we sat at the edge of the water and watched Handsome swim. A turkey sandwich, I remember, with avocado and sharp cheddar cheese. Homemade lemonade. I lay back, settling my head in Gerry's lap. The sun poured through the leaves, making patterns on the water. Gerry ran his fingers through my hair. "I love you," I said.

"Lauren," said Gerry, "will you marry me?"

It was an immediate reaction: I felt choked and could not breathe. I sat up. "I'm not marrying anyone," I said. I had promised myself again and again in the years following my mother's death. *I will never fall in love, I will never need anyone, I will take care of myself.* I locked away the agony as if it were a rabid animal. I made a set of rules, like armor—if I followed them, I believed, I could keep myself safe.

"I told you," I said, by the creek.

"I'm not your father," said Gerry.

I stood up, and walked down the path by myself. Handsome jumped from the water to follow me. I reached the car in about twenty minutes, and I unlocked it and put Handsome inside. I rolled down the back window, and used my water bottle to fill a Tupperware container with water for the dog to drink. Then I locked the car (Gerry had his own set of keys) and started walking home. It took me over an hour, and when I turned on Maplewood, Handsome ambled out to greet me.

I knelt down and rubbed his ears. Then I climbed the three steps to the front door. When I opened it, I saw Gerry sitting on the couch with a beer. "I get the picture," he said. "You've made your fucking point."

"I'm sorry," I said.

"Go to hell," said Gerry.

I moved out for a while, answering a Craigslist ad for a house share, but Gerry and I met for lunch every few days and took care of Handsome together. After two months, Gerry asked if I would come home.

Now I stared at the giant ruby ring. "Take it off," I said.

"Pardon me?"

"I'm not interested," I said. I grabbed the ring and pried it off my finger. I dropped it onto the velvet. "I'm here for research purposes."

The guy laughed. "Research purposes? That's a new one."

"You almost had me there," I said. "Phew, that's a nice ring."

"Women and jewels," said the guy.

"It's like a drug," I said. "Cocaine or maybe crack. I don't know. Fine white wine? Anyway, I'm trying to find out about someone who used to work here. A long time ago. I need to speak with her."

"Carole might be able to help you," said the man. "She's been here forever." The man pointed to a trim, white-haired woman staffing a display case in the far recesses of the store.

"Thanks," I said.

"You sure about the ruby?" said the man. I laughed. "When you find the right guy, send him in," he said.

"I've got the right guy," I said.

He looked at my naked fingers and shrugged, already scanning the room for a more likely commission.

I made my way toward Carole. She was talking to a couple about a watch. When they moved on, I stepped in front of her case. "How can I help you today, young lady?" she said. You could see the bones beneath her porcelain skin, and her eyes were deep brown. She wore heavy rouge and lipstick. Her wrinkles evidenced years of animated sales pitches.

"I'm trying to find out about a person who used to work here years ago," I said. "I need to ask her . . . something."

"Who are you looking for?"

"Pauline Hall," I said. "I have some . . . I have an earring of hers."

"Oh, Pauline," said Carole. She sighed and shook her head. "Poor old Pauline."

"Is she still working here?" I said.

"Pauline died a lifetime ago," said Carole. "Cancer. I went to the funeral with my husband, Ralph. Pauline had a hard life. You say you have her jewelry?"

"It's an earring," I said.

Carole squinted as if seeing a faraway place. "She was such a bookworm, Pauline."

"What do you mean about . . . when you said she had a hard life?"

"She fell in love with the wrong fellow," said Carole. "He got her pregnant, and then he left." She pursed her lips primly. "You have to be careful who you choose. I have three babies of my own. Three boys. Men now. But I waited until I was married, didn't I? Time flies, I tell you," said Carole. "Sweetheart, would you like to try on one of these watches?"

"Oh," I said. "No, thank you."

"Pauline's little girl was so sweet," said Carole. "She'd come in after school, do her homework in the break room. She had a little plaid uniform."

"Okay," I said.

"Her name was Sylvia," said Carole.

"Sylvia?" I asked.

"After Sylvia Plath, I think. Pauline fancied herself an intellectual." Carole shook her head. "I wonder what became of little Sylvia. Heaven only knows."

"Heaven only knows," I said.

Book Four

1

Mae Bright woke in her mauve-colored bedroom. For a moment she forgot that she was not alone in her apartment. Mae was a sixty-nine-year-old widow. She was accustomed to leisurely (if lonesome) mornings with the crossword puzzle and a pot of coffee. But as she yawned, she heard noise in the guest bathroom. With a start, she remembered: her daughter, Victoria, was getting a divorce and had moved into Mae's apartment with her two daughters until "things were sorted."

Divorce. Mae tasted the word—dead leaves in her mouth. No one in her Catholic family had ever gotten a divorce. As always, Mae thought drily, Victoria was breaking new ground. (She'd also been the first in the family to be arrested—for selling her own prescription Ritalin out of her high school locker.)

Mae sat up and sighed, tucking her white hair behind her ears. She'd recently had it cut into a chin-length bob, like Anna Wintour. It suited her, Mae thought. She donned a pink robe and walked into the kitchen, opening a can of Maxwell House and taking her favorite yellow mug out of the dishwasher.

In the sink was an empty wineglass (not rinsed), and on the

counter, an empty wine bottle and a discarded cork. Mae picked up the bottle and peered at the label: Victoria had drunk the 1995 Château Lafite Rothschild. Mae remembered her husband, Preston (may he rest in peace), choosing the wine at a shop in Virginia. It had cost some eight hundred dollars.

"What are you doing?"

Mae was snapped out of her reverie by the loud voice of her daughter. She looked up and there was Victoria, wearing a scarlet peignoir and socks. "Why are you staring at an empty bottle?" said Victoria, raising an eyebrow.

"This was one of your father's favorites," said Mae.

"He always had good taste," said Victoria.

"Victoria . . ." said Mae.

"Uli is such a jerk," said Victoria. "Don't blame me, Mom. I wanted something nice at the end of a horrible day."

Mae shook her head, trying to stay on track. Victoria often did this—derailed you while you were trying to admonish her. "Victoria," said Mae. "If you're going to be here awhile, we're going to have to . . ." She swallowed. "Are you going to be here awhile?"

Victoria rummaged in the refrigerator and pulled out a Budweiser. "I'm going back to bed," she said.

"Is that a beer?" said Mae.

"You know damn well it is," said Victoria. Mae pointedly checked her watch; it was eight-forty-five in the morning. Victoria took a bottle opener from a kitchen drawer and daintily opened her beer, then poured it in a glass.

"Would you like some melon?" asked Mae.

"Uli wants full custody," said Victoria. "He says I'm unfit. An unfit mother."

"Please don't drink that beer," said Mae. "I'll make you an English muffin, honey."

Victoria took a sip from the glass and set it on the counter. "What gets me is that it's all about him. He just wants to win. Greece! I'm not letting him bring up my girls in that backward shithole. Did I ever tell you about the toilets in that country? Fuck me."

A shudder ran through Mae: a wave of revulsion. She composed herself with a deep breath. "You can't be drinking, Victoria," she said with as much kindness as she could muster.

"I know, Mom."

"Just pour it down the drain," said Mae.

Victoria sighed, wrapping her hands around the glass. "It's only beer," she muttered, avoiding her mother's eyes. She added more loudly, "I can hide it from you if you want me to."

Mae felt deflated. "Is this a relapse?" she asked.

"My husband is divorcing me," said Victoria. "I am sad. I had some wine last night, and now I am having one fucking beer. That's what this is."

"By the way," said Mae, hoping that if she changed the subject, the pain in her stomach would go away, "did Sylvia reach you?"

"Sylvia?" said Victoria.

"She called here last night. She sounded sort of strange, come to think of it."

"She always sounds strange," said Victoria.

"At least she has that nice young man. What's his name? Raymond."

"Are you kidding me?" asked Victoria, picking up the beer and sipping it with measured nonchalance.

"What, dear?" said Mae.

"Is that some sort of pointed comment?" asked Victoria. "Because the last thing I need is my *own mother* turning against me."

"No, dear, no," said Mae.

Victoria snorted, a horrible thing to behold. Then she said, "God, with you and Dad as role models, what chance did I even have?"

"What does that mean?" said Mae. Though she should have been immune to her daughter's jabs, this one struck unhappily close to Mae's midnight worries. She had *not* been a good role model for her daughter. She'd always been a doormat—Victoria had seen her mother walked all over by her husband and life in general. Mae had not protested when Victoria herself treated her mother terribly. But it was not too late! The truth be told—and maybe it was high time to tell the truth, before she was labeled an old bat and everyone could call her opinions dementia—Mae didn't even like Victoria very much.

Victoria stared into space. She shook her head, her lovely curls reminding Mae of when she'd been a little girl. Victoria had loved those ribboned barrettes. "Maybe if I had told the truth," said Victoria, "things would have turned out differently for me."

"Victoria," said Mae, touching her daughter's arm.

"What?" said Victoria. The anger was gone from her voice, and she seemed disoriented.

"Honey," said Mae, but then, as always, words failed her—or she failed with the words. "It was so long ago."

"Right," said Victoria. She nodded as if convincing herself of something. "Right, right," she said.

And furthermore, thought Mae. It had been her mother's favorite expression; it meant: *end of conversation.*

Sunny, Victoria's twelve-year-old daughter, came into the kitchen. She was tall and painfully thin. Mae had begun to wonder if Sunny had an eating disorder, like the ballet dancers Mae had seen in a PBS documentary. Sunny wore a green tracksuit, her earbuds firmly in place. She looked like a skinny gym teacher. Without speaking to anyone, she filled a glass with water from the tap.

"Good morning, Sunny," said Mae loudly.

"She won't answer you," said Victoria, crossing her arms over her chest.

But Sunny took the earbuds from her ears and met her grandmother's gaze. "Good morning, Nana," she said.

"Would you like some eggs, dear?" asked Mae. "Some melon?"

Sunny picked up the empty beer bottle her mother had left on the kitchen counter, then set it down. "You promised," she said to Victoria.

"It's just one beer," said Victoria.

"Sunny?" said Mae. "Honeydew?"

"I'm not hungry," said Sunny, leaving the kitchen. A moment later, Mae heard the front door open and then shut.

After dressing, Mae sat in her room, looking out the window. *Unbearable.* The word came into her mind unbidden, but it was the right word. Mae simply couldn't bear the thought of Victoria going back to rehab. Uli would have ample evidence to take the girls to Greece for good; Mae would drain her bank account to pay for another six weeks of massages and meetings; and for what? Mae didn't believe that Victoria would ever get better, not anymore. That naïveté had been worn down to nothing.

Mae looked down at the park. It was a balmy day already, and people wore shorts and sleeveless shirts. Mae could see a couple sitting on a bench, deep in conversation. A woman pushed one of those expensive strollers, stepping lightly, a cell phone pressed to her ear. Mae squinted but did not see Sunny among the joggers.

They told you, in those depressing rooms, as you sat in a circle of metal chairs, they told you to hold fast to the person your loved one had been, before the booze. Before the booze? Mae could scarcely remember. Victoria hadn't had a chance to be much of anyone before the booze. When she was four years old, she'd taken sips from all the glasses left on tables after a cocktail party, done a little dance in the middle of the living room, and passed out. How they'd laughed that night. "Look out, skid row," a guest had joked.

Let go and let God, they said in that basement on Seventy-second Street, sipping tea from Styrofoam cups. She and Preston had attended the Al-Anon meetings for almost a year until one night he had stopped outside and said, "I'm done. I can't do this anymore." He had kissed Mae on the forehead, saying, "You keep going, sweetheart, but I'm done."

Mae had almost gone inside by herself but, in the end, had taken his hand. They'd eaten at Sardi's, she remembered, then had gone home and made love—tenderly, sadly. Victoria was in worse shape than ever that spring. Mae searched her bags every day after school, ransacked her room, but found nothing. It took Mae until midsummer to realize that Victoria's shampoo bottle was filled with whiskey, right there in the bathroom.

Mae had forgotten to buy new shampoo, had borrowed Victoria's Pert Plus one morning. With hot water running down her back, Mae had upended the bottle and watched, mystified, as amber liquid ran through her fingers. She smelled it but could scarcely believe her own nose.

She only drank it to go to sleep, Victoria confessed tearfully. She had nightmares, Victoria said. Southern Comfort! In a bottle of Pert Plus!

Unbearable. It was unbearable to give up on your baby.

Maybe this was all Mae's fault. Surely. Surely it was all Mae's fault. She had never given Victoria a moral center. She had loved her too much, or too little. She should have had another baby, a sibling for Victoria. Maybe she should have sat by Victoria's bed all night to calm her nightmares. Maybe Victoria drank to fill a void. Maybe it was the money. Maybe she drank to forget.

Mae stood and took her Bible from the shelf. It had been a gift from her mother on Mae's first communion. The Bible was bound in white leather. As always, Mae opened it to the passage that made her feel sick, Proverbs 19:5. It was like poking a sore tooth—she couldn't help herself. Sometimes she felt cleansed after forcing herself to stare at the words. There they were—small black letters. They were unyielding, simple, true:

> A false witness will not go unpunished, and he who pours out lies will not go free.

Mae hadn't been to confession in months, maybe a year. She wasn't sure she even believed the Catholic doctrine anymore. But her father had once told her that was what faith *was*—going to church even if you weren't sure. Following orders. Maybe she should tell the priest about Victoria, just lay it all out from the beginning: what had happened and what Victoria had confessed and what Mae had forced the girls to do. Mae could let it go and let God decide on her punishment once and for all.

Let go and let God.

She wished she had decided to confess when Father Gregory was in charge, before he retired to Palm Beach. Mae had known Father Gregory since she was a young bride, and he was a comforting presence, a kind old man. The new priest, Father

Richard, was a bit too attractive for his own good, too eager to please. In all honesty, Mae wasn't sure he was up to the job of absolving this big a mistake. It had been a mistake, after all! Just a terrible, brutal mistake.

Mae closed the Bible firmly and put it back on the shelf.

2

St. Gabriel's was a beautiful building, and inside, it was dim and cool, smelling of wood wax and incense. Mae was immediately calmed. The church had answers. It had rules and regulations. Her father had believed with his whole heart in Catholicism, which had to count for something.

"Mae! What a nice surprise." Father Richard walked toward her, his arms outstretched.

"I'm here for confession," said Mae.

Father Richard's face remained exactly the same—a genial, welcoming arrangement of his features. Mae had to admit he was a professional. "Of course," he said. "Follow me."

One of the things Mae could not stand about Father Richard was that he wanted parishioners to sit across from him in his bright office while they confessed their sins. Mae, whose husband had never seen her in the altogether, squirmed under Father Richard's aggressively benevolent gaze. She missed the old days, the shadowy figure behind the screen. She didn't know where to look: there was the picture of Father Richard on the golf course, and there was his dirty coffee mug.

Mae decided to focus on her toes, then the wall to her right. Mustard-colored stucco. "Bless me, Father, for I have sinned," she began.

Father Richard sat back in his ergonomic chair, which squeaked. He crossed his stubby fingers over his stomach. After a minute, he tilted his head to the right, toward the window. Outside, Mae could see, it had started to rain. "It has been over a year since my last confession," she said.

"Mm-hm?" said Father Richard.

Mae knew that this young (she didn't want to use the word *whippersnapper*—who was she, her grandmother?—but that was the right word, it simply was), this young priest was allegedly able to absolve her, but what could he possibly know of sin?

"Well," said Mae, "here's the thing."

"Go on, my child," said Father Richard.

"When Victoria was a teenager," said Mae, changing tack, "once, when she was a teenager, Victoria came home in a state." She took a deep breath, remembering the morning when Victoria and Sylvia had come home smelling of beer, looking uneasy and frightened. She and Preston had giggled in the kitchen, thinking the girls had sneaked a drink or two at their sleepover. How naive they had been. She remembered herself, winking at Preston. So stupid. She was so stupid.

"Mae?" said Father Richard, piercing her reverie.

"One morning, when she was seventeen, Victoria asked me for advice."

"Go on," said Father Richardson.

"It was August," Mae whispered.

"Okaaaay," said Father Richardson in a syrupy tone. He wanted her to share more, to expose her heart. But Mae felt as she had always felt during Victoria's stints in rehab, when she and Preston had to fly out to Hazelden or Betty Ford: all this disclosure was a bunch of hooey. What on earth was the point of blathering about your private affairs, your secrets? Saying them out loud didn't change the truth—didn't undo anything.

"I just wanted to say," said Mae, realizing the futility of trying to make peace with God using Father Richard as a conduit, "I did not attend mass on many Sunday mornings when Victoria was growing up. I was extremely busy, and some Sundays I just didn't get to church."

"I see," said Father Richard, lifting his index fingers, touching them to each other in the universal pose of someone who is trying to look as if they are smart. "I see, Mae. But I think God understands the trials of a mother."

"How comforting," said Mae.

Father Richard nodded. Why didn't he wash that disgusting mug? And there on his desk was a broken pencil, the lead tip smashed to the side. What kind of an adult man broke a pencil and didn't throw it away or sharpen it? Mae was seized with a desire to stand up and leave. "May I have my penance?" she asked impatiently.

"Say three Hail Marys, and try your best to attend mass regularly," said Father Richard. "You're not a young mother anymore," he said with an obnoxious chuckle.

"Thank you for pointing that out," said Mae.

Father Richard gave her the benediction, and Mae remembered the dark sacristy, the soothing voice of Father Gregory. Why hadn't she tried to atone when she'd had a real priest to unburden herself to?

"By the way," said Father Richard when he was done, leaving Mae frustrated and irritable, "please take a flyer on your way out. I'm starting a new rock-and-roll mass on Wednesday evenings to try to bring the youth back into the flock."

"The youth?" said Mae.

"I thought you might give a flyer to your granddaughters," said Father Richard. Mae pictured Georgia and Sunny, so worldly and disdainful that they scared Mae. There was something missing in them, and Mae lay awake some nights trying to figure out what it was and how it could be replaced. Father Richard's orange flyer filled Mae with pity.

"All right," she said. "I'll be sure to pass one along."

"The church is as relevant now as it always was," said Father Richard to himself.

"I'll let myself out," said Mae. She walked slowly downstairs, enjoying the dusky smell. The scent had brought her so much comfort once. Mae could remember coming to St. Gabriel's as a child, watching light pour through the stained-glass windows and filling with awe, clutching her mother's gloved hand.

Next to her favorite window (it was Mary, her arms outstretched), Mae stopped. Had Mae's mother, Dottie Pendelton, ever made a mistake? As far as Mae knew, her mother had died free of sin or complication. She was a strict Catholic and raised Mae to be the same. What would Dottie have done in Mae's place?

I never would have let her go out in the middle of the night! Mae could almost hear her mother's indignant voice. *And furthermore,* said Dottie.

Mae looked up at Mary Magdalene, who gazed back beatifically, though surely, thought Mae, Mary Magdalene had some secrets of her own.

Back out on the street, Mae saw a homeless person leaning against the wall. "Lady," the person said, "can you spare a dime?"

Mae squinted. "Are you a man or a woman?" she asked.

"I'm a woman," said the homeless person. "I have a mental problem."

"I see," said Mae, and she opened her wallet, took out eighty-some dollars in cash, and rummaged around in her purse. She unearthed a new tube of Clinique lipstick (Mulberry Morning) and handed the money and the lipstick to the homeless person.

"God bless you," said the woman.

"Let's hope so," said Mae.

3

Back on Madison Avenue, Mae tried to hail a cab. Across the street, she saw a subway station, and without much thought, she brought her arm down. Though Mae hadn't taken the subway in years, she felt drawn to the cavernous passageways, the stench of humanity.

She passed a few disadvantaged men and women as she descended the stairs, all with their hands out, begging. She lifted her chin and strode past. You couldn't help everyone, thought Mae, and this was the essential problem. If you gave your lipstick to one homeless person, you'd just be denying it to another (not to mention yourself). Lipstick, of course, being a metaphor for your money, your belongings, your heart. Though, also, your lipstick.

The subway car pulled up; Mae was surrounded by sweaty people. When the passageway was clear, she stepped into the car and found a seat next to an obese woman and her little boy. The boy looked up at Mae and smiled. He was missing one tooth. "Hello," said Mae.

"Hello," said the boy.

"What's your name?" said Mae.

"Deeshawn," said the boy (or it sounded like Deeshawn).

"You sure are cute," said Mae. "How old are you?"

"None of your business," said the boy's mother, glaring at Mae and yanking her son upright, lumbering away. Though the subway car was crowded, with many people standing up, no one filled the seat next to Mae. She rode for five stops, reading the subway advertisements, scanning the faces of strangers. Finally, a twitchy white teenager practically fell into the empty spot next to her. His face was thin, and he sat forward, resting his bony arms on his knees. He stared at the subway floor, and the train began moving again.

"Are you—" said Mae. "Are you all right?"

"What?" said the teenager sharply. His jacket was cheap, and his jeans looked dirty. He wore large sneakers patterned with red and black boxes.

"I was just asking if you were all right," said Mae.

The boy laughed, one quick bark. "I've been better, lady," he said.

"What's wrong?" asked Mae.

Incredulous, the boy sat back in his plastic seat, but his knee didn't stop moving. "I lost my job," he said. "I was working, and I lost my job."

"What happened?" asked Mae. She felt both excited and terrified.

"What happened? I'll tell you what happened," said the teenager. "I was walking to work and a man fell on me."

Mae nodded. Her heart hammered in her chest.

"He fell on me. From a platform. He was washing windows. I was just walking to work."

"Oh," said Mae.

"He still had the fucking wiper in his hand," said the teenager.

"Jesus fucking Christ, you know?" As he talked, some color came back into his face. Mae knew he could be lying, but he didn't seem like a liar. Then again, what did a liar look like?

"That's terrible," said Mae. Around them, a few other passengers were listening. Mae felt redeemed. *See? I wasn't preying on that little boy! I'm a good person. I care.* "What happened next?"

"The guy, he didn't even move," said the teenager, shaking his head. "I was just fucking standing there, you know? I was walking to work. Then blood started coming out the guy's head, like real slow, just fucking leaking out his head."

"What did you do?" asked Mae.

"So I, like, called 911 on my phone, you know? And I was late to work. But you can't just leave some guy who has his brains leaking out of his head!" The boy's voice rose in pitch. "So I stood there! And I was, like, should I talk to the guy?"

"Did you talk to the guy?" asked Mae.

The teenager looked up at Mae, his forehead creased with lines. "I bent over, you know? I said, 'It's gonna be okay, man.' But he didn't answer me."

"Was he dead?"

"I don't know," said the boy. "I don't know, lady. I think so, though. I think so, lady, yeah."

Mae watched him, a boy in pain. Tentatively, she touched his shoulder, wrapped her fingers around his shirt. The boy moved toward her. He smelled like a fried egg. "I think so, lady, yeah," said the boy, and Mae put her arms around him.

"I'm so sorry," said Mae. "It's not your fault."

"He just fell out of the sky," said the boy, and as he spoke, his breath was warm against her skin.

The boy got off a few stops later, thanking Mae for listening, even squeezing her hand with his own cold one. Mae walked home feeling light and somehow cleansed, despite her incomplete confession. But when she opened her purse to get her elevator card, she realized her wallet was gone.

"Can I help you, Mrs. Bright?" asked the doorman.

"I just . . ." said Mae. She stared into her bag, at the dark place where her wallet had been.

"Ma'am?"

"I forgot my key card," murmured Mae.

"Not a problem," said the man, swiping a card and handing it to Mae with a flourish.

In the elevator, a heavy sadness pressed her down. She should not be so upset. People stole, that was just the way of the world. People were dishonest and unkind. But Mae felt as if she'd been operating under a happy trance: the delusion that she mattered. In reality, she had mattered for a few years, when Victoria was young. Mae remembered the open-faced toddler who had run around the Maidstone Club with such joy, crying, "Mom-maaay, get in water! Me jump you, Mom-maay!" It had all been so easy—and she'd complained about having to get her suit wet. She could just slap her former self. *Pay attention,* she wanted to tell young Mae, checking her tan in the East Hampton sunlight. *Let her jump to you! Hold her, love her, look up. This is the best it will be.*

The apartment door was locked, which was surprising. Luckily, the boy hadn't stolen her set of keys on the silver chain. In her living room, Mae found Sunny and Georgia eating her Hammond's ribbon candy and watching people in leather pants play guitar on the television. "Girls!" she said. "What are you doing home on a school day?" They looked at her dully. "Where's your mother?" asked Mae. Sunny pointed to Victoria's bedroom.

Mae walked quickly down the hall, opened the door, and shrank back at the smell of . . . what was the smell? "Victoria!" she said, trying to sound firm but only sounding wavering and old. "Victoria, wake up this minute." Mae approached the bed and saw her daughter curled up.

"Leave me alone," said Victoria.

On the bedside table, Mae saw two wine bottles, empty. "Victoria, what are you doing? Your girls—"

"Oh, they're *fine,*" said Victoria, sitting up, pressing her hands to her face.

"They're not fine," said Mae. "They need you, Victoria. They need their mother. Why didn't you take them to school?"

"Why didn't *you* take them to school?" said Victoria. She was quiet for a minute, and then she shook her head. "They don't need me."

"Clean yourself up," said Mae. "Take a shower. I'll call Hazelden. We can work on this together. This is just a relapse. It happens, honey."

"No," said Victoria. "I'm not going back."

"You don't have a choice," said Mae.

"What's the fucking point?"

Mae sat down next to her daughter. "Come here," she said.

But Victoria moved away from her, climbing out of bed. "I'm going out," she said. "I'm getting out of here. I have an appointment."

Mae looked up and saw Sunny and Georgia in the hallway, holding hands. They looked much younger than twelve and ten.

Victoria pulled on pants and slipped her feet into shoes, and the girls watched Mae, waiting to see what she would do. They didn't seem hopeless, but they were wary, unsure, starting to lose faith that the world had simple joys in store for them. Mae could help them. She wanted to—more than she had ever wanted anything.

"You're not going anywhere, Victoria," she said.

"Watch me," said Victoria.

"This is my house," said Mae, "and I make the rules. Everything is going to be fine. You just need to pack a few things in a bag, Victoria. Do as I say."

"Do as you say?" said Victoria.

"Yes."

"You can go to hell," said Victoria. "I should have told you that a long time ago. Girls, we're leaving. Your grandmother doesn't want us here."

"That's not true," said Mae.

Sunny's and Georgia's eyes darted from their mother to their grandmother. "Nana?" said Sunny.

"Shut up," said Victoria. "Everything is fine. Come on, girls."

Mae felt her strength ebbing. "I can help you, Victoria," she said. "Let's just talk this over now."

"There's nothing to say," said Victoria. She went to her daughters and took them by the hand. "We'll be fine. I'm fine, girls. Let's go." She walked to the door, holding them firmly. First Sunny and then Georgia looked back, a question in their faces.

But Mae was silent.

"You can't take them away from me," said Victoria as she pressed the button for the elevator. "No one can."

4

By the time Sylvia's bus pulled in to Port Authority, it was past midnight. Sylvia was glad to depart the airless bus. She stretched and shouldered her duffel, stepped on a whining escalator. The shops were gated and locked, and no one in the terminal seemed up to any good. By the exit, a slight girl played a mournful song on a violin. Sylvia dropped a dollar in the case as she passed, and the girl whispered, "God bless."

Sylvia ached to see Victoria, to huddle together like they had as children, spilling secrets in Victoria's beautiful room high above the city. Sylvia craved the sense of belonging that only Victoria could give her. All these years, Sylvia had kept the secret about the night on Ocean Avenue so she could remain inside the circle of the Bright family. The terrifying dreams, the regret in the pit of her stomach: this was the cost of loyalty, the price Sylvia had to pay. Victoria had done it for Sylvia, after all.

Sylvia had almost told Ray once, in the twilight after lovemaking. She'd turned to him and almost come clean. But something stopped her, a shadow—the memory of how lonely her life had been before Victoria.

New York City was surprisingly desolate in the dead of the night. Walking toward Times Square, trying to find a taxi, Sylvia saw a twenty-four-hour Internet café. It was the only place open that wasn't a strip club or bar. Sylvia went inside, thinking she could rest and keep an eye out for a cab.

Sylvia found a crumpled five in her wallet and handed it to a young man at the front of the café. The man pointed to a computer.

Sylvia sat down and logged in to her email account. There were a few messages from her boss but none from Ray. There was a message titled IMPORTANT PLEASE HELP.

Dear Ms. Hall,

My name is Lauren Mahdian. If you are the Sylvia Hall whose mother was Pauline Hall, it is very important that I speak with you. I have tried to reach you by phone and left messages. Your biography on the Snowmass Club staff Web page says you grew up in New York City, so I have a good feeling you can help me. Please help me. My number is 512-670-2398.

Yours sincerely,
Lauren Mahdian

Sylvia's hands hovered over the keyboard, and then she did it. She typed L, and then A, and then the rest of the name: LAUREN MAHDIAN.

It took a fraction of a second, and a list of hits came up. Sylvia clicked on the first and was directed to the Web page of a real estate company, Sunshine City Realty, in Austin, Texas. Sylvia stared at the face of a chubby, dark-haired young woman with a shy smile. Sylvia had never met her, but the face—of course—was familiar.

Sylvia had thought about her father's other children over the years. She knew the names of her half brother and sister, though she had never searched for them. She hated her father for abandoning her. His being in jail seemed just punishment. But when Sylvia thought about his orphaned children, guilt and sorrow washed over her—guilt, sorrow, and shame.

Sylvia felt a sensation in her stomach, the smallest flutter, like a butterfly's wings. It was her baby, his feet, inside her. She put her face in her hands.

5

Sylvia pushed open the heavy door to Mae's apartment building. Despite not having received the welcome she had expected from either Mae or Victoria, where else was there to go? It was like traveling back in time—the lobby never changed, with its high ceilings and ornate light fixtures. In the center of the room was a large wood-paneled desk with a potted plant on either side. Along the walls were leather benches the color of coffee. As girls, Sylvia and Victoria had roller-skated around the lobby, falling hard and often on the marble floor.

The doorman, an older man in a burgundy uniform, was half asleep. "Free Bird" played at a low volume from a portable radio. When Sylvia said she was expected in Apartment 7L, the doorman turned the volume down further, straightened his hat, and said, "Lady, it's one in the morning."

"I know," said Sylvia. "Please. Will you just call up?"

The man sipped from a blue mug that said # 1 DAD, hesitating.

"Give me the phone," said Sylvia. "I'll call Victoria's cell." The doorman handed Sylvia an iPhone—his own, she presumed.

She sat on one of the leather couches to dial, remembering the number this time.

The doorman's radio began playing "Sweet Home Alabama." He watched her with suspicion. "I'm an old friend," she said as Victoria's phone rang. Sylvia ran her fingers through her hair, which she knew was flat and a little greasy.

"Hello?" said Victoria. There was loud noise in the background.

"Vee, it's me."

"What?"

"It's Sylvia."

"What do you want, Sylvie? It's the middle of the night."

"Just call the doorman. I'm in the lobby. Can you call down?"

"In the lobby?" said Victoria. She sounded confused. She yelled, "Can you keep it down! I'm *on the phone*!"

"Are you in your mom's apartment?" said Sylvia.

"No, no," said Victoria.

"Where are you? It's really important."

"Sylvie, now is not a good time."

"Tell me where you are," said Sylvia. The doorman was approaching her, his hands on his hips.

"The Lorraine," said Victoria. "But I'm not alone."

"The Lorraine?" said Sylvia. Victoria had already hung up.

Sylvia hit redial, but there was no answer.

A taxi approached the building and slowed. The doorman rushed outside and opened the car door. As Sylvia watched, two young girls climbed out of the cab. One was tall and slight, the hood of a sweatshirt pulled over her head. She had her arm around the younger girl, who had a powder-blue jacket. The children were unaccompanied; the doorman took their hands and led them inside.

"Please just don't ask," the girl in the sweatshirt said to the doorman as they entered the lobby.

"This lady's here to see your mother," he replied, gesturing to Sylvia. The light hit the older girl's face, and Sylvia saw that it was Sunny, Victoria's daughter. Sunny looked exhausted. She kept her arm around Georgia, who clutched a stuffed kangaroo.

"Aunt Sylvia?" said Sunny.

"Yay!" cried Georgia.

"Girls," said Sylvia, standing and hugging Sunny, who seemed resistant to her godmother's embrace. *My God,* thought Sylvia, *the girl is skinny.* Anorexic? She looked it. Georgia clasped her neck and hung on. Sylvia picked her up, and the girl nuzzled her neck. "Sunny," said Sylvia, "what are you two doing out at—"

"One-eighteen in the morning," finished the doorman, taking his phone from Sylvia.

Sunny shrugged, casting her eyes down at her high-top sneakers.

"We woke up in the hotel room," said Georgia seriously, her hand in Sylvia's hair. "We woke up in the hotel room, and Mommy was gone!"

"Be quiet," said Sunny. "Georgia, be quiet."

"Mommy wasn't gone," Georgia amended.

"The last time I saw you, it was your eighth birthday party," said Sylvia. "At the zoo, remember?"

Sunny nodded, tracing a circle with her toe.

"And now you're . . . what are you, eleven?"

"I'm twelve," said Sunny.

"Is everything all right?" said Sylvia, putting her hand on the girl's shoulder.

Sunny snorted, a sound that made Sylvia think of Victoria. "Define *all right,*" Sunny said.

"Sweetheart—"

"We have to go," said Sunny. "It's really late, and Georgia needs to brush her teeth and go to bed."

The adult words coming from Sunny's sweet face made Sylvia ache. "How about this?" said Sylvia, bending her knees to look Sunny in the eyes. "How about we have lunch tomorrow? Just you and me."

"I'm not really into lunch," said Sunny.

"We could go to Maria's," said Sylvia. "Do you still love those pepperoni rolls?"

"No," said Sunny. "Come on, Georgia." Georgia climbed down and took her sister's hand. They stood awkwardly in the lobby, and then Sunny said, "Aunt Sylvia, what are you doing here?"

"I'm here to visit you," said Sylvia. "You and your mom."

Sunny's face closed. "Let me know if you find her," she said, turning away and walking toward the elevator.

"Bye," said Georgia, holding the paw of her kangaroo and making him wave.

Sylvia was so tired. She wanted to follow the girls upstairs, but she asked the doorman for a taxi. When she told the driver she was going to the Lorraine, it seemed to make sense to him. As she sped downtown, Sylvia stared out the window, replaying Sunny's every word.

"Wake up!" said the taxi driver. "Wake up! You want the Lorraine?"

"Oh," said Sylvia. She reached into her pocketbook and paid the driver. The Lorraine Hotel was an old stone building with a sleek neon sign and a pink and black awning. Sylvia wasn't sure if it was really a hotel at all, but the music thumping into the street advertised that it was a nightclub. Leave it to Victoria, thought Sylvia, to find the newest, hippest spot.

A steel door led to an entranceway lit by wall sconces. Sylvia could smell hamburgers and expensive perfume. She blinked, trying to get her bearings. A bald woman in leather pants and a silk top approached Sylvia. "Can I help you?"

"I'm looking for someone," muttered Sylvia, lugging her duffel bag past the hostess.

"Aren't we all?" said the woman, crossing her arms over her chest but letting Sylvia by.

Many of the tables were filled, though it was late. A live band played at top volume, the singer screeching in a language Sylvia could not identify. She felt underdressed and ridiculous as she wandered past tables of club kids and older people with faces that were unnaturally expressionless and waxen. She remembered her friend Carlos, a bartender at the Snowmass Club, who joked about giving drink specials to especially taut women on "Face-lift Fridays."

Victoria was nowhere to be found. After searching for what felt like an hour, Sylvia gave up. She exited and sat down on the steps outside the club. For the love of God, she was tired. She could try to book a room at the Lorraine—if it was, in fact, an operating hotel—but she didn't want to go back inside. Maybe she could find somewhere cheaper. After a good night's rest, things might seem clearer. Sylvia sighed and stood up. Her duffel bag seemed heavier with each step.

She was not in a great neighborhood. It was very dark, and Sylvia saw three figures emerge from an alleyway ahead of her. She heard the wail of a police cruiser or an ambulance. She felt a flame of fear, but there were no taxis in sight.

Sylvia stood still and said a silent prayer. She had never believed in God, but she had never *not* believed in Him, either. *Please help me,* she prayed. As the words formed in her mind, she felt warmer. She felt as if someone were holding her, wrapping her up. *I am here,* Sylvia thought, or thought she heard. Sylvia opened her eyes and saw a pay phone under a streetlamp about a block or so away. The three figures were gone.

The phone booth was next to a bar. The name of the bar was painted in black on the heavy door: Claiborne's. It was a rough place, from the looks of it: dirty brick exterior, sidewalk littered with cigarette butts and broken glass. Above the bar, a light was on in a dingy apartment. Sylvia lifted the receiver. Miraculously, there was a dial tone. She could call information, she thought, or a car service.

And then, through the window of the bar, Sylvia saw Victoria. She almost didn't recognize her old friend sitting in a lonely corner. Victoria looked old, bony. It was as if her skin had sunk into her cheekbones. She stared at her drink. As Sylvia watched, Victoria brought the glass to her lips, drained it, and called out for another. When a man placed a fresh drink on the table, she did not look up.

It was cold. Standing in the street, holding her duffel, Sylvia understood: Victoria was broken. Sylvia was on her own—Victoria was not going to save her. Still, the number she dialed into the keypad was her best friend's phone.

Sylvia watched as Victoria drew her cell from her purse, squinting to see who was calling. *Please,* thought Sylvia. *Please.* But after looking at the phone for a minute, Victoria placed it on the table without answering. She set it next to her glass, and then she drank.

Sylvia remembered the first day she had been invited home to the Brights' apartment on East Eighty-sixth and Park. A uniformed maid had met them at the door, taking their after-school snack orders ("chocolate Yoo-hoo and Cheetos" for Victoria, "Um, the same" for Sylvia) and then bringing the food on a tray with folded napkins.

Victoria's room was enormous and had a four-poster bed with a canopy made of pink fabric. When Mae popped in to say hello, Victoria treated her with complete disdain, a revelation to Sylvia, who gave her own mother cowed respect. Mae wore a crisp tennis dress; she was on her way to "hit some balls with the girls." As she left, shutting the door firmly behind her, Victoria yelled, "And don't forget, *I need new shoes*!" in such a demanding tone, Sylvia almost gasped.

Victoria's room had floor-to-ceiling shelves filled with hardcover books and wooden toys in wicker baskets. There was a table with small pink chairs and brand-new art supplies lined up in a row—markers, paints, fat brushes. Kennebunkport, a medium-sized goldfish, was housed in an aquarium built into the wall. Victoria slid open a drawer underneath the tank and removed a plastic container of foul-smelling fish food. She pinched a few flakes and sprinkled them over the water. Kennebunkport ate greedily.

"Eat some fish food," Victoria had said, turning to Sylvia. "I dare you."

Sylvia would have done it—she would have done anything—but felt nauseous from the pet-store smell of the flakes. She lied feebly, "I have food allergies." She walked over to the tank and peered in. The fish darted playfully. "I'll get sick," said Sylvia.

Victoria moved closer to her, holding up the open container. Her chocolate-colored hair was held back by pink barrettes; her eyes were seductive, mischievous, inviting. "Do you dare me?" she said.

"No," said Sylvia quietly. She leaned toward Victoria, readying herself. If having a friend meant eating something disgusting, she could do it. Life was full of challenges to be surmounted, as Pauline always said.

"Why don't you dare me to eat Kennebunkport?" said Victoria. She was inches from Sylvia, who felt invisible waves between them. *Do the right thing,* she heard her mother tell her. *Do whatever you have to do.*

Victoria gripped Sylvia's fingers. For a moment, Sylvia thought Victoria was going to kiss her, and the thought was thrilling.

With her free hand, Sylvia took the cover off the tank and reached in. The water was viscous and cold. It took her a minute, but she trapped Kennebunkport in a corner and grasped his tiny tail. She pulled the fish—so defenseless!—from the water and held it next to Victoria's lips.

"I dare you," said Sylvia.

Victoria opened her mouth, her focus never leaving Sylvia. Sylvia lowered her hand, placing the shock-still fish on Victoria's tongue. Victoria closed her mouth and swallowed.

"I can't believe you did that," said Sylvia.

"Believe it," said Victoria.

Now, decades too late, Sylvia turned her back on Victoria. Putting more change into the metal slot, she dialed another number. Lauren Mahdian. The phone rang three times, and then a sleepy but scared voice answered.

"Is this Lauren Mahdian?" asked Sylvia.

"Yes."

"My name is Sylvia Hall. You . . . you asked me to call you?"

"Oh," said the girl. She cleared her throat. Sylvia thought of the picture she had seen in the *New York Times* after Lauren Mahdian's mother had been killed. It was a grainy shot: a girl in pigtails holding the hand of her skinny brother.

"I . . . This is going to sound crazy," said Lauren.

"I don't mind," said Sylvia.

"Do you know anything about an earring that belonged to your mother? Pauline Hall?"

"An earring?" said Sylvia. She felt her lungs seize up—she could not breathe.

"It's made of jade, let me get it," said Lauren. "Okay, it's jade and silver . . ." Her voice trailed off, and then she sighed. "I don't know. I don't know what I'm trying to ask you."

"My mother's dead," said Sylvia.

There was a silence, and then Lauren said, "My mother's dead, too."

"I'm sorry," said Sylvia.

"It happened a long time ago," said Lauren.

Sylvia didn't answer. Something in the pure sadness of the girl's voice brought tears to Sylvia's eyes. The girl was her half sister, though she didn't know Sylvia existed. "That must have been terrible," said Sylvia. "Growing up without a mom."

"What can you do?" said Lauren.

What could you do? This seemed like an important question to Sylvia, even essential, though Lauren had said it with a mix of bravado and sarcasm. Sylvia could do *plenty* for Lauren. She could tell Lauren about the earring, about the murder. She could bring a measure of peace to someone, to her blood sister—*that* she could do. "I've always wanted a sister," said Sylvia; she just blurted it out.

"What?"

Sylvia glanced briefly at Victoria, shadowed in the corner of the bar. "I've always wanted a sister, I said," said Sylvia. "I think a lot of things I did that were wrong were because I wanted . . . someone. A family."

"Yeah," said Lauren. "But we're alone, really. We all are."

After a moment, Sylvia said, "That's so sad."

"Sad but true," said Lauren. Then she repeated, "Sad but true."

Despite the serious tone of their conversation, Sylvia laughed. "You make me think of this quote I heard once. 'She was born with the gift of laughter and a sense that the world was mad.' "

Lauren snorted. "You said it, sister."

Sylvia grinned. She liked Lauren's dark sense of humor. She liked Lauren, which was nothing she had expected.

"Listen, do you know anything about this earring?" said Lauren plainly.

Sylvia wanted to keep talking to Lauren, wanted to know her, to be her friend. "It's jade?"

"Yes."

Sylvia drew a deep breath but could not bring herself to speak.

"I'm sorry," Lauren said finally. "This is . . . I don't know why I'm doing this. There was an earring . . . I thought that maybe it would help explain what happened. My father's in jail, and now my brother . . . I think my brother's gone."

"I don't know about an earring," said Sylvia. The lie was bitter in her mouth.

"I'm sorry," repeated Lauren.

Sylvia wanted to be honest before the memory of that night burned her up from inside. Instead, she murmured, "I'm sorry, too."

"I'm done with this," said Lauren. Maybe she was talking to herself. "If you think of anything, call the Holt Police Department," said Lauren. "I'm done."

"I wish I could help you," said Sylvia.

"Oh well," Lauren said, her voice flippant in an obvious effort to mask pain. "Goodbye."

"Bye," said Sylvia, and Lauren hung up. Sylvia stood in the dark, holding the receiver. She thought of Sunny shrinking into her hooded sweatshirt. She felt Georgia's soft arms embracing her. And then she conjured a vision of herself comforting a boy with a nightmare. A boy in his own room, with a window full of stars. Sylvia saw her hands pulling up a Superman comforter, tucking it around her child. "I'm here," she would say, kissing his cheek, his forehead, his nose.

"Mommy's always here," she would say.

Through the bar window, Sylvia saw Victoria stagger to her feet. For a moment Sylvia thought Victoria had seen her and was coming toward her, but Victoria was just going to the bathroom.

It seemed an easy decision, finally. *What can you do?* Lauren had asked, and to Sylvia, it was a challenge. What can you do to save a stranger, a young woman who makes you laugh? What can you do to help someone who deserves kindness and the truth of the story that you have to tell?

Sylvia picked up the pay phone a last time and called the operator. "Collect call, please," she said. She swallowed, gathering the strength to turn Victoria in to the authorities. Maybe Sylvia would go to jail herself for what she had done. She didn't know, but the path forward was suddenly—blindingly—clear.

"I'd like to place a call to the police department in Holt, New York," said Sylvia.

"One moment, please," said the operator. "One moment, please, and I'll connect you."

6

Somebody's parents had a house in the suburbs, on the beach. The parents were away, and there was going to be a massive party. Someone filled a 7UP bottle with vodka, and they started drinking in Grand Central Station. First Sylvia felt nothing, then jubilant, then a combination of wary and wanting more. She was seventeen.

Victoria had taken something else, some pills. Every time Sylvia was wild, Victoria was wilder. She wore a dress the color of blood. She leaned her head against the train window. She put on big sunglasses, her hair blew around her face. She wore no makeup; none of them wore makeup. Makeup was for nouveau riche, for bridge-and-tunnels.

By the time they got off the train, they were wasted. It was afternoon in the suburbs. Rich men were walking Labrador retrievers and buying ice cream. The dogs had collars printed with sand crabs and starfish. The men wore loafers without socks. Victoria was already too far along, her pupils wide and frightening.

They took a taxi to the address Victoria had written on her

hand, the address of the house where the party would be. First they stopped at the Getty Mart for cigarettes, then drove along a road that turned into sand. The house had shingles that were bleached-out gray. Everything in this town had been in the sun too long.

Victoria and Sylvia put their bags in a guest room on the third floor. "This bed is *so small,*" Sylvia said. She was learning to complain—to expect more, always.

"We'll snuggle up, then," said Victoria. She was sitting at an antique dressing table, staring at her beautiful face in the mirror. Sylvia took up a silver hairbrush and ran it through her best friend's tangled hair. Victoria leaned back against Sylvia. She smelled like Camel Lights. Then Victoria pushed Sylvia away and stood up to rummage in Sylvia's bag. "Did you bring them?"

"Yes," said Sylvia. Victoria had gone through Pauline's drawers and found the jade earrings, the ones from her blood father. Victoria wanted them, wanted to wear them, and that was one small favor Sylvia had to give.

The party had already started. There were seniors in lounge chairs around the pool, juniors by the barbecue grill, sophomores making fruity drinks in the kitchen. When Victoria started dancing, Pauline's earrings caught the light.

Sylvia started talking to a boy, a senior, Matthew Cohen. (Robert had dumped her the year before.) She could tell Victoria didn't like it. Victoria kept walking by them, waving. Finally, she took Sylvia's hand and dragged her outside. "What is it?" said Sylvia. "Vee, I like him."

"I got some car keys," said Victoria.

"What?"

"Let's go," said Victoria. "Let's go to your dad's house."

"My dad's house?"

Victoria's face was animated, brilliant. She was looking for a fight. "We can talk to him, tell him that you need him," she said. "Your father! He lives a few streets over. Ocean Avenue, I can find the house. He'll listen to me. Trust me."

"What are you talking about? No!" said Sylvia. She dropped her cigarette on the lawn and turned to walk away.

"Don't leave," yelled Victoria. "I can help you, Sylvie! I can make him see you!"

Sylvia hissed, "You're being crazy."

"I'll fix it for you," said Victoria.

With a boozy clarity, Sylvia realized she was sick of Victoria and her dramatic pronouncements. Victoria didn't want Sylvia to be with Matthew or anyone.

Sylvia shook her head. "Come on," she said. "Let's just go back to the party." As she walked across the lawn, leaving Victoria seething, unsaid words echoed in Sylvia's mind: *This isn't a Nancy Drew book, Victoria. This is my life.*

It was easy, so easy, to forget about Victoria. Time swung forward, and Sylvia was sitting in Matthew's lap. He kissed her neck, and she picked up handfuls of sand and watched it run through her fingers. She felt a small flickering of desire, eclipsed fully by a flame of wanting more to drink. Matthew brought her a glass of something; maybe it was gin. There was no more tonic, he said. By this time she was lying on the beach, looking up at the sky.

Sylvia thought Victoria would find her when it was time for sleep. At some point, with Matthew passed out next to her, Sylvia realized it was time for her to say her good nights and go to sleep. There was a row of houses along the beach; Sylvia almost went into the wrong one but heard music from the right one, Blues Traveler's "Alone." A few people were still awake, either drinking or having sex, but most were passed out. There was a circle of people around a bong in the living room, but Victoria wasn't there.

Sylvia found their room. It was empty. She got into the bed and entered a black passage of sleep.

By the time they found the dead woman on her bedroom floor, Sylvia and Victoria were back in the city. The owner of the house where the party had been held made his son give the police a list of everyone who had been to the party, and everyone on the list was interviewed.

As she had promised Mae, Sylvia told the police that Victoria was sleeping with her in the attic bedroom. Sylvia told them she had drunk two wine coolers.

The truth was that Victoria didn't come back until dawn, and when she did, she woke Sylvia by flinging open the bedroom door.

Victoria's dress was wet. She took it off and climbed into the bed, putting her face close to Sylvia's. Her limbs were cold, and she was shivering. Her hair, too, was drenched. When Sylvia asked what had happened, Victoria said, "Please be quiet." When Sylvia asked why she was wet, Victoria said, "Promise me you will never ask me that question again." She said, "I love you so much, Sylvia, and I'm the only one who loves you, and you know that. You asked me to do this, and I did it. I did this for you." Sylvia lay awake then, afraid to say another word.

In the morning Victoria handed Sylvia one of the jade earrings. She had gone for a midnight swim, said Victoria, shrugging without apology. The other earring, she said, must have fallen off in the waves.

Book Five

1

The days moved like molasses. In Baghdad, they kept sorting through rubble, trying to find something of my brother. In Austin, I went through the motions of living. Gerry and I ate and we slept, even made love. But I was not present. I was paused, praying that my brother would somehow come home. I began to understand the parents of missing children who said they just wanted to find a body, even if it meant their son or daughter was dead. It was so awful to wonder and wait.

One afternoon Jonesey stopped by my desk, where I was staring into space. I was supposedly on floor duty, but no one had come in all morning. I felt like crying, though there were no tears left.

"Request for you," he said. "Line two."

"Send it to voice mail," I said, rolling my stiff neck back and forth.

"No," said Jonesey.

I looked up. "I'm about to go to lunch," I said dully.

"You haven't had a client in days," said Jonesey. He put his hands on his hips.

"Oh, jeez," I said, but Jonesey had whirled around and was walking purposefully to the front desk. He put the call through, and my extension rang.

"Lauren Mahdian," I said. "Sunshine City Realty."

"Oh, hello," said a woman. The connection was bad; I could scarcely make out what she was saying. "I'm . . . Um, I'd like to find a house. Or maybe an apartment. I don't have a job yet, but I've sent out my résumé."

I rolled my eyes and mouthed *Thanks a lot* to Jonesey. "I'd be happy to show you around," I said. "Is there a date and time that works best for you?"

"How about now?" said the woman.

I pursed my lips and breathed in, but Jonesey was watching. "Sounds great," I said. "Right now sounds great. Why don't you come by the office? We're located in Hyde Park, at Forty-second and Duval."

"Okay," said the woman.

"What's your name?" I asked, my pencil poised, but she had already hung up.

"Good luck," said Jonesey, tossing his blazer over his shoulder. "I'm meeting Gil at Lucinda's."

"Have a great lunch," I said. I played Scrabble online until I heard the front door open. A pregnant woman in a rumpled black dress stood in the front of the office, touching her hair. Her face was puffy. I stood and made my way toward her. I felt like I knew her somehow, though I did not know her.

"I'm Lauren," I said, holding out my hand.

"Hi," she said. She held on too long.

"Have we met?" I said.

"No," she said. "I just— I've heard of you. The website. You look like your picture."

"So you're new in town?" I asked.

She sighed. "I just got here. Literally."

"Great," I said. "Would you like to sit down here? Or we could grab some lunch."

"I'm really hungry," said the woman.

"Fair enough," I said.

We walked next door to Hyde Park Café. Aaron, one of my favorite waiters, sat us in the front room by a window. "I don't think you've told me your name," I said after the woman had ordered a lemonade and I'd ordered a Fireman's Four.

"It's Syl— It's Sarah," she said.

"Nice to meet you," I said.

"Likewise."

Aaron returned with our drinks, and the woman ordered a burger and fries. I said I'd have the same, though I really wanted another beer. "Can you tell me what you're hoping to find?" I asked.

She looked out the window. "I like it here," she said.

"Hyde Park Café?" I said.

"Austin," she said. "It strikes me as a good place."

It seemed I had hooked a nut job. "Would you like me to tell you about some of Austin's premier neighborhoods?" I said.

"Where do you live?" said Sarah.

"I live east of I-35," I said. "It's called French Place."

"Do you belong to a health club?" she asked.

"Um, no," I said. "I don't."

"I think I'd like someplace in the country," Sarah said.

"Westlake is very nice," I said. "Or if you go south, there's Circle C."

"It's just me and my baby," said Sarah. "But I want him to have his own room. That's very important. Two bedrooms. And a kitchen."

"That seems reasonable," I said.

"I want to be somewhere quiet," said Sarah. "I want to stay home as much as I can. I want to be with him, you know?"

I had no idea what she was getting at. Had this person been abused? "Let's talk about price range," I said.

"I think I can be happy here," said Sarah, staring out the window.

My phone buzzed, and I glanced down. (Gerry called it "getting figital" when I played with my phone in restaurants.) Detective Brendan Crosby was calling me from Holt, New York. I hadn't talked to him since my fruitless visit.

"Excuse me," I said. Sarah nodded and looked teary. I rose, bumping the table, and I went outside as I answered. I stood in the sunshine and watched a bus drive down Duval Street. A man pedaled past on a bicycle. He had two kids in a little buggy attached to the back. Though the father had no helmet, both the kids wore plastic saucers strapped to their heads.

"Lauren," said Detective Crosby.

"Hi," I said.

"I'm calling with some news," said Detective Crosby. "Are you sitting down?"

"No," I said. I looked around for a bench, but an amorous couple was wedged into the only available spot. I sank down on the front steps of Hyde Park Café. "Yes," I said.

"Lauren, we just arrested a woman for the murder of your mother," said Detective Crosby. "She's in police custody. Her name is Victoria Bright."

"What?" I said. I put my hand to my throat.

"We're still getting all the facts," said Detective Crosby. "We got Victoria's name from a woman who contacted us with very convincing new evidence. She decided to come forward after all this time. And, well, it looks like Victoria Bright's fingerprints match a set that was found at your house."

"What?" I said.

"This is a really good day, Lauren. We have a call in to your father. There will be a new trial."

"My father?" I said. I started laughing and crying at the same time. I waited for the smoky feeling, but things stayed clear.

"I'll be in touch, Lauren," said Detective Crosby.

"Oh my God," I said. I repeated, "Oh my God." The sun was hot on my face. I heard the bus pull away from the bus stop, and I saw a little girl standing by the ice cream shop next door, holding a strawberry cone. The pregnant woman came outside and sat down next to me.

"Excuse me," I said. "I'm sorry."

"I'm going to go now," she said. "I hoped I would be here when you got the call."

"My father . . ." I said.

"Thank you for telling me about Austin," she said. "It seems like a good place."

"I can't believe this," I said.

"Believe it," said the woman. Without asking, she leaned over and embraced me. Surprising myself, I leaned in to her. I felt comforted, peaceful, in this woman's arms. Her belly touched mine, and I thought I felt her baby—an elbow or a foot—although that may have been my imagination.

Sarah let me go and stood.

"Please be in touch," I said.

"I'd like that," said Sarah.

As I watched, she began to walk south on Duval Street. Something in her stride was familiar. She held herself like Alex, I realized—the way she moved seemed to convey an inner confidence. She turned back and met my eyes. I lifted a hand in farewell. I hoped we would meet again.

2

In the cavernous church, Mae bowed her head. She pressed her hands together in prayer and saw that they were old, the veins prominent and dark. She remembered her mother saying, as she shuffled slowly to take communion, *This isn't me, honey. This old person isn't me.*

Mae was an old person now. But she could still remember the August morning when she'd unpacked Victoria's overnight bag and found a red dress, soaking wet. "Victoria!" she'd called. "What on earth is *this*?"

Victoria had stood in the doorway of the laundry room, pale. She was wearing a bathrobe. Seventeen! She was just seventeen.

"Why is your dress wet?" asked Mae.

"I went swimming," said Victoria.

"Swimming! Where?"

"We went to a party on the beach." Victoria held up her hand as if to stop her mother from talking. She was shaking. "Listen," she said. "Mom, something really bad happened."

"Tell me," said Mae. She sank back onto her heels, the dress falling to the floor. Victoria came to Mae and sat in her lap like a child. Mae ran her fingers through her daughter's hair. Victoria began to cry, racking sobs.

"What happened, baby?" said Mae.

"It was a party," said Victoria. "I was drinking. I drank so much."

"It's okay, honey," said Mae. "Everyone makes mistakes."

"No," said Victoria, turning her face to her mother. "No! No, Mom! No!" She balled her hands into fists and shoved them into her eye sockets, saying, "No, no, no . . ."

"Get ahold of yourself, Victoria," said Mae.

"I was drunk. We were at a party on the beach," said Victoria.

Mae shook her head, trying to take it in. Her daughter on some beach, drunk . . .

Victoria went on, "I went to find Sylvia's father—it was the same town. I thought I could just *talk* to him. I wanted to make him understand. Sylvia needs him!"

"Sylvia's father?" said Mae. Her head spun. "What are you talking about?"

"I— I found some whiskey," babbled Victoria. "It was in a glass bottle—a decanter. I just thought . . . I don't know what I thought. I was going to drink some. I was going to talk to Sylvia's dad. I went upstairs. I thought maybe I would find a place to sleep or something. I forgot which house . . ."

"Good Christ," whispered Mae.

"Listen to me," said Victoria, seizing her mother's shoulders painfully. "Listen to me." Mae nodded, her mind already a few minutes ahead. Victoria would finish this story, and Mae would call Preston, who would know a lawyer. *Breaking and entering, unlawful trespassing . . .*

"I went upstairs," said Victoria. "There was a lady. She got out of bed. She was mad. She came toward me. I . . . I was scared. I thought I'd get in trouble. I just— I wasn't thinking. I thought

I'd knock her down so I could run away. I hit her. I hit her with the decanter. I hit her really hard, and she fell."

Mae gasped.

"I ran. I ran to the beach, and I swam out with the . . . with what was left of the decanter. I swam as far as I could, and then I dropped it."

"Was this woman," said Mae, her hand over her mouth, "was this woman okay?"

"I don't know," said Victoria, pushing her fists into her eyes again, shaking her head. "I don't think so," she whispered. Then she looked up at her mother. "What do I do? Mom, what do I do?"

In that moment, Mae made a decision. She saw the possible avenues, and she chose one. "Don't ever tell anyone else what you've told me," she said. "This never happened. Don't say a word."

Victoria pressed her lips together and nodded. Mae held her tightly.

And until she was arrested, twenty-four years later, Victoria never again told the story. When the police came to Lark Academy, when the woman's death was in the paper, when the husband was arrested and sent to jail. They were silent, the both of them.

And furthermore.

Now, staring at her hands, Mae listened to Father Richard talk about sin. She thought about her husband, who had died of a heart attack on the golf course. She did not feel he surrounded her and watched over her. Nor did she believe he was in hell. He was simply gone.

When the police came for Victoria, they handcuffed her in

front of her daughters. Mae drove behind the cruiser to the Holt station. As they interviewed Victoria, Mae sat next to a soda machine in a long hallway. She stared at her wedding ring, twisted it around and around on her finger.

Finally, between two police officers, Victoria emerged. She was still shackled. Mae stood. She almost hoped Victoria had told the police what she—Mae—had done in advising Victoria to stay silent. Then Mae would be arrested as well.

"I told the truth, Mom," said Victoria. She looked almost relieved. She held her mother's gaze, and the police did not move toward Mae. She had told the truth, her eyes said, but not the whole truth. She had protected her mother.

Mae embraced her daughter. "I should have saved *you,*" she whispered.

"You tried," said Victoria.

A child was being baptized in St. Gabriel's, a boy. As he poured the water, Father Richard said, "I baptize you in the name of the Father and of the Son and of the Holy Spirit. May the Almighty God, the Father of our Lord Jesus Christ, Who hath regenerated thee by water and the Holy Spirit, and Who hath given thee the remission of all thy sins, may He Himself anoint thee with the Christ of Salvation, in the same Christ Jesus our Lord, unto life eternal."

Winter sunlight shone through the stained-glass windows with a cold intensity. Mae would spend Christmas with her granddaughters and their father. After the New Year, they would move to Greece without her. Mae had bought them books that they would not read. She had unpacked the crèche, laid the wooden baby Jesus in his hay-bale bed, and set his mother next to him, watching over him, her head bowed in reverence.

Mae rose and walked toward the altar, though she did not know the family. The baby began to cry as his original sin was washed away, and the sound pierced Mae's heart clean through. She reached toward the infant, and he looked at her. His eyes were as green as jade.

3

Sitting, stunned, on the front steps of Hyde Park Café, I marveled at the fact that everything looked the same, though my whole life had changed. My father was innocent. He had loved my mother. Also, he loved me.

The afternoon sun warmed the top of my head and my shoulders. Jesus H. Christ, I was happy. I felt like my childhood night-light, glowing. Joy, I supposed—this was what joy felt like—your body filling with light. I wanted to run into the street, screaming the news. I tilted my head upward, focusing on a lone, wispy cloud. I whispered, "Thank you."

I was never taught to believe in God, in anything. Our family did not go to any religious services. We did not celebrate Ramadan or Hanukkah, and we celebrated Christmas only in a secular way. But on Sunday mornings, when I was small, my mother would fix Alex and me bowls of cereal and settle us on the couch for cartoons. My parents would retreat to their upstairs bedroom and lock the door.

I loved Froot Loops and Cap'n Crunch. On Sundays, we were allowed as much cereal as we could cram in our mouths, and we lay on the couch for hours. When our parents came downstairs, our mother was freshly showered, flushed, and ravenous. The joy our parents found in each other was undeniable, and their passion never waned.

The pleasure they found upstairs, while Alex and I munched sugary O's, was what bound them. But after my mother's death, I believed that my father's passion for my mother had made him capable of something awful. I had seen his face when my mother admired Mr. Schwickrath's present, his eyes narrow with anger. I had imagined they fought, and their love had exploded into something that could lead my father to pick up a heavy glass object and swing.

But I had been wrong. Now the knowledge washed over me: my parents' love had not changed into something dark. It had been complicated, like all love, but our family's happiness had not been a mirage.

My father, with his imported cigarettes and his fancy stereo, trying to fit in. He had written me for years, and I had not had the courage to read one letter. I felt guilty. I felt happy. I felt like going inside and finishing my lunch—so that is what I did.

Later, I called my father. Gerry sat next to me on the couch with an open bag of SunChips. The person who answered the phone (a guard? an operator?) told me that Izaan would have to call me back.

"Please tell him it's his daughter," I said. "Please tell him . . ."

"What?"

"Tell him I called," I said.

"Okay, lady," said the man on the other end of the line.

I hung up the phone. "What's going to happen?" said Gerry.

"There's going to be a trial," I said. "A new trial."

"Would you like a SunChip?" asked Gerry.

"Thank you," I said, "but no."

Gerry put his hand on the side of my face. "He didn't do it," he said.

"I know," I said. Gerry smiled. "It feels so good," I said. "It feels impossibly great to have a father." I put my arms around my boyfriend and I held him tight.

The sky was luminous outside the windows of our house. On the coffee table were two glasses of sweet tea. Handsome wedged his nose into the space between us. The phone rang, and I took a breath before lifting my head from Gerry's shoulder. "I'm scared," I said.

"It doesn't matter what you say," said Gerry. "That's the point of love."

"Really?" I said.

"Yes," said Gerry.

I picked up the phone. "Hello?" I said.

"Is this Lauren Mahdian?" said a strange voice. It was a man's voice, but there was nothing about it that was familiar. I felt a sinking sensation in my gut. The voice did not sound right.

"Yes," I said. "Who is this?"

"Ms. Mahdian," said the man. "I'm calling about your brother, Alex Mahdian."

"Oh, no," I said. "This is the wrong call." I dropped the phone and stood quickly. "It's not him," I said to Gerry. It took seven steps to reach the front door, which I flung open. "It's not my father!" I yelled as I ran outside. I looked wildly up and down Maplewood Avenue. There had to be a direction I could turn, I thought. There must be a place I could go where I would not have to hear what the man on the phone was going to tell me. Going west on Thirty-eighth led downtown, past a coffee shop, a piñata store, and the Fiesta grocery. If I turned east, I would hit

Patterson park and pool and the neighborhood surrounding it. I chose east, and began to sprint.

Gerry came outside. I head him yell, "Lauren!" I didn't turn around. "Lauren!" called Gerry. "Come back, Lauren!"

I was barefoot, but I kept going. I felt the blood pumping through my body. I turned onto Ashwood Road, passing broken-down houses, very nice houses, yards that were cared for and yards that were a mess. I ran without a destination in mind, just away, just away.

But Gerry was faster. He overtook me at the corner of Ashwood and Green, grabbing me around the waist and pulling me down. I fought him, I screamed, I bit his arm and said, "No, no, no!"

"Stop," whispered Gerry. "Stay still," he said, "shhhh."

"Please," I said, looking into his clear blue eyes.

"They found him," said Gerry. "They found Alex. He's alive."

4

Everyone loves their siblings. Gerry has a brother and a sister, and when the three of them get together, it's like a reunited tribe—Gerry gets giddy, goofy, he's completely understood. But I can scarcely describe how I felt when I first heard Alex's voice on the phone from Baghdad. It was as if I'd completed the most arduous journey, and was taking my last steps toward a golden door.

I began crying as Gerry handed me the phone.

"Is this Lauren?" Alex's voice was shaky, confused in a way that reminded me of Gramma.

"Alex," I said, and my voice broke.

"Lauren," said my brother. "Alex," I repeated, and then we were quiet. There was nothing else to say.

I called Gramma after Alex's nurse made him hang up the phone. When I told her Alex was okay and coming back to Texas, she said, "That's the best news I've had all week."

Alex came home on Thanksgiving Day. You would think he'd have a parade to welcome him, trumpet players and high-stepping girls in bright skirts. But it was only Gerry and me, clutching helium balloons and a six-pack of Shiner in the arrivals area. We watched the escalator silently.

I almost didn't recognize my brother. He was very thin—emaciated. He wore loose clothing, so the change was most pronounced in his face. His skin was discolored and raw. I guess I had imagined he'd be the same.

Alex stood on the escalator, not running to greet us, not even scanning the crowd. He didn't have the floral duffel or his books; all that was gone. As we approached Alex, he looked up. When he saw me, his face brightened, and I began to cry. "Why the hell are you crying?" said Alex.

"I thought you were dead," I said.

Alex shook his head tiredly. When I hugged him, he hugged me back. "I'm not dead," he said.

We drove home on Airport Boulevard. Alex was silent in the passenger seat. He opened a can of beer but took only a few sips. He stared at the pawnshops, strip clubs, gas stations. "I called your landlord," I said. "I told her to kick out the new guy. Or girl. I told her you're home."

"I can find another place," said Alex.

"Oh," I said.

"What do you want for dinner?" said Gerry.

Alex shrugged.

"I know!" I said. "Crown and Anchor. Your favorite. Cheeseburgers for Thanksgiving!"

"Okay," said Alex.

"Don't order wine there," said Gerry. "Remember, Lauren?"

"Right," I said. "I once ordered wine there and it was terrible! A mini-bottle. They just unscrewed the little cap and handed it to me."

Gerry chuckled desperately. "Right," he said. "That was really funny."

"It was so funny!" I said.

Alex didn't respond. Gerry took a left on Thirty-eighth Street, then another left on Duval. The Crown and Anchor was packed—students spilled into the parking lot, drinking beers and throwing Frisbees for dogs. We parked on Harris Park Avenue and walked over. Alex's hands were in his pockets. He seemed folded into himself.

There were no tables available, so we ordered glasses of beer and stood between a pool table and the dartboard, sipping and ducking to avoid being hit. "This is really not relaxing," said Alex after a while. The music in the pub was loud. It sounded like Pearl Jam, but I wasn't sure if it was Pearl Jam. It might have been John Mayer trying to sound like Pearl Jam.

"Do you want to leave?" I said.

"I don't know," said Alex.

"Let's go," said Gerry. "Come with me." He put his beer down on the bar, and Alex and I followed him out the door. In the parking lot, Gerry said, "Eat or drink?" to Alex.

Alex lifted his bony shoulders. "I don't know."

"Come on, Al," said Gerry.

"Both," said Alex.

"Done," said Gerry. We got back in the car, and Gerry drove south on Lamar, all the way to Artz Rib House. "Wait here," he said. He went inside.

"Are you okay?" I said, once Alex and I were alone. "You seem kind of down."

"I'm just getting used to it all again," said Alex.

"Can you believe it," I said, "about Dad?"

"I knew all along," said Alex.

"I know you did," I said.

"Have you talked to him?" asked Alex.

"Yeah," I said. "Every day, actually."

"Me, too," said Alex. I looked out the window at a man in only a thong bicycling up Lamar, at a dog gnawing a rib in the parking lot. "Now I guess I need a new mission in life," he said.

"Or you could relax awhile," I said. "I'm actually pretty happy hanging around. I made pasta from scratch last night. But Handsome ate half the noodles while I was taking a shower."

Alex nodded seriously. "Ah," he said. "There is rapture to be found in the ordinary."

If he wanted to be pretentious, he had certainly earned the right, so I bit my lip. "You need to eat," I said after a minute. "You're really skinny."

"I know," said Alex. He had been knocked out by the bomb blasts, burned badly on the face, and transported with many of the sick and injured to a small hospital over an hour from the city. It had been complete mayhem, and patients from Ibn Sina had been relocated wherever beds could be found. Things moved slowly, and a month later, some Iraqis were still unidentified. Unbelievably, it wasn't noted that Alex's comatose body was American. Maybe because of his Arabic tattoo, no one connected Alex to the missing American doctor the State Department was trying desperately to find.

"It just seems impossible," I said to Alex on the phone, the day before he flew back to Texas.

"A clerical error," said Alex. His laugh was bitter.

"I guess they happen everywhere," I said.

"I don't know," he said. "I just want to come home."

When Alex had finally come to, he was disoriented, bandages

covering much of his healing face. A nurse spoke to him in Arabic, and he was confused and frightened. But then Alex remembered who he was, and spoke his name.

Gerry came out of Artz, carrying two big bags. He got in the car. "Now more beer," he said. Neither Alex nor I answered him. Gerry drove to Barton Springs Road, stopped at a gas mart, and ran inside. When he returned, he handed me a six-pack of lemonade. Then he drove to Zilker, paid three dollars, and parked. "Come on," he said. "Carry something."

Trailing Gerry, we went to the water. Gerry paid for a canoe and tossed paddles and life preservers inside. The river was shot with golden light; we slid the canoe down the bank. The metal seat burned my thighs, but I said nothing. Gerry and Alex paddled toward the Congress Avenue Bridge. Once we were underneath and could smell the guano, Gerry passed around cold cans and hot meat.

The brisket was perfectly cooked, tender and slightly sweet with sauce. I ate sausage links, pickles, smoked turkey. Gerry had remembered that Alex liked the giant pork ribs. We finished the beans and the potato salad. Alex ate listlessly, then with vigor.

The sun went down slowly, and still we waited by the edge of the bridge. The sky turned scarlet, deep blue, the orange of a marigold. Gerry touched my hair. Alex almost looked happy, one hand in the water and one around a beer. The paddle rested on his lap. "Here they come," he said, looking up.

It was like another river twisting toward the heavens: the bats—hundreds of them, thousands. A flood of beating wings, streaming above us, breathtaking. They flew from the bridge into the fire-colored night, looking for food. Above us, people clapped and shouted. The bats came out every night, but you would never know it from the cries of celebration. I looked at my brother, and he had tears in his eyes.

"And now," said Gerry, reaching into the last bag and handing us plastic spoons, "bread pudding for dessert."

"With brandy sauce?" asked Alex. I looked at Gerry, hope like a balloon in my chest.

"Of course with brandy sauce," said my love.

Epilogue

It was dim in the motel room, the thick shades drawn. Beside me, Gerry dreamed, but I remained awake. In an Econo Lodge in upstate New York, I let myself rest in the space before sleep. Handsome lifted his head, then settled back down as I ran my fingers through his fur.

Cars drove by, scattering squares of light along the wall. I tried to remember my father as a young man, a glass ashtray at his side. He had been striking, commanding, his hair the color of licorice.

I must have fallen asleep eventually. When I awakened, Gerry and Handsome were gone. My head felt scraped out and strange, but it wasn't a hangover or Tylenol PM—I'd switched to chamomile tea and scalding baths. I sat up and stared at the motel desk, yellow with faux-bamboo edging. A white and yellow lamp, a giant mirror. The last time I had seen my father, I'd been a girl in pigtails, a bathing suit in my hand, frosting from a cinnamon bun on my lips, taking the stairs two at a time. In the mirror, which was edged in the same bamboo pattern, I was an adult—thick, messy hair, circles under my eyes.

Meeting with my therapist the week before (I had gone back to therapy after I called and apologized, and Jane Stafford told me no apology was necessary), I had felt myself sink into the couch. My voice had come from me, hoary with tears, high-pitched. "I've always felt alone," I'd said. "I've felt that way since the morning of the murder. I'm alone, and no one can take care of me."

"You are not alone," said Jane.

"I am not alone," I had repeated, and I tried to believe it was true.

The door banged open, and Gerry entered. "This town," he said, "it is *rough*."

"What do you mean?"

"Pawnshops and bars," said Gerry.

"Perfect for Mr. Cheapskate," I said.

Gerry smiled tiredly. "I know—the whole thing is so stupid."

"No," I said.

He held my gaze. "I want to do something important."

"Like selling houses to people?"

"That's important," said Gerry, sitting backward on the bamboo-edged chair. "Finding a family a home?"

"I guess," I said.

"I know I have to go back to a real job," said Gerry.

"I don't know," I said.

"I don't know, either." He stood and opened the curtains. We sat for a moment and stared at the parking lot. At the edges, the snow was three feet tall. We were a long way from Texas. "Where's he going to live?"

"Jesus, who knows," I said.

"He's famous," said Gerry. "Infamous, anyway."

"Maybe he'll teach," I said.

Gerry looked at me steadily. "We'll make it work."

"What do you mean?"

"I think he should stay with us. In Austin."

I sighed. "We don't have room."

"Yes, we do," said Gerry.

"It just seems like too much all of a sudden."

"I think you owe him," said Gerry.

I tried to temper my fury. "It's not my fault."

"I know," said Gerry. "But it's the right thing."

I had been scared of my father, angry with him for so long. My emotions hadn't caught up with the circumstances. "Let's take him to lunch."

"Seems like a good start," said Gerry, nodding.

"Is there a diner somewhere?"

"There is."

"Okay," I said. I took a shower, using the thin bar of soap to wash my hair. I dried off and smeared lotion from a small bottle on my arms and legs and face. Shivering in a towel, I lay next to Gerry on the bed.

The phone rang, and I answered. It was Alex calling from Austin. He had gone back to work at the hospital and didn't have time to spare, so he was planning a big welcome meal for our father when we all returned to Austin. Alex might invite his new girlfriend, he'd told me earlier, and he might not invite his new girlfriend. I had finally pried the new girlfriend's name from him. It was Mary-Anne.

"Hey," Alex said.

"Hey," I answered.

"You got Dad?"

"Not yet."

"I can't miss this, I decided. I'll be there tonight," said Alex.

"Oh," I said, feeling flushed with pleasure. We would all be together: my family. The joy was edged with fear; I supposed it always would be for me. But I could try to enjoy it while it lasted—that, at least, I could do. "Alex?" I said.

"Yeah?"

"I'm glad you were right," I said.

"Oh, zip it," said Alex.

Attica, New York, was not a welcoming hamlet. Deserted storefronts gave way to houses long past their prime. Broken plastic toys littered the snowy yards, and some windows were no more than plastic bags adhered with duct tape. The wind was brutal, but teenagers in only sweatshirts stood on street corners. Some pushed grocery carts through the streets. It was like *The Road,* for God's sake, but these kids weren't headed anywhere. From my toasty car, I saw their red faces and hopeless eyes. Attica, New York, was a town that was dying. My father had been here for twenty-four years.

The prison was a half hour out of town. We drove to the front gate, and a guard told us to pop the trunk, then he peered inside.

We parked in the visitors' lot. Gerry turned off the car and unlatched his door. "No," I said. He looked at me and sighed. "I'm doing this alone," I said. He bit the inside of his cheek and nodded. He turned the ignition, adjusting the heat to high. I opened my car door. "I love you," I said.

I climbed out of the Dodge, then bent to breathe on Gerry's window. I drew a heart with my finger. Gerry smiled. "Put on your damn gloves," he said loudly. I exhaled again, then wrote, *Will you.* Gerry raised an eyebrow. I blew on the glass and wrote, *marry.* Gerry watched steadily as I took a last breath, then wrote, *me?*

He stared at me through the glass. "You're really asking?" he said.

I nodded, finally sure of something.

Gerry smiled. He fogged up his side of the window and wrote, *Yes.*

There was a large black door at the front of the building, and I put my shoulders back and walked toward it. The door opened, and a guard and an old man came out. The man lit a cigarette and laughed at something the guard said. The guard laid his hand on the old man's shoulder and went back inside. The man wore a cheap windbreaker and jeans. His hair was thin, combed over a pale skull. My feet crunched through the snow. I was afraid I would slip, but I did not slip.

The old man turned to face me. He froze, cigarette halfway to his mouth.

I remembered the way I had adored him as a child—unthinkingly, with complete faith. I didn't think I was capable of that sort of love anymore. I was too hard, too old, for that, now.

I started to run. I ran until I reached him, my father. He closed his arms around me. He was slender, but he was strong. In his embrace, I felt a long-dormant flood of need and devotion rush through me. I wanted to be held, and my father was holding me.

"Little One," he said.

I said, "Daddy." I spoke so quietly I wasn't sure I had spoken at all, so I said it again, and louder.

Acknowledgments

For reading one or more of the many, many drafts of this book—and for inspiring me with their own work—I would like to thank: Jami Attenberg, Anika Streitfeld, Masha Hamilton, Allison Lynn, Mark Lane, Juli Berwald, Ellen Sussman, Mary Helen Specht, Sarah Bird, Dalia Azim, Vendela Vida, Hyatt Bass, Leah Stewart, Emily Hovland, Clare Smith, Marc Parent, Jenna Blum, and Beth Howells.

All my love, as always, to my beautiful mother, Mary-Anne Westley; my sisters, Sarah McKay and Liza Bennigson; and my grandmother, the lovely Lorraine Ward.

Laurie Duncan and Clay Smith, you're wonderful. Michelle Tessler is the best agent anyone could hope for in these confusing times. Thank you, Jennifer Hershey, for your razor-sharp insights, cognac chicken, and an encouraging card in the mail when I most needed one.

Tip Meckel, thank you for your kindness, your brilliance, your margaritas, and the best office in the world. I love you, and I can't wait to see your "Amanda" tattoo.

My favorite moment every day is bringing my boys home. THM and WAM, you fill our house with noise and my heart with joy.

Close Your Eyes

AMANDA EYRE WARD

A Reader's Guide

A Conversation Between Amanda Eyre Ward and J. Courtney Sullivan

J. Courtney Sullivan is the author of *Commencement* and *Maine*. Her website is jcourtneysullivan.com.

J. Courtney Sullivan: Lauren and Alex have such a special bond. While reading, I was struck by the thought that we don't often see extremely close brother-sister relationships in literature. What made you want to write about one?

Amanda Eyre Ward: Often, my novels begin with an image, and in the case of *Close Your Eyes,* one of the first images I saw was a young brother and sister, alone in a tree house, about to discover something that will change their world.

When I was sixteen, there was a murder in a quiet town near my suburban home. A husband and wife were brutally stabbed to death on New Year's Eve. For years, the murder was unsolved, and it's always haunted me. I'm not sure why I honed in on the perspective of two children left behind. (The children of the real-life couple were also a brother and sister—both grown and married at the time of the murder.) But from the very start, *Close Your Eyes* began on the night of Jordan's death. In writing Lauren and Alex's story, I believe I was trying to make sense of a crime that so unsettled me.

I think *Close Your Eyes* would be a different story entirely if

Lauren had had a sister, or if she'd been an only child. I have two sisters, and I'm extremely close to both of them. But I've always imagined that having a brother would be different: you could lean on a brother, and he would protect you. Perhaps Lauren takes this too far, even relying on Alex as a father figure. Over the course of the novel, Lauren learns to look to other people (and herself) for security.

I now have two sons (and I just had a baby daughter) and am always amazed by the ways they interact. There's so much richness in the relationships we share with our siblings. I love exploring that terrain. That said, I never really made a conscious decision for Lauren to have a brother—he was always just there, next to her.

JCS: In the stories of Lauren, Sylvia, and Victoria, you perfectly capture the ways in which childhood trauma follows us into adulthood. Can you speak to this?

AEW: We all want to create a life that is free of past hurts, but I have found that our childhood experiences can return to us in unexpected ways. As a novelist, I'm interested in the year (or week, or day) when a person's smooth life becomes choppy and confused. For the characters in *Close Your Eyes*, it is past events that throw them into a tailspin: unresolved questions, unexplored friendships, unacknowledged loves.

Each of the characters in *Close Your Eyes* needs to confront the past to move on. In Lauren's case, she needs to open herself to the possibility that her father is innocent, and in doing so, acknowledge that true love is possible . . . even for her. Sylvia, who carries so many burdens from her past, is able to see beyond her own pain and give the truth of the worst night of her life to someone who desperately needs her story: Lauren.

My French editor wanted me to write more about Victoria, who never finds peace. She's fascinating to me—she is the character I most identify with. I'd love to revisit her story someday, if only to give Mae a happier ending. [Visit Amanda's website at amandaward.com/Close_Your_Eyes.php to read "Victoria in Rehab," an earlier draft depicting Victoria's struggles.]

JCS: Why do you think Lauren and Alex come to such different conclusions about their father's guilt?

AEW: It's almost as if they both hold onto what they need from that night. Alex needs to believe in his father's innocence, while Lauren needs to believe that she's not crazy: that what happened was awful but unalterable. We tend to seek ways of telling our stories that bring us comfort, and I think this is what Alex and Lauren both do.

JCS: What is it about secrets that make for such great reading (and writing)?

AEW: One of my favorite writers is Alice Munro. In her stories, characters often hold secrets not only from each other but from the reader. In one of my favorite Munro stories, "Carried Away," we are introduced to the dreams of the town librarian, and then told that they will be dashed . . . but she doesn't know it yet. This astonishes me—the way that Munro can let the reader in on a secret that her own characters are not privy to. I tried to emulate this in *Close Your Eyes.* I wanted the reader to have the experience of putting the story together, even as the characters might not see the whole picture. Each of the characters in *Close Your Eyes* holds a piece of the story of the night on Ocean Avenue, the night Lauren's mother was killed.

In early drafts of the novel, I had many more characters with insight into the murder: a woman who wrote to Izaan in prison; friends and family members whose points of view proved too distracting. In one version of the novel, Victoria even had a brother who married Sylvia! But those characters are gone now, joining many more in my "Character Graveyard." [Visit amandaward.com/Close_Your_Eyes.php to read "Desiree's Fantasy," which introduces Izaan's pen pal.]

JCS: Even before her father is imprisoned for her mother's murder, Lauren feels like an outsider because of her Egyptian background. As an adult, living in an age of anxiety about terrorism, she feels judged for her ethnicity even more acutely. What made you build this into her character?

AEW: It's hard not to think about stereotypes these days, the way we judge each other. In 1995, the year after I graduated from college, I was living and teaching in Athens, Greece, and visited Egypt for the first time. The country made a strong impression on me; I've always wanted to write about it. My friends and I took a train from Cairo downriver to Aswan, and we were warned to be very careful—anti-American sentiment was high, especially in some of the more rural areas of Egypt. We were staying in Aswan, trying to hire a *dhow* (sailboat) to float up the Nile, when we heard there had been a bombing in the United States, in Oklahoma City. We were confused and scared, unsure who had bombed the Alfred P. Murrah Building. I remember being afraid to leave the boardinghouse in Aswan.

As we know now, it was an American—Timothy McVeigh—who had bombed the building. In my many visits to Egypt,

I've never been hurt or even insulted (though I don't speak Arabic, so who knows!); I've always felt pretty safe (if often disoriented).

Izaan is such a complicated character. In many ways, he is a devoted family man, and he also acts (toward Pauline) in ways that are unforgivable. Perhaps his upbringing has something to do with his machismo, but I wanted to explore how easily we can see people of other ethnicities as completely different from us, capable of acts we don't understand. Izaan didn't fit in in suburban New York, and his outward looks most certainly affected the outcome of his trial. Lauren, who just wants to disappear, wrestles with her looks and her heritage. To me, it all plays into the story.

JCS: Early in the book, Alex leaves home to join Doctors Without Borders in Iraq. Why was his absence so essential to the story?

AEW: If he had stuck around, Lauren would never have fallen apart in a way that would force her to look at her mother's murder. I needed Lauren to be unbalanced, to seek out the truth. Without Alex, she is broken.

JCS: *Close Your Eyes* manages to be both a literary novel and a whodunit. How were you able to build suspense, and create such a truly surprising conclusion? (I gasped so loud, I woke my dog up from a very deep sleep!)

AEW: Courtney, I love the vision of you gasping and waking your dog!

My brilliant editor, Jennifer Hershey, sent me a card when I was in the thick of rewrites (and despair). "There are three rules for writing the novel," it read. "Unfortunately, no one knows what they are." (This is a quote from W. Somerset Maugham.)

I realized why so few writers attempt character-driven mystery novels. Often, revealing the mystery of Jordan's murderer seemed to pull against how the characters were evolving. For example, Lauren *had* to go to New York to look at the case files of her mother's murder. But I also had to make sure a trip to New York was in line with her character development—she wasn't just going to go where I needed her to! I was often torn between character and plot, and the book took a very long time and many drafts to come together.

JCS: One of the most painful aspects of the book is Alex's disappearance. Why did you choose to end that plotline as you did? Did you ever think of having it turn out differently?

AEW: Yes—in early drafts of the book, Alex died in Iraq. It seemed to make sense to me that Lauren would be alone in the world, but when my husband read the book he asked whether it was really necessary for Alex to die. The book seemed too unrelenting, he said, too grim. I thought about this for a while, and realized that the focus of the book didn't have anything to do with Lauren losing Alex—the book is much more about how she opens herself up to love and trust.

While I was considering the possibility of bringing Alex home, I found out I was pregnant. The happy news inspired me to resurrect Alex. [Visit amandaward.com/Close_Your_Eyes.php to read "Alex's Body," which explains how things might have turned out very differently for Alex.]

JCS: I know how much you love living in Austin. One thing I loved about *Close Your Eyes* is the way in which the city itself is almost a character. We get such a great sense of the place. Was that an intentional decision?

AEW: I don't think it was intentional; I do love my city, and it continues to fascinate me. I've lived in Austin for almost fifteen years now, on and off, but I try to see it with the eyes of a visitor when I'm writing. I ask myself what a tourist might notice: what food, what expressions, what details? Every time I leave my house, something (or someone) surprises me. Yesterday, a Spanish-language radio station was sponsoring a party at the 7-Eleven a few blocks from my house. While I filled up the car with gas, my sons rolled giant foam dice and won plastic cups with Mexican wrestlers on them. Everyone cheered. My four-year-old clutched his Slurpee cup and said, "This is the best day of my life."

JCS: Tell me a bit about your writing process. Do you make yourself stick to a set schedule each day?

AEW: I write best in the morning, still in pajamas, with plenty of coffee. I used to write whenever I wanted (even if it was in the middle of the night), but now I am a mom, and have to budget my time more wisely.

When my first son was born, I remember thinking, "I'll just write when the baby naps!" This was so impossible; it makes me shake my head now at my former naïveté. Both writing and motherhood seem to require such complete concentration that I almost have to divide myself—choosing times that I am wholly a mother, and times that I write without distraction.

Whenever I try to do both at the same time (or even in the same hour), it's awful.

I now write three days a week, and two days a week I try to put the work aside and be with my children. It's hard, especially when I'm in the middle of a difficult scene or rewrite.

In the course of writing *Close Your Eyes,* there was a point where I knew the book was off-course, but I simply couldn't get to the heart of the problem in the time I had for writing. I tried, but it wasn't working. I ended up staying home alone while my husband visited his family over Thanksgiving, and I lay on my living room rug next to my dog for a few days and just thought, fitting all the pieces together in my imagination (and ordering Chinese). If I had an idea at two in the morning, I went and wrote for a few hours, to see where the idea would lead. Finally, by being able to hold the entire book—and nothing else—in my mind, I saw that Sylvia needed to bring Lauren the truth of her mother's murder.

At this point, Sylvia was a fairly stable person. She worked at a Manhattan prep school. There was no reason she would be driven to find Lauren. So I had to completely reimagine Sylvia's character. I'm not sure why I didn't change her name.

When Sylvia became a desperate woman, pregnant and on the run from her boyfriend and her past mistakes, frantic to start anew, the book came together. And that wouldn't have happened if I hadn't had sustained time to reenvision the book and then scrap Sylvia's former self and create a new character.

In my dream life, I would have my home and family; a motel room nearby to work; and a way to bend time and write for five days straight, then pick up my kids after school. [Visit amandaward.com/Close_Your_Eyes.php to read "The Woman

Formerly Known as Sylvia," which introduces an earlier draft of the character.]

JCS: What's next for you?

AEW: I am working on a new novel about ten years in a marriage and a mysterious fire.

Questions and Topics for Discussion

1. How did you feel about the relationship between Sylvia and Victoria? Did you feel like they both took advantage of each other equally?

2. Were you surprised to find out how Lauren's mother was killed? At different stages of the novel did you think of different scenarios?

3. The Innocence Project estimates that as little as 1 percent or as many as 7 percent of inmates in jail are actually innocent. How do you feel about this number? Do you think there are things we should be doing as a society to prevent this or is it a hazard of our system?

4. Race and class were two subtle but important themes that appeared in the novel. In what ways were they handled and what do you think the author was trying to say about them?

5. Why do you think it was important that Alex goes to Iraq for most of the novel? Do you think it was crucial to Lauren developing an identity of her own? Was his possible death also important in shaping who Lauren became?

6. How do you feel about the fact that Lauren believed her father did it? Do you think he forgave her too easily for believing the worst in him?

7. If *Close Your Eyes* was made into a movie, who could you see playing each character and why?

8. On the surface, Sylvia, Lauren, and Victoria are very different people from different backgrounds, but were you able to see some similarities? Was there something else besides the murder that tied them together?

9. How did you feel about Lauren's father's relationship with Pauline? Did it make you change your perspective of him?

10. So much of the novel deals with ambiguity: Lauren's dreamlike recollections from the night of her mother's murder, Victoria's rash deed enacted in a drunken trance; even the title, *Close Your Eyes*, hints at the tendency for characters to perceive things through varying levels of consciousness. Explore the element of uncertainty that runs throughout the narrative. How might some characters use this as a means of shielding themselves from the truth, or as an excuse for their actions? In addition to Lauren and Victoria, can you think of others who use the foggy details of their lives to concoct their own version of reality? Is this part of human nature?

PHOTO: © CORY RYAN

AMANDA EYRE WARD is a graduate of Williams College and the University of Montana. She is the author of the novels *Sleep Toward Heaven, How to Be Lost, Forgive Me,* and the short-story collection *Love Stories in This Town*. Amanda lives with her family in Austin, Texas.

www.amandaward.com